Praise for Naomi Hirahara's Novels

SUMMER OF THE BIG BACHI

*Named one of "The Ten Best Mysteries and Thrillers of 2004" by the *Chicago Tribune**

*A *Publishers Weekly* "Best Books of 2004" pick*

"Hirahara has a keen eye for the telling detail and an assured sense of character uncommon for a first-time novelist. . . . Both mystery fans and readers of L.A. fiction will eagerly await her characters' further adventures."
—*Los Angeles Times*

"Naomi Hirahara's story of forgotten men who share an unforgettable past sweeps the reader into a world most of us know little about. . . . A complete original."
—S. J. Rozan, Edgar Award–winning author of *Absent Friends*

"[A] seamless and shyly powerful first novel... Peppered with pungent cultural details, crisp prose and credible, fresh descriptions . . . this perfectly balanced gem deserves a wide readership."
—*Publishers Weekly* (starred review)

"An intriguing mystery [whose] plot and characters are as fresh as a newly mown lawn . . . . A unique voice in a genre cluttered with copycats."
—*Rocky Mountain News*

"Hirahara uses a wealth of fascinating historic and social details . . . to create an original and exciting mystery. [A] poignant story of loyalty and betrayal, full of real people who could be ourselves."—*Chicago Tribune*

"Packs a considerable wallop." —*San Francisco Chronicle*

"Naomi Hirahara is a bright new voice on the mystery scene. *Summer of the Big Bachi* presents an intriguing puzzle written with a true insider's eye for Japanese-American life."
—Dale Furutani, author of *Death in Little Tokyo*

"Hirahara has crafted an intriguing mystery, full of earthy, subcultured richness.... An impressive first novel."
—*Old Book Barn Gazette*

"Debut novelist Hirahara's prismatic writing nails a Japanese American subculture and a troubled past few of her readers have ever confronted directly."
—*Kirkus Reviews*

"A fascinating portrait of Japanese American society... Captivating." —*Mystery News*

"An impressive and moving mystery." —*Pasadena Weekly*

"A novel about social change wrapped inside a mystery... Reveals the hopes and compromises that lurk on the fringes of the American Dream."
—Denise Hamilton, author of *Savage Garden*

GASA-GASA GIRL

"Hiroshima survivor Mas Arai is a man of few words: luckily, readers are privy to his thoughts.... What makes this series unique is its flawed and honorable protagonist.... A fascinating insight into a complex and admirable man." —*Booklist* (starred review)

"The plot of *Gasa-Gasa Girl* is as knotty as a root-ball and reaches deep into the history of Japanese Americans.... Affecting." —*Washington Post*

"A taut, quick read." —*San Francisco Chronicle*

"[Mas Arai is] a fascinating and unusual lead character. . . . Hirahara writes with passion for her characters and a real touch for genuine human feelings and relationships. . . . A satisfying story."
—*Chicago Sun-Times*

"[Hirahara] brings heart and elegance to a nifty whodunit." —*Kirkus Reviews*

"The endearing, quietly dignified Mas, supported by a cast of spirited New Yorkers, as well as the distinctive Japanese-flavored prose, makes this a memorable read."
—*Publishers Weekly*

"A terrific who-done-it starring a wonderful protagonist. . . . Readers will demand more Mas novels from refreshing author Naomi Hirahara."
—*Midwest Book Review*

"[Mas Arai is] a memorable character, and Mari is totally believable." —*Chicago Tribune*

"Compelling and unique . . . The complex and layered story blends together character, setting and plot in a satisfying harmony." —*Romantic Times*

SNAKESKIN SHAMISEN

Edgar Award Winner

"Hirahara's well-plotted, wholesome whodunit offers a unique look at L.A.'s Japanese-American community, with enough twists and local flavor to keep you guessing till the end." —*Entertainment Weekly*

"A shrewd sense of character and a formidable narrative engine . . . Hirahara knows [Mas] Arai intimately."
—*Chicago Tribune*

"The third in a charming and earthy series."
—*Wall Street Journal*

"Hirahara's sharp ear for dialogue and keen sense of place mark this as a superior read, but it's her intimate view of the Japanese-American community and her wry portrait of the endearing Mas, with his fondness for gambling and Spam, that really make this series stand out." —*Publishers Weekly*

"Hirahara has the distinction of writing a mystery series that is unlike any other. As her latest novel proves, she is truly one of a kind . . . . Mas Arai is one of the freshest, most realistic and fascinating characters in the mystery genre. Every book featuring him is a joy to read." —*Chicago Sun-Times*

"Hirahara's complex and compassionate portrait of a contemporary American subculture enhances her mystery, and vice versa." —*Kirkus Reviews*

"This is a winning series." —*Seattle Times*

"Hirahara has created a wonderful character in Mas and lets us into his world, which is so influenced by his Japanese roots." —*Library Journal*

BOOKS BY NAOMI HIRAHARA

Summer of the Big Bachi
Gasa-Gasa Girl
Snakeskin Shamisen

SUMMER

of the

NAOMI HIRAHARA

BIG BACHI

A Dell Book

SUMMER OF THE BIG BACHI
A Dell Book

PUBLISHING HISTORY
Delta Trade Paperback edition published April 2004
Dell mass market edition / February 2008

Published by
Bantam Dell
A Division of Random House, Inc.
New York, New York

Cover design by Royce Becker

Title page photo by Lynn Newmark

Library of Congress Catalog Card Number: 2003055538

ISBN: 978-0-440-24154-6

Printed in the United States of America

Published simultaneously in Canada

www.bantamdell.com

OPM 10 9 8 7 6 5 4 3 2 1

To Mom and Dad,
for dreams and laughter, and to
Chiyoko Mukai
(1912–2003)

ACKNOWLEDGMENTS

First of all, I credit my early readers—Marilyn Lowery, Sandra Mizumoto Posey, and Thelma Seto, the latter two who listened to drafts while on a houseboat docked in Marina del Rey. Virginia Stem Owens, my mentor in more things besides writing, helped to rein and guide the revisions, while Brian Niiya, who only gets sharper with age, gave valuable input, as did Joyce Nako, my kindred spirit, and Momoko Iko. I thank the California Community Foundation for its Brody Arts Award and Hedgebrook on Whidbey Island in Washington State for both the space (an incredible one at that!) and time to write. I'm also indebted to the Milton Center in Wichita, Kansas, and its supporters for its writing fellowship program.

Additional acknowledgments go to my former colleagues at *The Rafu Shimpo* newspaper, UCLA Extension Writers' Program, Pacific Asian American

Women Writers–West, and the Little Tokyo community in Los Angeles. Evergreen Baptist Church, First Baptist Church of Wichita, and New Life Christian Church all provided spiritual guidance and encouragement.

Mas would have never made it in the New York City publishing world without the insight of two literary professionals: my agent Sonia Pabley and editor Abby Zidle. Thank you for seeing the potential of this series and helping to make it better.

Again, there were many who provided tangible and emotional support during this process: Martie Quan, Coleen Nakamura, Sindy Saito, Diane Ujiiye, Jane Yamashita Shirk, Amy Ota, Elaine Kimura, Essie Sappenfield, Grace Choi, Jeroo Sinor, and, of course, my parents, Isamu and Mayumi Hirahara, and my brother Jimmy.

Most importantly, I could not have fully pursued the writing of Mas's stories without the enthusiasm and sweat of my husband Wes, a poet and storyteller in his own right.

On August 6, 1945, at 8:15 A.M.,
an atomic bomb was dropped on the naval base
of Hiroshima, Japan.
Approximately 140,000 individuals
were killed instantly or died within months.
At least 210,000, however, survived.
Of the survivors, more than 500 eventually
returned to their birthplace—the United States.

July 1999

Mas Arai didn't believe in Jesus or Buddha, but thought there might be something in *bachi*. In Japanese, *bachi* was when you snapped at your wife, and then tripped on a rock in the driveway. You didn't suffer your punishment in another lifetime, but within the same life, even within the next few minutes.

Bachi came to Mas's mind when he heard the news at Tanaka's Lawnmower Shop, in Altadena, California. The news had spread a hundred miles in less than an hour; by the time it reached Tanaka's, it was eight in the evening, and unusual for Mas and two other old gardeners to be there so late.

The lawn mower shop's owner, Wishbone Tanaka, was the one to tell it: Haneda was dead. No one had liked this man called Joji Haneda, but then, they hardly liked anyone at all. He had been tall, with a hooked nose, strange for a Japanese, and a keloid scar splashed across his neck like a spidery starfish. They knew basic things about him: He owned a nursery in Ventura County and was born in Los Angeles but had spent some time in Japan. And although he had a wife and two children, he was no family man. Far from it.

Nobody knew any other details of his life; nobody aside from Mas Arai. So really, Joji Haneda, U.S.A., could have disappeared that instant, his existence erased. Whether he would be remembered for who he really was depended entirely on Mas, who bowled well enough to know that you could handle a split effectively in either of two ways. If you are right-handed, tap the left pin gently on the left side so that it pushes down the right pin. Or else bang the right pin hard enough so that it ricochets from the back to the left. Beginners, on the other hand, don't know about these things. They usually release the ball right down the middle. It is no wonder they end up hitting nothing.

Mas knew that they all were expecting him to come up with an explanation. Tell them why this man had turned on them so hard, like a beaten dog. But it couldn't be told to those who hadn't been there. As much as Mas had hated the man, he knew that they were two of a kind. For them, keeping secrets was a way out. But while Joji had escaped, Mas was still around, waiting for *bachi* to strike at any second.

CHAPTER ONE

June 1999

Tanaka's Lawnmower Shop was where it all started, at least this time around. Buried in a town called Altadena at the base of the purple San Gabriel Mountains, it was the closest thing to home for Mas Arai. When Mas was younger and his hair jet-black, he spent most of his nights after his gardening route in the shop's back room. They cleared the worktables of screws, pliers, and invoices and got out a case of plastic poker chips in red, yellow, blue, and green. Wishbone Tanaka would plunk down a new pack of playing cards, a sticker still keeping the virgin lid in place. Someone would toss in a bag of red-dyed pistachios; after a night of cards, everyone's fingertips would be pink and salty.

Even after he got married and his daughter, Mari, was born, Mas continued these late-night outings. Most of the guys were still single, or had wives who didn't care, but Chizuko called every night. When Mari was old enough to say "Dad-dy," she was the one who was on the other side of the line. Then Chizuko was pregnant again, and Mas thought twice about gambling at Tanaka's. "One day it's all going to catch up with you," Chizuko shrieked. "You going to get big *bachi*."

One late weekend night the *bachi* did come. Mari kept calling and calling. Mas refused to take the phone, because he didn't want his successful run to be ruined.

"I got me six hundred dolla," he announced, stumbling into the bedroom that night.

"I don't feel so good, Masao-*san*," Chizuko moaned.

Mas flipped on the light. Chizuko's permed hair was damp against her forehead. He turned over the flowered bedspread and cotton sheets to reveal Chizuko's plump belly extending over her tight panties. Next to her was a spot of blood, fresh and dark.

"I called you, Daddy." Mari, dressed in a flannel nightgown, stood in the doorway. "I kept calling and calling."

After Chizuko's miscarriage, Mas stopped playing cards. Chizuko kept her nagging, but it took on another tone. The words were the same, but all their power was gone. It continued like this for twenty more years, two decades filled with one *bachi* after another. In the end, he was the only one left in their three-bedroom house at the bottom of the San Gabriels, the purple peaks now barely visible due to the smog. Even their mutt dog was gone.

But it seemed to always work out this way for Mas. He was the ultimate survivor, whether he liked it or not. It was a distinction that Mas hated and lately had begun to test. He resumed hanging out at Tanaka's, first just once a month, then once a week. Within a year, his Ford truck was on automatic. After Mas finished his gardening route at noon, he headed for Fair Oaks Boulevard, which pushed up into tiny streets like the thin veins that traced his brown fingers. While the main town, Pasadena, was full of wide boulevards and fancy streetlights, Altadena, to the north, was scrawny like a chicken that didn't get enough feed. It had a slight wildness to it—hardly any sidewalks—as if the town weren't even worth taming. Mas liked it that way.

Tanaka's Lawnmower Shop was a small shack between an abandoned gas station and a discount grocery store that used to be a chain called Market Basket. In any other city around Los Angeles, Tanaka's would be long gone. The advent of huge home building supply stores meant survival of the fittest. And Tanaka's was anything but fit.

It was the beginning of summer and hotter than hell. Wishbone's air-conditioning had broken down, and the door to the shop was wide open. A few flies circled the heads of the men whose graying hair was slicked back with Three Flowers oil.

Wishbone was behind the counter, like usual. Wishbone's real name, given by his immigrant parents from Kumamoto Prefecture, was Wallace. Strangers who met Wishbone for the first time thought that his nickname meant that he was lucky. But it had nothing to do with luck. When he was a skinny teenager, his legs were terribly pigeon-toed, resulting in the nickname from his East L.A. classmates. At age sixty-seven, the name still stuck.

He and three others were talking about the gardeners' association meeting the night before. "Hardly anyone there, *ne*," said one of the guys, a gardener in San Gabriel. "A lot of fines to be paid."

"Took just about thirty minutes, datsu all. Was even home for the horse race broadcast," said Stinky Yoshimoto, also a gardener who lived in Pasadena.

Mas, at first, didn't notice the man standing in the corner by the loops of garden hoses. He was quiet, and it was his silence that attracted attention. He was in his fifties, younger than the usual crowd. He wore a tan turtleneck, even though it was ninety-eight degrees outside, and a pair of tinted glasses with golden tips. Must be straight from Japan, Mas had thought, studying the man's flat, manicured fingernails. Definitely no gardener.

"You not at the meeting last night, Mas." Stinky held on to the handle of a lawn mower on display.

The man in the tinted glasses and the two gardeners stared at Mas as if they had just noticed him in the doorway. He fumbled with a button on his khaki shirt and adjusted his Dodgers cap.

"Mas don't go to meetings. He's not that kind of guy." Wishbone grinned, wrinkles covering his face like a Mojave lizard's.

Mas bit into an old toothpick he had found in his jeans pocket. The guys always made a big deal about the gardeners' association meetings. But what was it, really? A bunch of old guys in folding chairs, listening to speeches on the latest drought or blower ban. The heyday of the Japanese gardener had passed them by years ago. Once, there had been hundreds of them on the front lawns of practically all Southern California homes and businesses. Now they were replaced by their former helpers, the Mexicans, with shiny new trucks, eager family members, and cut-rate prices.

"We were just tellin' this fella—what your name again?" The gardener from San Gabriel turned to the stranger.

"Nakane." The man squeezed the right tip of his eyeglasses.

"Yah, Nakane-*san*, yah, tellin' him that we saw Haneda last night."

The toothpick broke in Mas's mouth. His heart pounded, and blood pulsed through his head.

"You know Haneda Joji?" the stranger asked in

Japanese. His tinted glasses had turned a shade or two lighter in the dark shed, and his heavy eyelashes fluttered.

"Yah, he knowsu Haneda." Stinky's eyes were bloodshot and milky yellow like a stirred raw egg. "Knowsu each other back in, what, Wakayama?"

"Hiroshima," Mas corrected Stinky.

"Oh, yah, that's right. Hi-RO-shima."

"Longtime friends," Nakane stated, more than questioned.

"No, I neva say friends." Mas chewed on the broken toothpick until it splintered into even smaller pieces. What kind of stranger comes around and makes noise like this?

"Shitsurei," Nakane apologized. "Don't take offense. I'm just looking for him."

"Heezu right ova there, in Ventura," said Stinky.

"Yah," the gardener from San Gabriel interjected, "got a fancy nursery right there by the ocean. 'The beach clean there,' he say. 'Best sashimi in California. Better than the ones down here, any day.' "

"That's the thing." Wishbone smoothed a dollar bill on his wooden counter. "He's not in Ventura anymore."

"Oh, yah?" Stinky looked greedily at Wishbone. Wishbone was the king of local gossip, which seemed to sell better than his lawn mowers.

"He left his wife and his kids, although they all are

pretty much grown now. They say he's with a mistress down here in North Hollywood."

North Hollywood? Mas felt like spitting the tiny splinters of toothpick onto Wishbone's floor. While it took at least an hour and a half to drive to Ventura, North Hollywood was only twenty miles away.

"Happen to know her name?" Nakane's eyes looked shiny and bright, but Mas couldn't tell if it was just the reflection off of his glasses.

"No." Wishbone's smile diminished slightly. "Just know that she's younger."

Atarimae, thought Mas. That much they all could figure out.

Another gardener walked into the steamy shed, and the conversation switched from Haneda to gossip about a Japanese mechanic whose son had been arrested for drug dealing. The turtlenecked man retreated into the back storage area, and Mas remained with the others. It was only a matter of time before the man in the tinted glasses made his way toward Mas. "So, you know where Joji-*san* is?"

"Why you wanna knowsu?" The man spoke as if he were straight from Japan, and Mas was suspicious. He smelled like high-tone cologne, not the familiar scent of Old Spice that Mas splashed on special for a funeral.

The man bent his head. "I'm working in conjunction with the government. Trying to restore some lost records. We thought that Joji Haneda died in 1945,

August. But here's one, right here in Southern California."

Mas tossed the chewed toothpick on the floor. "Lotsu of Jojis, I betsu. A dime a dozen." Mas made sure he spoke in English. "And Haneda. Probably a load of themsu, too."

The man squeezed the tip of his glasses again. "Yes, it could be so. But they never recovered his body."

Mas almost laughed out loud. How many thousands were never found? How many were tossed in piles like charred, useless logs? "You gonna track down every dead sonafugun? You gonna be one busy man."

The man did not smile back. Instead, he flipped out a thin gold case and removed a business card. SHUJI NAKANE, INVESTIGATIONS, it read. Underneath the title was an address in Hiroshima. "You call me if you remember anything. My local pager number's on the back," Nakane said.

"Wait a minute," Mas said before Nakane left the shed. "How you knowsu a Joji Haneda in America?"

"Television," said Nakane. "On an American news program."

Mas remembered. It had been a couple of years ago in August. He had been flipping through the television channels after eating a burnt Swanson's chicken pie, and there was that ugly face, the hooked nose. He was sitting next to a *hakujin* man reporter, one of those generic ones with neat hair, not too good-looking, but not so bad, either. They were on the shore of a beach; must have been Ventura. "I was with two friends that morning," he said. Below him, on the screen, were the video letters JOJI HANEDA/SURVIVOR.

Mas felt sick to his stomach. "You nuts," he practically spit at the 12-inch image of video dots. It was just like him to run after attention. Couldn't he keep quiet after all these years?

"How many of them survived?" the reporter asked.

Haneda's eyes watered, like those of a trapped fish. "Only me," he said, "and one other."

Mas promptly turned off the television and smashed his hand against the fake wood console. The worn-out antenna, which he had reattached with metal telephone wire, sagged down to the floor. *"Baka,"* Mas cursed. He couldn't believe this man could be so stupid. It would be just like him to talk after fifty years, when it felt deceptively safe. And now that recklessness had resulted in this fancy investigator nosing around.

"So, were you able to help the man out?" Wishbone had left his counter to stack some cans of snail killer on a shelf next to Mas.

Mas shook his head. "What youzu know about dis guy, anyway?"

"Just came in this morning. Never laid eyes on him before."

Strange, thought Mas. Wishbone didn't care for these white-collar types from Japan. If he had his way, none of them would be allowed into the United States, much less his Altadena lawn mower shop. Before Mas could ask any more questions, Wishbone had returned to the rest of his customers.

Standing beside the cans of snail killer, Mas studied the investigator's card. This Shuji Nakane was no government man; that was for sure. No such person would set foot in Tanaka's Lawnmower Shop. This man was used to getting down and dirty, digging in places he should not be. What would happen if he uncovered the truth about Joji Haneda?

CHAPTER TWO

Mas's best friend, if he could call him that, was Haruo Mukai. He was scrawny and a little shriveled, like a piece of fat that you couldn't quite chew through. He had a shock of white hair that usually covered the left side of his face.

What was underneath that hair made Mas's stomach churn, even to this day. A keloid scar, puckered and webbed, from the eyebrow to the chin. And the fake eye, which needed to be adjusted. *Ron-Pari* eye, they called it. While one faced London, the other looked toward Paris.

Haruo never talked about it, at least to Mas. Didn't have to. That's the way they operated, and it had worked for more than forty years. They had met at the Pasadena DMV, where they both happened to stand in line, struggling with the paperwork to get their new driver's licenses. Turned out both had spent time in Hiroshima, and both were gardeners trying to make their living from the lawns of *hakujin* people.

They soon became track buddies—sometimes even going in between gardening jobs during the weekdays. Type of lunch break, Mas told himself, didn't have to tell Chizuko. But of course Haruo got found out by his wife, Yasuko. Yasuko seemed as gentle and pliable as a willow branch, except for her eyebrows. It was these eyebrows, or rather her lack of them, that revealed her true character. She had plucked every single hair and replaced the brows with two hand-drawn black strokes—ominous crows in the swaying willow branch.

When she discovered ten betting stubs in Haruo's back jeans pocket, all hell broke loose. She even brought Chizuko into the picture, claiming Mas was a corrupting influence. The lunch breaks to the track ceased, and Mas saw Haruo only when they got together on a sprinkler job.

Haruo had lost out to the sweeping eyebrows, and come clean. That's why Mas didn't believe the lawn mower shop gossip several years later. The talk was that Haruo had collected money from his *tanomoshi* but had failed to show up to the meetings to make his monthly contributions. The *tanomoshi* clubs served as private banks among the Japanese. It was through their *tanomoshi* that Mas and Chizuko were able to buy their home, replace their old refrigerator that had wheezed like an aging dog. There were no contracts, just an understanding that you—in time—would replenish the pool of money.

Occasionally, someone would take off with the money and disappear into the far northern or eastern suburbs, or maybe back to Japan. But Haruo wasn't like that. If he borrowed a power drill—bam—it was back the day after, in addition to shiny homegrown eggplants and prickly long cucumbers. "Nah, got story wrong," Mas told the guys at Tanaka's Lawn-mower Shop.

But then, two days later, Yasuko called for Chizuko. "He took a second mortgage on the house," she wailed. "That good-for-nothing. Bookies callin' every hour. Nothing. We have nothing now." The house was lost. Eventually Yasuko packed up the teenagers and furniture and walked out. Haruo was now living in a small apartment in Los Angeles's Crenshaw area, and regularly seeing a Japanese counselor in Little Tokyo to get gambling out of his system.

Haruo was trying to purge himself from his past, but Mas needed the old Haruo for a moment—at least until he could find out more about another old gambler, that one called Joji Haneda.

✣ ✣ ✣

Mas navigated his Ford truck to the right side of the Santa Monica Freeway, toward the Arlington Exit. He didn't like to go to Haruo's anymore, especially after the riots. It wasn't like anyone treated him bad, but it wasn't quite the same. It was a feeling that hung out there, like the smog. Other drivers seemed on edge, like if you went a little over the yellow line, you would pay dearly—if not with your life, then at least with your car.

"You too nervous," Haruo had told him, launching into the same story of a small Japanese eatery called Kiku's that sold plate lunches of fried breaded pork and dollops of sticky rice. During the torching of other businesses, mostly liquor stores, the neighborhood people came out and hung makeshift signs that said "Black-owned" all over the barred windows. "They save that business."

"Yah, yah," Mas replied. He had heard it all. L.A. was always mixed up. Even here on the boulevard, next to a large church for blacks, was a sign in Spanish for a dentist named Hernandez. Inside the local grocery store, pink fish cakes would be stacked up beside white Mexican cheese, fleshy pigs' feet, and chorizo sausage. But people weren't like food and billboard signs. They didn't like to rub up against one another, and Mas was no exception.

Mas drove past a tiny barbershop, a clothing store with racks of discounts outside on the sidewalk, a Chinese restaurant with a police car parked along the curbside. On the corner was a gas station operated by a Korean family—the son, wearing a blue short-sleeved shirt, manned the pumps, while a grandma-looking woman sat inside, dispensing change through a hole in the bulletproof glass.

Mas turned and parked his truck in the driveway beside Haruo's apartment. It was a two-floor duplex. Haruo lived downstairs, on the left-hand side. Occasionally, the upstairs unit would host samba parties on Saturday nights, causing the whole building to pulse like a pumping heart.

All was quiet today, aside from a shoddy lawn mower down the street. "Hallo." Mas rattled the metal gated door. His back felt a bit stiff, and he was reminded of the pain he used to feel when he rolled his thirteen-pound bowling ball down Eagle Rock Lanes twenty years ago.

After a few minutes, Haruo appeared, wiping his hand on a rag. "Oh, Mas." He seemed surprised. "Come on out to the back."

They walked into the backyard, which was mostly full of weeds and dirt and an old metal incinerator. It was illegal to light those things up now, something about polluting the air. Now weeds encircled the contraption, and Mas noticed that a bird had started a nest at the top of the long pipe.

In the far corner of the backyard, only about five feet by five feet and practically hidden by the weeds, was Haruo's pride and joy: a vegetable garden with rows of eggplants, tomatoes, cucumbers.

"I'm growing *gobo* now." Haruo raised a tangle of

long roots from a sheet of newspaper he had spread out. "You want some?"

"What am I going to do with that?"

"I dunno. Make some *kimpira*."

Mas glared. The only thing Mas cooked was rice, eggs (over easy), and hot dogs. He barely knew what was involved in making *kimpira*, which looked like a batch of old brown weeds tossed together. He had seen Chizuko make it from time to time, grating the *gobo* and salting it with chili pepper.

Haruo lowered the snarl of dirt-clumped roots and sat back down in a lawn chair. "You look worn out, Mas. Not sleepin' too good again?"

Mas sat in the other lawn chair. "I'm sleepin' fine," he lied.

"Gettin' those bad dreams, huh?"

"No bad dreams," Mas lied again. One night of sharing a room at the Four Queens in Las Vegas, and Haruo thought that he was an expert on Mas's sleeping habits. So what if I yell a couple of times in the middle of the night? Mas thought. It had to be from his daily habit of eating pickled plums before he went to bed. Or maybe at the Four Queens, it was because he hadn't had his plums. Anyway, if those dreams were so bad, he'd be able to remember them, wouldn't he?

"So, you busy?" Haruo tried again.

"Always busy."

"Hmmm."

Haruo seemed to be waiting for something, but didn't have the guts to come out and say it. "So, you playing the horses, Mas?"

"Go over Santa Anita for offtrack. But not the same watching them on TV."

Haruo nodded. "Pincay not doin' so hot right now."

Mas looked suspiciously over to the sweat dripping from Haruo's long white hair. His fake eye drifted, while the good eye was yellow and bloodshot.

"My counselor says itsu *orai*," Haruo explained. "Can watch on TV. Not like I have money down."

Mas stayed quiet and pulled a piece of old skin on his callused thumb. He could hear kids on the street calling out to one another. "So, you see anybody?" he finally said.

"Huh?"

Mas felt his head grow hot. You couldn't be roundabout with Haruo. "I dunno. Just wonderin' if you run into anyone these days."

"Who youzu talkin' about, Mas?"

"There's lot of people in town. Summertime."

"Huh?"

"Just wonderin' if somebody call you."

"Whozu gonna call me?"

"Forget it. I gotta go."

"Who, Mas? You talkin' about Joji Haneda?"

Mas's chest tightened. "How come you say him?"

"Dis guy came by the other day. Even give me a

meishi." Haruo went back into the house and came out with a plain white business card. Mas immediately recognized the name. Shuji Nakane. "Not him," Haruo clarified, turning over the card. The name David Hawthorne was scribbled on the back. "Was a *hakujin* guy. This guy tole me Haneda's in North Hollywood. You know him, Mas?"

"Whatcha tell him?"

"Tole him what I could. That we used to gamble. Play cards. But that I don't do that no more. Then he started askin' me about Hiroshima."

"Hiroshima?"

"Yah, if I know him back then, stuff like that."

"Whatcha tell him?"

"What can I tell him? Nutin'. I dunno Haneda back in Hiroshima. If dis Hawthorne wanted to know that stuff, he could talk to you."

"You went ahead and say that?" Mas felt betrayed.

"No, I don't involve you. I know you not the type of guy to talk about ole times, Mas."

Mas gripped the armrests of the lawn chair hard, so hard that the plastic began to separate from the metal.

"You neva liked him, huh?"

"What?"

"You neva liked Joji. I neva knew why. Did sometin' happen?"

"Don't even remember his face anymore." As soon

as Mas had said that, he knew that it was true. It was as if Haneda had been a bad sickness and Mas's memories of the symptoms had faded over time.

"Well, you never liked him," Haruo repeated.

"He stole that business deal." Mas frowned, trying to contain his impatience. "That nursery, my idea."

"Nah, I mean back then—" Haruo continued, and Mas felt the hairs on his neck begin to rise.

"What the hell, Haruo."

Haruo straightened his back, and glared at Mas through the strands of his graying hair. "I dunno . . . just sometin' *okashii*, strange, I feel in the gut. I talked to Joji Haneda long time ago—"

"What long time ago?"

"He tole me you close, like brothas. Then sumptin' happen."

Mas felt his stomach and head churn, like a rickety old washing machine.

"I dunno why you got sometin' against that guy." Haruo stuffed his hands in his pockets. "You know each other since you little. That's not natural. You need to talk about it. That's what my counselor would say—"

"Look, you're the one need counselor, not me. Just because you make life bad with Yasuko . . ." Mas paused with regret.

Haruo became quiet and returned to shaking off

the dirt from the *gobo* root. "You sure you don't want some?" he said after a while.

Mas got up. "No, no need."

✣ ✣ ✣

After Mas got back on the Santa Monica Freeway, it was already eleven and the sun was blazing hot. Mas wiped his wet forehead with the back of his hand. What was Nakane doing with this *hakujin* man, David Hawthorne? It was one thing to have Nakane at Tanaka's, but a *hakujin* in the Crenshaw district? They were either fools or fearless. And if they were without fear, it was because they had backup, plentiful either in numbers or in brute strength.

What was Joji thinking? When Mas had last seen him face-to-face, almost thirty years ago, they had come to an agreement. "I stay in L.A.; you stay in Ventura," Mas told him. "I knowsu nutin' about you." And with that, Mas pressed down on his memories so hard that they lay thin and almost invisible. America was again his home; there was no place for Hiroshima anymore.

Mas tried not to let his mind attempt to connect Nakane with Joji and with Hawthorne. Nothing to do with me, anyhow. If Joji's in trouble, that's his business. If he falls, he can fall alone. Mas squinted his eyes and focused on what was before him this day. Work. Work always managed to remove the sting of deep thoughts, at least for a short time.

When he first started in Altadena, he'd had a total of three customers—all young *hakujin* couples living in small bungalows. Their lawns were tiny, rocky, and square, usually rimmed by hedges and gardenias. At first he had only a rusty pair of hedge clippers and a push mower. He would get a lift from his cousin, but dreamed of owning his own Ford, his own Custom Car. He had saved some money from his truck farming days, lost some on craps, but kept enough of a hefty sum to put down on a long-shot horse, Sweet Sister. His friends told him that he was crazy, that he should send for a wife from Japan instead. But the truck—a vehicle that would free him from his cousin's crowded home of wailing babies and hormone-stinky teenagers—that was the ticket out on his own.

Thanks to Sweet Sister, Mas had bought the Ford, which gained him more customers—so that finally he could afford his own studio apartment in Altadena and, what the hell, finally get hitched. His wife, Chizuko, sensed his devotion to the horses. *"Uma, uma, uma,"* she used to scream at him during their dinnertime arguments. "What about us—your wife and own daughter?"

Mari sat in her booster chair, her silver-capped front teeth shining as she chewed a piece of liver. Like always, she remained quiet, her eyes focused on a large crack on the wall. Soon the argument would escalate;

plates shattered against the wall and ceiling, soy sauce dripping over the crack like black blood.

He would escape, get into the Ford, and drive for hours. Friends could come and go—disappear in a puff of black smoke—wives got sick and died; children left home. But his Ford and its tough metal hide could survive accident after accident, the blazing L.A. sun, hail, gunshots, and domestic strife. Unlike the aluminum-can Japanese cars, his Ford truck was solid, reliable, and, perhaps most important, a friend.

Each year Mas added something new to his truck. In the old days, he merely secured hollow metal pipes in the back, which held lassos of green hoses. Mas remembered the times when he would drive home to McNally Street and see those dark eyes behind the backyard gate. "Daddy, Daddy," Mari's high-pitched voice would ring out. Mas saw a flash of yellow and then felt a slight weight in the rear. In the side mirror, he could see Mari's then-tender fingers wrapped around those pipes.

Later Mas got more elaborate and replaced the pipes with metal guards with holes to hold his rakes and push brooms. He also built runners for his lawn mowers from planks of wood, which he tied down with frayed rope.

His star lawn mower was his thirty-nine-year-old Trimmer. The signature lawn mower of all Japanese gardeners in the 1960s, the Trimmer had blades twisted into a cylindrical reel, which provided lawns with the closest shave. The handle resembled a sawed-off pipe, and it lay low—good for men like Mas who were nowhere close to five feet six inches.

His Trimmer was now faded and scratched, but its blades were razor sharp and its insides still roared like a tiger, thanks to Mas's handiwork. He had replaced the engine with a Honda—the best—and every gear and spark plug was new and in top condition.

His friends warned him about maintaining an open bed on his truck: "Get a cover," they told him, "so danger, *abunai*, these days." He even heard of one guy who kept a loaded gun in his glove compartment. Mas compromised by locking down the Trimmer with a heavy chain and a Master Lock. He preferred the openness of the truck, liked that when he looked in his rearview mirror, he could see his equipment against the expansive blue-gold sky.

Lately, though, the sky looked brown, heavier than usual, and Mas's tools seemed flimsy and cheap as he rattled over spilt gravel on the boulevard.

Since his back was acting up, he knew that he should drive past Pine Street, just to take a look. But it was so late; today's were truly a sorry-looking lot. He slowed the Ford and stared down at the men crowded at the curb on Pine. Frayed T-shirts. Chapped elbows. Twisted legs. He recognized most of them—Eduardo, Joe, Juan . . . family men, good enough, yet the meat on their arms lay limp and stretched.

Some newer men leaned back against the graffiti-covered taco stand, their hands shoved in their pockets, their eyes narrowed against the morning sun. Their faces showed the betrayal and disbelief as well as the faint flicker of hope that Mas knew only too well.

Mas's gray-black eyes finally stopped on a tall, lanky teenager. The boy's sinewy arms lay crossed, daring Mas to hire him, daring him not to.

Mas took a puff from his cigarette and then smashed it down into his metal ashtray.

"Mista Arai," someone called out. A mustached man with thinning hair broke out of the crowd and looked into Mas's open window. "You need helpa?" he asked, wrinkling his forehead into thick lines. "I come."

Mas shook his head as he tore back the clear plastic wrap hanging from his pack of cigarettes. "Sorry, Eduardo. Some other time, okay, but need a young one today. That one, ova there." Mas gestured with a fresh, pungent cigarette toward the teenager with his arms crossed.

Eduardo shrugged and turned to the boy. Mas could make out about half the Spanish words rolling off the young man's tongue.

The boy showed no expression but sauntered over to the car window. Mas examined the boy's fingernails on his right hand. The nail on his pinky was long and sharp, revealing a faint ring of dirt. Probably didn't work yesterday, noted Mas, but had done hard work sometime this week. Would have energy today. His eyes, although suspicious, were still bright; Mas knew that the boy had not been in America long.

The young man then took his turn looking over the mold-green truck. He surveyed the bed of the truck, the makeshift dividers and wire metal hooks holding rakes and green hoses, the greasy lawn mowers and gasoline-powered blowers. He dragged his finger along the dent on the side of the truck and then approached the front.

He focused on Mas's dark, leathery face—the prickly white whiskers, thin eyes—and then down to the brown arms laced with distended veins. The teenager licked his thick lips and then turned toward Eduardo. "No," he said, the deep darkness of his left eye flashing toward Mas. "No, *demasiado viejo*."

Mas waited a minute, letting the words sink into his gut. Old. Yeah, he was. He pushed back his cap, arched his spine against his slippery, worn upholstery, and chuckled. Sixty-nine, but I can still beat your *oshiri*, you little sonafugun, Mas said to himself. I've probably mowed enough lawns to circle the entire world, maybe even two times, he thought. The kid was brazen, but Mas had to admire some of that; after all, hadn't the boys back in Hiroshima call Mas mini-dynamite, an explosion packed in a five-foot-two-inch body.

Eduardo, on the other hand, wasn't taking it well at

all. His eyebrows seemed matted together like tangled fish netting as he chastised the boy for his impudence. All Mas could make out for sure was the boy's name, Raul.

"Okay, okay, Eduardo. Tell him go in truck. Fifty dolla."

"Sorry, Mista Arai. His mother—my sista—no good. Don't live him right."

"Hell, I know I'm old. But no heart attack. *Corazón* good."

Eduardo's bushy eyebrows turned up. "Not you," he said, "the car. He say your car old, too old. He ride in a new Dodge van yesterday. Power windows, everything."

What the hell. Mas spat out his cigarette onto the cracked cement and felt the steam rise to his fatty ears. He shoved the door open, almost hitting Eduardo's back. He stood face-to-chest next to the young boy. "Listen, you, *Escucheme*. This truck old—damn yes—but insides better than any Dodge van, you hear me?"

Mas walked over to the truck's bent hood, which reached his chin, banged it three times on the left side, and screeched it open. "See this engine? Rebuilt it. Come here. Look," Mas ordered. The boy's square shoulders were slightly stooped. He dutifully walked over to the truck's open mouth and hung his long head toward the oily black engine.

After Mas rattled off the parts that he had worked

on during the past thirty years, he slammed the hood shut and climbed back into the truck. "Mista Arai," Eduardo called out, but Mas merely muttered something under his breath and turned the key to the ignition. The motor rattled apologetically until it fired up into a roar with Mas's right foot.

The men on the curb looked up curiously, the smoke from their cigarettes curling in waves. Raul had returned to the group; he leaned against the building and stroked his chin with his one long fingernail.

I'll do the work myself, thought Mas, glancing back at the men in his rearview mirror. He narrowed his eyes and focused on a face—a long, hooked nose—and then it disappeared amid the brown faces. The blast of a horn startled Mas. How had he wandered into the middle of the road? He hit the accelerator, passing the graffiti-covered taco stand. His hands, slick and wet, slid around the skinny steering wheel, and as he changed gears, he heard metal scraping against metal. He remembered the words of his wife, Chizuko: "No need to lose your head over *nandemonai mono*. Your father, your brother, all die of stroke, lung cancer. Smoking no good, too, Masao-*san*."

"Outlived you, didn't I, old woman," he muttered, and took another drag on his Marlboro. He kept driving on and on, and before he knew it, he was nowhere close to his customers—one an East Indian couple who had a shar-pei dog that always pressed its pitiful wrinkled face against the window when Mas trimmed the hedges. Another customer was a doctor, a young one, who sometimes came home in the middle of the day, wearing green scrubs and paper-covered tennis shoes. And last of all, there were the broken branches. The dog, the doctor, and the broken branches would have to wait, because today Mas was going to North Hollywood.

✣ ✣ ✣

Mas didn't know North Hollywood well—but then again, who did? It was just a blip in the smog, a short sprawl somewhere near another blip, Van Nuys. Beyond the haze you could see the outline of the Hollywood Hills and the white blocky Hollywood sign that always turned out better-looking on postcards than in real life.

Mini-malls on every other corner, old-fashioned gas stations, and looming apartment buildings. No wonder he didn't have any customers around here—no lawns.

One place in North Hollywood Mas did know about was Keiko's Ramen House. She advertised on the local UHF television station that broadcast Japanese programming on Sunday nights. In the commercial, Keiko looked like one of those dish-washing brushes—skinny body, with short, spiky hair that could probably clean out any filthy glass. She wore a yellow apron with a drawing of a hot steaming bowl of noodles. "Please come," she said in a cute, high-pitched voice, bowing outside her establishment. The address then flashed below her in video letters and numbers. Mas couldn't remember it exactly but knew that it was somewhere on Sepulveda.

After almost forty minutes of driving back and forth, Mas spotted it. Shaped like a giant shoe box, the restaurant had a small, unassuming sign. But the neon letters displayed in the window cinched it: RAMEN.

Mas parked his truck and went inside. It was three o'clock—too late for the lunch crowd, too early for dinner. Aside from a *hakujin* boy, sweat pouring down his shaven head as he slurped down noodles, the place was empty. A bookcase by the door was filled with fat Japanese comic books and women's magazines. Day-old newspapers were neatly folded on the bottom shelf.

Mas immediately looked for the spiked head of Keiko but saw only a Latino man in a paper hat behind the counter.

"Hai, irasshaimase," the cook said.

Mas narrowed his eyes and sat down at the counter. Maybe coming here was not a good idea after all. A laminated menu was in front of him, between a bottle of black soy sauce and a cylinder of red pepper. He didn't even bother to look at the choices, and ordered a bowl of miso ramen, as basic as a ham-and-cheese sandwich.

Mas hated to eat out, especially now. He didn't like to talk to strangers. He didn't like to look at a long list of food items with foreign, fancy names. He didn't like multiple pieces of silverware, two forks, two spoons. All you needed were a pair of chopsticks and a pair of hands to wrap around a hamburger or a *carne asada* taco.

When Mari was growing up, they went to only one restaurant: Entoro in Little Tokyo. Entoro was also known as Far East Café, a chop suey house, the old kind before the new Chinese came to town. There, you got greasy *homyu*, looking like day-old Cream of Wheat in a tiny bowl; almond duck, slippery, fat, and buttery, with a crunch of fried skin and nuts; and real sweet and sour pork, bright, stinking orange like the best high-grade motor oil. Everyone went to Entoro, crowded around tables separated by wooden dividers like a giant maze of horse stalls. The upstairs area was open and reserved for special occasions. Someone married, go to Far East. Someone dead, go to Far East. It was simple and predictable. Same set of waiters, who doubled as the cooks, who happened to own the joint. And the menu—who bothered to even look? Mas wasn't even sure they had menus, but he seemed to remember a bewildered *hakujin* family, probably visiting from out of state, looking lost while they perused some kind of stained sheet of paper in front of them.

Far East Café closed right after the Northridge earthquake. Later, Mas heard that one of the waiters/cooks/owners had passed on. No sense in going out anymore, Mas figured. But now, against his better judgment, he was here, in Keiko's Ramen House, in the middle of North Hollywood.

The boy with the shaven head had left, leaving only murky broth at the bottom of the bowl. Mas felt strange here alone with the mustached cook, who was tossing tangled noodles into the vat of boiling water. What was he doing here? How could he expect to find someone he hadn't seen for thirty years?

It was that *meishi*, with its sharp, clean edges, fancy printing, and Hiroshima connection, that nagged at Mas. Why was this straight-from-Japan fellow looking for Joji Haneda? It meant trouble, a kind of trouble that Mas knew would touch him, too. His only hope was that the man everyone here knew as Haneda kept running, and stayed the hell away from L.A.

The miso ramen, looking as limp as the sweaty chef, was surprisingly tasty. It certainly beat those instant ones that Haruo insisted on buying at his local grocery store.

As soon as he slurped up the last bit of soup, he smelled something sweet behind him. It was Keiko, the Ramen Lady on the television commercial. The points on her spiked hair glowed bright yellow.

"How was it?" she asked. Her voice was low and husky like a middle-aged barmaid. It didn't match the high-pitched one on the television commercial, and for a moment Mas was too stunned to know what to say.

Keiko then switched over to Japanese. "How did you find it?" she repeated.

"*Oishii.* Very good," Mas answered.

"First time?"

Mas nodded.

"How did you hear about us? *Terebi?*"

Mas nodded again. "Saw your commercial."

Keiko smiled, obviously pleased with her public presence. "My voice too low, too sexy, they told me. Used a twenty-year-old who was working at the station on her summer break. Nice to be young, *ne.*"

Mas didn't dare to say anything more. He wasn't used to snooping around, especially out here in the San Fernando Valley. This wasn't his part of town, and it knew it. Mas was waiting to be tossed out, rejected like those broken branches he tended at one of his longtime customers'. They called it grafting, an attempt to attach something strange and new to an established tree. It usually didn't work, either with plants or with people.

"You don't live around here," Keiko said before Mas could get away.

Mas shook his head and took out his wallet.

"What, you have some friends out here?"

Mas was thankful that his face was already sweaty and red from the hot noodles. She wasn't going to give up, so Mas gave her what she wanted. "Yah, friend."

"Oh, really? Well, tell him to come try."

Mas grunted.

"Maybe I know him. What's his name?"

Mas stared into Keiko's eyes. What the heck? he thought. What did he have to lose? "Haneda," he said finally. "Joji Haneda."

"Haneda-*san*? Junko-*san*'s friend? They were coming here almost every day last week. Told Junko she should try cooking herself once in a while."

Mas's chest lurched. So it was fate after all that he was in this sweaty ramen house in the middle of North Hollywood. He had come this far. No sense in backing off. "Yah, Junko," he said. "You don't know where she lives, do you?"

Keiko's eyes flashed for one second. "Just a minute," she said, disappearing into the back kitchen.

Now I've done it, thought Mas. I'm not cut out to do this kind of sneaking around. He picked up the check and placed a crumpled five-dollar bill and a couple of ones on the plastic plate. She's probably on the phone now, warning this Junko about a dirty old *ojiichan* at the ramen house.

He pulled open the door, and almost walked smack

into another Japanese woman, who was maybe around Mari's age. Her eyes sloped downward like two tadpoles; her left one curved more than the right. At the bottom of the left one was a black birthmark, looking like one of those tattooed teardrops on some of the boys Mas picked up as day laborers. Only this mark was natural, not branded.

"Excuse," mumbled Mas.

The woman flared her nostrils in irritation. She was one of those who hated old men, Mas figured.

"Wait," Keiko called out. "She let me borrow this. Her address is here." She waved a shiny magazine titled *Cosmopolitan* and pointed to a mailing label. Mas walked over, and sure enough it had a name, Junko Kakita, and a North Hollywood address.

Mas tried to make out the numbers and letters without his drugstore reading glasses, which he'd left in the truck. "Sank you, *ne,*" he said, reciting the address in his head.

The tadpole-eyed woman stood close behind them. "Oh, Rumi-*chan.*" Keiko finally became aware of the woman's presence. "This man is looking for Joji-*san,* Junko's friend."

The young woman froze, aside from her left eye, which began to twitch. Mas was close enough to also see that her hands were trembling.

Keiko didn't seem to notice. "Tell Haneda-*san* that

I hope he's feeling better," she said to Mas. "And come again."

✣ ✣ ✣

Mas went back to the truck and pulled out his Thomas guide, which was under some rope behind the seat. It was 1987, published before the Century Freeway, but good enough for North Hollywood. He pulled his glasses out of the glove compartment, flipped through the pages, and found the street. It was a small one, and dead-ended before it could get anywhere.

Driving over to Junko Kakita's, he saw more of the same, plain apartments that looked like mini-motels. He finally spotted the address, a two-story unit with a line of doors and windows. Must be a Japanese owner, thought Mas, looking at the shaped juniper trees, or at least a Japanese gardener.

"Numba D," Mas muttered to himself. He looked at the line of metal mailboxes. There were only eight; the fourth one over bore the name KAKITA.

It was on the second floor. A couple of rolled-up advertisements were hanging from the screen door. Heavy curtains were drawn. Mas tried to peek through the window but heard a male voice behind him. "She's not there."

A Latino man in his fifties and about Mas's height stood against the second-floor railing. "She left a couple of days ago."

Again, Mas didn't know what to say. The whole thing looked suspicious, he was the first to admit. If he had caught a dried-up old Japanese man looking through his customer's windows, he would have kicked him out, right on the spot.

"You the one who going to take care of her plants, right?" the man, probably the manager, said.

Before Mas could respond, the manager was opening the door and leading him inside. The living room was dark, aside from light coming through the open door and the edge of the drapes.

The manager walked over to rows of at least twelve bonsai plants arranged on wooden planks over cinder blocks by the window. "Why she make such a fuss over those little plants?" he said. "Last time she accuse me of killing two of them. Said she was going to take fifty dollars out of her rent. I told her, 'Next time, find someone else.' "

Mas stuck his finger into the soil of one of the planters. Pretty dry. As he walked over the kitchen, he made a mental note of everything on the counter, table, and floor. Roll of aluminum foil, rice cooker pot soaking in the sink, stack of newspapers in the corner, with, yes, crib notes from Hollywood Park racetrack on the top. He filled an empty water jug with lukewarm water and proceeded to water the plants. There were juniper, pine, even a miniature maple. To look further authentic, Mas got out his pruner, which was dangling from his belt, and clipped some wayward leaves.

The manager soon got bored waiting for Mas and went outside for maybe a smoke or who knows what. This was Mas's only chance. He quietly crept down the hall. As he passed by the yellow tile bathroom, a smell hit his nostrils. Menthol, strong enough to burn the insides of your lungs. Mas knew that smell well. Salon Pas—thin pads that old gardeners like him stuck to sore backs and battered knees. Would a woman named Junko use those for her achy joints?

Her bedroom was a typical woman's, with a pink bedspread, even stuffed animals tucked in by the pillows. Simple dresser with a jewelry box, heart-shaped. But next to the box was a black plastic Casio watch. Strange, thought Mas. This woman, judging from her taste in furnishings and miniature plants, wasn't the type to wear a cheap man's watch that you could buy at the local drugstore for $9.99.

He returned to the hallway, where a series of photos were displayed on the wall. Many were of a middle-aged woman with long hair and a rubbery face with too much makeup. In most of them, she was posed with other women—Mas recognized one of them as the tadpole-eyed girl he had run into at the ramen shop today. Another photo had a lot of girls and men in suits, holding beers and smiling like at a New Year's party.

The last one on the end was different. It wasn't in a

frame, just taped onto the wall. The woman was wearing a visor, sitting in front of a slot machine, with an old man. Mas tried to make out the man's face. Japanese, with age spots. Hooked nose. Damn, there was no mistake. The resurrected Joji Haneda.

The blood seemed to drain out of Mas's fingertips, and his hands felt cold and clammy. Before Mas could figure out his next step, the screen door banged open and shut.

Mas adjusted his eyes to the brightness emanating from the doorway. It was a woman dressed in all black, with a pair of huge sunglasses crowding her round face. She dropped her black duffel bag onto the floor. "You're Joji's friend, *desho,*" she stated more than asked. "I had heard that you'd be coming."

CHAPTER THREE

Mas thought that the ramen lady had talked, but he soon figured out that something else was going on.

The mistress went into her bedroom, closed the door, and then came out with a long white envelope. She plopped it down on the kitchen table and perched her sunglasses on top of her head.

She was not a pretty woman. Her skin was blotchy and covered with blemishes. Her large eyes—her best feature—were ringed with dark makeup. Her hair looked like the mane of an *obake,* a ghost in those Japanese fairy tales. She was about fifty, trying to look like twenty-five.

"There," she said with a slight accent. "You check it."

Mas remained silent and picked up the envelope. Sure enough, a stack of twenty-dollar bills—must have been at least fifty of them. And some sort of receipt, folded in half.

"You lucky to get that," she said. "The bastard."

Mas pulled out the piece of paper, then pressed the envelope closed. He thought the woman was cursing him, but soon figured out she was talking about Joji Haneda.

"He owe me at least that much. Probably more." She went over to her bonsai and stuck her finger in the soil as if she were measuring the temperature. "Was going to take that money. But then, I don't need Joji's trouble. You know what I mean?"

Mas nodded. He knew well what trouble Haneda could cause. But was that the same kind of trouble the woman was talking about?

The mistress returned to the kitchen and opened her refrigerator. Smelling packages of wrapped raw chicken and white boxes of Chinese food, she hurled some food into the garbage can before pulling out a long, rectangular bottle of yam wine.

Mas was confused, but somehow he fit into the confusion. He unfolded the receipt from the envelope. On the blank side was a map written with a crude hand. There was a square for a building and then a Los Angeles address on Second Street. Mas checked the intersection. Little Tokyo, blocks away from the chop suey house he once frequented.

Mas stuffed the strange map deep into his jeans pocket and returned the envelope to the kitchen table. The mistress sat down and poured the clear liquid into two cups filled with ice. *"Shochu,"* she said. "From my hometown."

Mas declined. He didn't like drinking that stuff. It gave him a mean headache, and he needed to think clearly right now.

The woman took a long sip of the yam wine and pulled the sunglasses off her head. "So, how do you know Joji? From his Little Tokyo days?"

Mas nodded.

"You better be careful. He's not right in the head right now." The ice in the woman's glass clinked as she finished off her drink. She then started on the other one.

"Whatcha mean?"

"He left me in Las Vegas. Right there in the casino. Said he had to go to the toilet. Then never came back."

"Didn't say anytin'?"

"Well." The woman circled the rim of the glass with her finger. "We did get into a fight."

"You fight?"

"You know, at first it was all fun, exciting. We go to Las Vegas or Laughlin, and he would keep going and going—craps, blackjack, whatever. I'd keep stacking those chips up, higher and higher. 'Keep on, keep on,' I tell him. Trade them in for hundred-dollar chips, two hundred dollars. Can you believe one piece of wood could be worth five hundred dollars?" The woman finished the second drink and waited for Mas to pour her another. "When we went to the strip, the hundred-dollar tables, the people didn't take us serious. Thought we were just *nandemonai mono*, trash. But Joji-*san* would take out those bills, and they all changed their minds."

The woman cupped the glass as if it were a wounded bird. "But he kept going. Like he couldn't stop. Like if he stopped, something terrible would happen. That night I told him to stop. Take a rest. It wasn't fun anymore."

Mas licked his lips. They were dry again, and he suppressed the urge to drink some of the wine.

"I thought the whole point of him coming to Los Angeles was to spend more time with me. But I could tell that it was for something else. 'What, Joji?' I'd ask him."

The mistress emptied her glass while Mas traced his finger around a dark spot, probably spilt soy sauce, on the tablecloth. "I know what people were saying about us, about me. That I was only with him to get a green card. But it wasn't like that. Really. We were close, like brother and sister. I knew things about him that you all could never even imagine."

Mas felt a coldness on the back of his neck.

The mistress must have sensed his reaction, because she turned away abruptly. "You just like the rest of them. You believe what you want to believe."

Mas stayed silent for a good minute. "So when youzu gonna see Joji again?" he finally asked.

"Who knows? Who cares?" The mistress poured more yam wine into her glass. "I'm going back to Japan, you know."

"Oh, yah?" Mas waited, but the woman's long eyelashes, coated with black flakes, began to flutter. Mas knew that within ten minutes, the mistress, Junko Kakita, would be fast asleep beside her empty bottle. There wasn't too much more Mas could get from her right now. She wasn't letting on, but Mas knew she had the key to why Joji Haneda was in Los Angeles County. He excused himself and left the apartment, the map still in his pocket.

Mas sat in his truck for a while before leaving North Hollywood. What was Haneda into now? Drugs? It would be nothing new. Mas remembered Haneda happily supplying young *chinpira*—wannabe gangsters—with syringes of heroin and homemade alcohol made from car gasoline. But that was back then, when war orphans had little choice for survival. Whoever heard of a seventy-year-old drug dealer, anyhow? Haneda had the nursery, pretty successful, at least from all accounts at the lawn mower shop. To risk it all for more money didn't make sense.

Mas wiped away some sweat from his forehead when he saw a figure crossing the street. Skinny, wizened, almost bent over, and wearing a baseball cap.

"Haruo," Mas called out from the open window.

The figure turned and then scurried back to the other side. Mas's eyes stung from his sweat. He leapt out of the truck and then ran to the corner. It was all quiet, aside from a homeless man pushing a grocery cart filled with flattened cardboard boxes. It had been Haruo, hadn't it? Or was Mas just seeing things in the brown haze of North Hollywood?

"Gotta get outta here," muttered Mas to himself. He needed to get where he belonged—back to San Gabriel Valley and his customers.

✣ ✣ ✣

In L.A., there were two kinds of customers. One was the short-term ones, who basically wanted a "mow and blow," a clip of side hedges, and an occasional spray of insecticide. They were usually young or on the move and jumped from one house to another. You couldn't count on these people, but work was work. Mas looked at them like extra change you find in the corners of your pocket.

The other kind of customer was the lifer, the one you actually tried to hang on to. They gave hundred-dollar Christmas bonuses, plus maybe a box of See's chocolate candy or a small trinket for Mari. They had large estates in shady neighborhoods of oak trees and ARMED RESPONSE signs. Get a couple of customers like these, and you know that you've finally made it.

At the height of Mas's career, he had a half a dozen of these customers. Hollywood doctors, actors, big businessmen. But now there was only one. Mrs. Witt. When Mas first worked at the San Marino estate, there were two Witts, the missus and the mister, a tight end for the old Rams football team. As the mister's sports career began to fizzle out, his sex life grew, and he eventually left the missus for a *Playboy* centerfold. That was when Mrs. Witt became obsessed with her grove of fruit trees in the back of the house.

With a saw and a knife the size of an apple slicer, she attacked each tree, cutting off branches and creating monstrous tree figures that looked like mutilated fingers. Mas was afraid. Who knew what a rejected middle-aged *hakujin* woman would do next? But then he noticed that she was attempting to do some amateur grafting. With Mas's help, she attached different kinds of branches to the stumps, mixing a lemon with a tangerine, an American persimmon with a Japanese variety. Wrapping each wound with wax, string, or tape, Mas and Mrs. Witt became medics in the orchard recovery unit.

Not all of the grafts were successful. Sometimes a stump would reject a branch, and Mas would find a broken branch lying forlornly on the ground. This upset Mrs. Witt to no end. She would curse and sometimes even scream, muttering the name of her ex-husband.

Mr. Witt had been an immense man who almost filled the entire doorway of his San Marino home. His sandy-colored hair was almost the same shade of his skin, a bland background for his round, sunken eyes the color of blue slate.

Most of his customers mailed their checks in, but Mr. Witt had insisted that Mas come to the door on the last Friday of the month. Mas often felt like Mari's dog, Brownie, waiting for leftovers from their grilled teriyaki steak dinner.

One day Mr. Witt handed Mas the usual cream-colored check and an additional treat, two tickets imprinted with the blue-and-yellow swirl of the Rams.

"Sank you." Mas's fingerprints left green stains on the tickets. He preferred UCLA basketball on television, but it wouldn't be bad to go to a Rams football game once in his life.

"Wait a minute," Mr. Witt said, disappearing from the doorway for a moment. "You have a son, right?"

"No, girl. Mari."

"Well, she may like these anyway." Mr. Witt brought out three black-and-white photos of himself in uniform. There was a posed shot of him, knee down on the field, helmet at his feet. In a candid shot, he was snarling as he blocked a defensive guard. Finally, a full head shot, his sandy hair teased up and eyes shining like marbles.

Mr. Witt unfastened the top of a permanent ink marker with his teeth and scrawled on each photo: "To Mary, Good Luck and Good Playing, Bob Witt."

Chizuko wasn't sure if they should let Mari go to

the game: After all, she would be missing Japanese school, held every Saturday in a bare two-story building next to a nursery.

Mari herself didn't seem that excited. It was night, and she was wearing her headgear, apparently one of the last stages of her orthodontic work. A hideous contraption, the headgear had hooks and bands that tightened around her skull and stretched down to her metal braces. She pulled her long hair out from underneath the bands into rectangular sections, hanging spongy curlers from the loose strands.

Even when Mari remained unresponsive, Mas insisted. "Mr. Witt give to me. An insult if we no use."

"Get one of your friends. How about Haruo?" Chizuko said, cutting out an article on high school SAT scores in the *Los Angeles Times*.

"No. Mari."

"But she has perfect attendance so far."

Mari clipped the last curler in place. "Who cares, Mom? It's not like real school."

On the day of the game, Mas bought everything. He purchased the three-dollar color program, Rams banners, hot dogs—cotton candy, even.

Mari didn't seem that interested in the game. She instead kept adjusting her hair, which rippled in lines where her headgear was positioned at night.

Mas tried to get excited about the game. But the plastic seats seemed too hard, the sun too bright, and the men in front of him drank too much. They yelled and hooted at the cheerleaders, analyzing the merits of each one. The Rams weren't doing so well, either; balls were intercepted or else thrown out of bounds, hitting the green field beyond the chalk lines.

It had been easier to be with Mari when she was younger, around five or six. When Mas brought home an old Cinderella book that he'd found in a customer's trash can, her face brightened. She ran into her bedroom, reciting the story of the two evil stepsisters and the mice that helped the poor servant girl.

At Christmastime, she waited for Mas to come home with cheap gifts wrapped in red-and-white paper, gifts of fruitcake and chocolate-covered almonds from his customers. She didn't care that inside was just junk; she still arranged the presents under the flocked Christmas tree as if they were treasures of real gold and silver.

But as she grew, her breasts peaked, her *mensu* started, and she became more and more distant, a stranger with secrets behind her bedroom door.

They left the game early. As they turned back onto McNally Street, Mas parked the Datsun in the driveway, behind the Ford truck.

"Oh, wait a minute," he said, going into the garage. "Here, he gave you this." The three black-and-white photos with the personalized message.

"He spelled my name wrong. And he wasn't even very good." Mari frowned, flattening a bump in her hair. She left the photos on the car seat. Eventually

Chizuko found them on the floor, underneath the car mat, and stored them in a box with other old photos that they knew they had, but never saw.

✣ ✣ ✣

There were no photos of Mr. Witt in his former house now. Mas stood in the hall and smelled something that made his nose itch, probably some perfume from an aerosol can.

"Mas, I'm glad you made it." Mrs. Witt placed her hand on her hip. Her arms were freckled and leathery like old snakeskin. "I have something to discuss with you."

"Dis so?" Mas pulled back his Dodgers cap. He had a feeling that he wouldn't like what Mrs. Witt had to tell him.

"Well, first of all, I wanted to discuss the trees, the ones we grafted last spring." Mrs. Witt's reading glasses hung from her neck.

"The broken branches."

"Yes. Well, Mas, it's a disaster. I think it may be the combination. I don't know."

Mas followed Mrs. Witt into the grove in the back of the house. The trees, spaced out about three feet away from one another, stood like thin, emaciated bodies. Branches lay on the ground like amputated limbs. Only one tree seemed not to have rejected the grafted branches.

"It's a damn killing field," said Mrs. Witt. "I haven't had time to do anything with them."

Mas examined the bandages of the branches still connected to the root stock. "You've been cutting regular?" He pointed to the buds growing below the grafting tape.

"Like I said, I haven't had the time."

Mas took out a pair of clippers from his belt and cut off the invading buds.

Mrs. Witt played with the tips of her glasses. "Actually, Mas." Her voice grew higher, the rhythm faster. "I wanted to talk to you—"

Mas looked up from a grafted branch. Mrs. Witt looked paler than usual. She took a deep breath, as if she were entering an ice-cold pond. "I wanted to tell you—oh, I guess I just need to spit it out. I'm going to sell the house, Mas. I wasn't quite sure until a few days ago."

Mas blinked, hard. "What, you move?"

Mrs. Witt nodded. "I'm going to move into a condo in Colorado Springs. My daughter lives there. I don't get to see the grandchildren enough. So my real estate agent insists on digging up this grove and putting in Bermuda grass. I know that it's a job for many people. But can you come over next week, survey, then maybe we can come up with some ideas?"

Mas's hand slipped away from a grafted branch.

"Well, of course I'll recommend you to the new owners, whoever they are," added Mrs. Witt. "I mean, they may have their own gardener they like to work with, so I can't make any promises. And, of course, there's Mexicans who do mow and blow at any price. It'll just depend."

Mas returned his clippers to the leather case on his belt.

"I just need to get out of here, Mas. Make a new start. There's just so much of him, everywhere. I mean, I love this house. But then, all it is, is a house. It can't give me my grandchildren. You know how it is, Mas." Mrs. Witt leaned against the trunk of the only healthy tree. "How's your daughter, by the way? What was her name—Mary, was it?"

"Ma-ri," Mas said clearly. "And she fine."

✣ ✣ ✣

Mas spent the rest of the afternoon collecting the rejected branches. He threw them down in a large pile on top of a tarp in his truck. As he stared at the broken branches jutting out in all different directions like severed arms and legs, he felt sick to his stomach. Must be the heat, he thought. Maybe I am getting too old for all of this.

The thing about gardening was that you had plenty of time to think. Mas figured that's why so many gardeners turned out to be gamblers, philosophers, or just plain crazy. The younger ones who dropped out said that the work was just too darn hard on their bodies, but Mas knew better. They didn't know how to fill their heads.

Today Mas felt numb, as if someone had banged him good. Nothing seemed to go right, like a gear had jumped to the wrong place. He tried not to think about the income lost if the new owners decided not to keep him on. Extra cash in the empty coffee can that he kept on the bottom of the closet was getting low; he would have to hit it big at the track just to come out even this year.

As he loaded his equipment back in the truck, his thoughts returned to Haneda. Why was he blowing his money like some big-shot gambler? Mas hoped that he had stayed in Las Vegas, but he knew Vegas was only a place where vultures landed for a few days before coming back home.

✣ ✣ ✣

As Mas turned onto his street, he saw a black, shiny Lincoln Continental parked alongside the curb. A few neighbors had the same car, but theirs were twenty years older, with a generous share of dents and scratches. This one looked all wrong in front of his house, and when Mas walked up to his porch, he found his hunch was on target. Standing by the door was a man wearing large, gold-rimmed glasses and a turtleneck sweater. Shuji Nakane.

The high-tone fellow didn't waste any time. "You lied to me," he said straightaway. Mas felt the anger flush up to his earlobes. What no-good Japanese man would call a stranger a liar in front of the stranger's own house? He could push this Nakane off the porch into a long-abandoned rock garden filled now with broken glass and gravel.

"You told me that you weren't friends with Haneda-*san*," Nakane said.

"I have no business with you." Mas made it a point to speak English. He didn't want Nakane to get the wrong idea that they shared anything in common. He tore open the screen door, which flapped off its hinges. Mas had meant to fix that someday.

As Mas fumbled with his keys, Nakane was unrelenting. "In fact, you knew him very well. Like brothers." He pushed a photo in front of Mas's nose.

It was an old-fashioned black-and-white photograph, about wallet size. At first Mas made no connection to the image, but then he began to focus more carefully. It was a stone bridge, the kind that you often saw in Hiroshima before the war. This one had been near the train station, Mas remembered. Three boys in black school uniforms stood on different spots on the bridge.

"That's you." Nakane's manicured finger pointed to the boy in between the other two, taller and lean. Those other two, in fact, resembled each other. Lookalikes with strong noses. But one was born in California, like Mas, while the other was a native Hiroshima boy.

"Where you get dis?"

"That is not your concern."

"Well, then, I have no concern." Mas finally opened his front door and attempted to close it behind him, when the screen door fell down, almost knocking Nakane's glasses off his face.

"We can give you money for information," hissed Nakane, stepping over the torn screen.

Mas kept the door open a crack. "Whozu we?"

"My associates and I. We are prepared to make you a generous offer."

"You be wastin' money. I have no information."

"You were with him, weren't you? When the *pikadon* fell. What happened to him? Where is he now?"

"I don't know no Joji Haneda. Don't come round here anymore, Nakane-*san*. There's nutin' I can help you with." His chest pounding, Mas slammed the door shut. He waited to hear the hum of an engine and pulled back the curtains an inch to see the Lincoln Continental drive away. After a good five minutes, Mas took a deep breath and went back outside.

✣ ✣ ✣

When Mas felt trouble coming, he usually closed his eyes a few seconds in hopes that it would pass him by. He had done so when the doctor, almost all green in his surgical scrubs, had told him that Chizuko had stomach cancer, stage four. Mas had blinked hard, yet the green doctor was still in front of him, and the tumor still in his wife.

This other trouble was more familiar. It chased him through the corridors of his life, turned when he turned, flew over ocean and land. Mas, in fact, had gotten used to it, like a pebble in his work boot. Soon the sole of his foot would get so callused and blistered that he couldn't feel a thing.

Mas made it to the dead-end street faster than he had earlier in the day. An Impala with its bumper detached was parked in front of the apartment. Mas eased the truck right behind it and jumped out, not even bothering to check the door.

The mistress's apartment was dark, but a window was open and the drapes were pulled back. Mas pressed his face against the window screen. The duffel bag had been moved from the living room floor.

"Kakita-*san*," he called out. "Kakita." No answer. Mas could only hear muffled sounds of a television and a clatter of pots and pans from a neighboring apartment. Damn woman. Sleeping off the power of the yam wine, he figured. He pounded on the door. "Missu Kakita."

There was the click-clack of high heels below on the concrete. Who was that passing by the foot of the stairs? A woman with long, dark hair? "Hallo . . ." Mas called out.

The woman disappeared. Mas rushed down the

concrete steps and out to the street. A child wailed from one of the open windows, and the smell of onions and spices soaked the air. This was one no-good place, thought Mas. Faceless people coming and going. The sidewalk was still, too still. Mas's body pulsed, down to even the tips of his fingers.

Then he heard it. It shrieked at first, as high-pitched as an air raid siren. Then a rumble like a summer thunderstorm. He knew the familiar music, a morning ritual. It was the song of his Ford Custom Car truck, now hurtling from its resting place in the hands of a stranger.

In the darkness, Mas struggled to see the driver, but everything was happening too fast. He grabbed hold of the truck's bed, as Mari had done years ago, and ran forward, desperately trying to keep it from leaving. His gnarled hands grasped for anything, the rakes with missing teeth, the loops of garden hoses, the Trimmer lawn mower, which was being tossed about with the stacks of broken branches. The truck squealed and squeaked before gaining speed and tearing up the road. Yell, he thought, yell. But all that came out was spit and air and wheezing. The ends of the rake were cutting into his palms, and the edge of a blower pressing into his forehead. *Sonafugun, you not going to leave. You not leaving.* But as the truck turned, Mas tripped into a pothole and felt a burning in his back. His face smacked against the concrete. Mas tried to look up. He heard the truck abruptly stop. With the motor still running, the door of the Ford was creaked open, and then footsteps, hard heels of a man's dress shoes. The thief's knees popped as he knelt down. All Mas could see was the tops of his brown leather shoes—a fancy kind with silly-looking tassels. "Keep your mouth shut about Haneda, or next time it'll be more than your beat-up truck." A male voice—but young, old; *hakujin*, Japanese, black, or Mexican, Mas couldn't tell. Then something cracked against the concrete close to Mas's head. The foot-steps returned to the Ford, the door closed, and the engine revved one last time before the truck left the street. Mas struggled to turn his head, but saw only a broken branch with a piece of gauze bandage hanging from one end.

CHAPTER FOUR

"You needsu to see docta, real docta, Mas."

Mas glanced up at Haruo, who stood by the sheetless bed. Haruo's hair, which covered the left side of his face, looked freshly washed and dried, even electrified, by the dry summer heat. Next to him was Stinky Yoshimoto, listening attentively. Why he was here, Mas had no idea. Stinky's mouth was half-open, making him look like an eel awaiting its prey.

"Acupuncture enough, *yo,*" Mas replied. He lay on the bed, staring at his peeling bedroom ceiling. A gauze bandage was wrapped around his torn hand, while the bruise on his left cheek ached.

"Too bad about the Ford," Haruo said. Mas still couldn't quite believe it. How could he be without the Ford? The theft had done something serious to him. An anger, one he hadn't felt in years, burned in his gut.

"*Sugokatta, ne,* Mas," Haruo continued. "You lucky. You could've caught them and gotten your head blown off like Morishita-*san*."

"Probably young ones, eh, Mas," Stinky said, blinking furiously. "Maybe *kurochans*. Or those Mexicans."

Mas ignored Stinky—he wasn't worth wasting time on.

"Maybe the police will be able to find," said Haruo, the forever optimist.

"Ah." Mas spit into a tissue and tossed it on the floor. "Not counting on them." As it turns out, the police barely spent ten minutes asking their few questions. Name. Year of car. Model and make. Employer. Mas was going to say that he was self-employed, but gave Mrs. Witt's name and her San Marino phone number instead. Never know if her connection would help things along.

They did ask whether Mas saw anything, and he knew that this would be the time to come clean with the threat: "Keep your mouth shut about Haneda. . . ." But then more questions would follow. "How is he connected to all of this?" It was much easier to keep it all inside.

Haruo pulled a strip of hair behind his ear, revealing a bubbled keloid by his sunken cheek. "Whatcha doin' ova in North Hollywood, anyhowsu?"

Pain jolted up Mas's spine, and he turned on his side, grimacing. I should ask you the same question, he thought.

"You there to find Joji Haneda, huh?" Stinky greedily asked, folding his hands together.

Mas clamped down on his dentures. He didn't know who he could trust, even somebody as worthless as Stinky. Haruo didn't say anything either, so Mas knew that he was guilty. Stinky filled the silence with the time he had witnessed a liquor store robbery, the same story they had heard again and again. Every foolish word seemed to aggravate the pain in Mas's back. Finally, he moaned, low but long.

"I tell you, Mas." Haruo bent over the bed, and Mas could see a fringe of his friend's long hair. "You should see those docta, *tada*."

Stinky's interest was piqued. "Free?"

"They only come once . . . every two years," Haruo stammered. "They here . . . this week—you know, the *hibakusha* doctors. Whatcha got to lose? Japan doctors, they good."

Mas felt for his box of cigarettes on the nightstand by his Budweiser. "Those Hiroshima doctas, what do they know?"

"They're *wakai*, Mas, but they're educated."

"Young? Babies. Raised on Kentucky Chicken. They know nutin' about the war, black market—nutin' about it."

"That don't matter. . . . They're not history professors. It's the *karada* that they're interested in. Mas, I've been four times. They found nutin'," Haruo continued. "Strong as a horse, they say. And it's free for everything—blood test, *shikko* test. . . . Go to regular docta, cost you two hundred dolla, I bet."

"Easy," interjected Stinky.

Mas shooed away an especially large fly. "We're just guinea pigs for them. They want to find sometin' wrong, cancer, *gan*, in our eyes, ears, liver, hearts. So they can go back to the big shots and say, 'Look what we found in these atom bomb survivors. Nasty, huh?' "

"This the thing that happens, what, every other summer?" Stinky asked. Haruo nodded.

Every other year in June and July came the doctors, a month before the television reports on the Bomb. It was for an international study on radiation exposure.

What was the big deal? wondered Mas. He had survived Hiroshima and smoked a pack a day since age fifteen, yet still outlasted his wife and many others in their sixties. When you died, you died, and that was all there was to it.

Mas turned to his side and tapped his cigarette ash into the tab of his Budweiser. It was no use arguing with Haruo. He could be like an untiring mosquito, buzzing around one's ears until he sucked up what he wanted.

"*Honto,* Mas, I take you. No problem," Haruo insisted, while Stinky excused himself and went to the bathroom.

Mas waited until Stinky had closed the bathroom door. "Forget the doctas. I don't care about none of that. I saw you, Haruo."

Haruo averted Mas's gaze and began scraping some dirt under his fingernails. "Saw me where?"

"North Hollywood. You were there. The lady's place."

"What lady?"

"Haneda's lady."

"I have nutin' to do with Haneda."

Mas couldn't always tell if someone was telling the truth, but he could smell a lie fifty yards away. Right now the stench was unmistakable. "What does he want?"

Haruo looked back at the closed bathroom door on the other side of the hallway. "I just talk to him on the phone," he finally said.

"He wants sumptin'. I know that guy."

Haruo shook his head. "Just wanna see ole friends. Thatsu all. Even asked about you."

Mas pinched his cigarette stub. "There's nutin' he needsu to know about me."

"I knowsu that. I don't say nutin' about you." Mas heard the bathroom door open, and Stinky, zipping up his pants, reentered the bedroom. Mas wasn't going to keep talking about Haneda, and Haruo seemed to understand. He straightened his hunched back. "Well, Mas, how about the exams? You gonna go with me?"

"Can't go. Got plans."

"You can't work. No condition—"

"Me no work."

"The races, Mas? Just call your bookie."

"Bookie? Who said anytin' about gamble?"

"Mas, whatsa matter? Just go few minutes—"

"Dammit, Haruo, I don't wanna see those sonafugun Hiroshima doctas." Before he realized what he was doing, Mas flung one of his Budweiser cans just a few inches away from the wisps of Haruo's white hair. It ricocheted against the mirror of the dresser, spurting out cigarette ash, and then landed on the floor.

Mas immediately regretted his actions but said nothing. The North Hollywood incident had shaken him more than he cared to admit. The fly began to buzz and circle the room like a small aircraft losing gas. The three of them remained silent for about a minute.

"*Orai*, Mas, have your way." Haruo pushed back his hair. "Tomato in kitchen. Good ones, real red." He walked past the bed, then out of the room, with Stinky following, peppering him with questions.

I don't want your pitiful tomatoes, Mas wanted to yell out. He couldn't stand the puppy dog, his eternal friend. Why didn't Haruo ever fight back, tell him where to go? Mas wondered. Be a man, a real man, for once.

Mas lay back on the mattress and finished off the stub of his Marlboro. He should have asked Haruo to help him put the sheets on the bed. The buttons on the mattress were dark and soiled from sweat and dirt. Flies whizzed into the room from the broken window screen and landed on Chizuko's old jewelry box.

"Sonafugun flies," murmured Mas, who could only follow them with his eyes. After a few hours, the flies just buzzed in the corner of the ceiling. They were just plain worn out and afraid to move.

❖ ❖ ❖

When the phone rang, the room was shadowy and dark. Mas flung his arm, knocking his beer can and television remote control from the nightstand.

"Hallo," Mas mumbled.

"Yeh, Mas, it's Tug. Tug Yamada. Hope I didn't wake you."

"Oh, hallo, how are you." Mas pictured the tall, sturdy Japanese American man who entered a room like a tugboat fighting a storm. Tug's real name was Takashi, but like other Nisei, the second-generation Japanese Americans, he had to have a more "American" moniker worthy of veterans and Sunday golfers. Mas always hated to call a grown man Tiger, Wimp, or Fats, but what could he do? A Nisei was a Nisei, and there was no changing them.

"I heard what happened to you. I can't believe how bad things are today. To have your truck stolen right underneath your nose." Tug's voice boomed over the line.

"Yah," Mas said.

"Well, Lil made a tamale pie, and we want to drop it off. You just sit tight; we'll be there in fifteen minutes." The line clicked, and Tug Yamada was gone.

Mas groaned and slowly pushed himself up. Tug's wife, Lil, and Chizuko had met years ago, when their daughters were in the same preschool class. The Yamadas were Mas and Chizuko's first full-blooded American friends. Tug had fought in the U.S. Army over in France—even had a missing half a forefinger to show for it.

That shortened finger both terrified and entranced Mas; he tried time after time to avoid looking at the severed appendage, but his eyes were inevitably lured to it. It was a mark of citizenship, reminding him that while Tug was a red, white, and blue American, Mas was only a bloody *Kibei* born in Watsonville who had spent most of his early years across the Pacific in Japan.

Mas eased himself to his feet and stared at the image in the dresser mirror. Large bags drooped from his black, beady eyes, and his long, outgrown hair stood up like a rooster's crown. His cheek looked bad, like someone had tried to hull out a piece of flesh with a spoon. He groaned again, not for himself but for his duty to be presentable, a curse he learned from the always proper Chizuko.

After changing his T-shirt and jeans, Mas surveyed the living room. His fishing gear lay sprawled on the scratched coffee table, and stacks of junk mail and unopened bills littered the floor. Mas swept everything together and threw the mess into the hall closet. Better, almost, thought Mas. He went to the midnight-black piano and wiped the edge of his T-shirt over the layer of dust. Framed photos of Mari—as a baby in a pink pinafore, as a high school graduate wearing a lopsided mortarboard—stared back at Mas. But there were no others after that. Mas had picked up a kindergarten photo, when he heard a knock at the door.

"Your screen door's broken and doorbell's stuck, Mas." Tug's thick hands were wrapped around a casserole dish covered in aluminum foil. He plowed into the house, leaving the dish on the kitchen counter, while Lil followed ten steps back.

"My gosh, Tug, you're acting like you live here," Lil said from the porch.

"Come in, come in." Mas held the door for the slight woman in the flowered dress. Her dark eyes were enlarged through her slightly tinted bifocals.

"Got a screwdriver?" Tug had returned after circling the living room.

Before Mas could answer, Tug was out the door. "It's okay. Got one in the glove compartment," he called from the porch.

"He's been like this ever since he retired." Lil sat down on the brown couch. "I don't know what to do with him, frankly," she added, laughing.

"What you want, Seven-Up, Coke?" Mas stiffly stood by his black easy chair.

"Oh, no, Mas, just finished with dinner. We were so worried. What kind of world are we living in?"

More evil than you can imagine, Mas thought to himself.

"Was it just one person?"

Mas nodded. "A man, datsu all I knowsu."

"You see his face?"

Mas shook his head. "His shoes. Saw his shoes. Looks like the kind O.J. wore."

"The fancy Italian loafers? With the tassels?"

Mas nodded again.

"That's strange," Lil said.

Mas had to agree. He said nothing about the warning issued by the thief. He bit down on his dentures to contain his anger. It was one thing for him to decide to stay out of somebody's business; it was quite another for someone to steal his property to keep his mouth shut. Mas had no desire to dredge up old memories, but he wasn't going to let some fancy-heeled sonafugun try to push him down.

"So, is there any chance that they'll recover your truck?"

"Maybe in pieces." Mas tried to lower himself in his easy chair but felt another sharp jab of pain in the middle of his spine.

"You okay? Is it your back again?"

"A little." Mas looked out toward the backyard of withering eggplants and wilted cymbidium. "I'm a ole man, Lil."

"Have you gone to a doctor?"

"Nah, what do they know?"

"They don't all have to be bad, Mas. Chizuko was an unusual case."

Just stomach problems, Mas remembered Chizuko saying. Probably clear up in a few weeks. "So how about your daughter? She docta now?"

"Joy's finishing her residency in South Carolina. She might have a job back here in L.A."

"Yeah, *sugoi, ne*. She smart one, eh. So quiet." Mas remembered the plain girl with a moon face and thin eyes like her father's. The brother took after Lil—bright, round eyes and big white teeth.

"Well, it's taken her long enough to get to this point." Lil smoothed out her flowered dress. Joy had been on her way to a Ph.D. in physics before she'd switched over to medical school. "But she's no Mari. She can't put words together like Mari can."

"That girl talks too much." Too much back talk, no good, Mas had told Mari time after time. Those fiery black eyes had burnt holes through Mas's forehead all through her junior high and high school years.

"But that's not bad." Lil paused, and they both listened as something metal fell on the outside concrete steps.

Lil's rose-colored glasses glimmered. "I know it wasn't easy, Mas, that Mari went through her stages. But I knew that she would make something out of herself. I mean, Joy's doing well, and we're proud of her, but Mari—she has something special. I tried to deny it, mind you. I guess I never wanted to sell Joy short. But I can admit it now, especially since Chizuko . . . Well, Joy has always played by the rules, but Mari, her spirit, that's going to take her places."

Mas's spine began to tingle, as if Lil's warm, soothing words were lapping at his back. He never understood what "freelancing" was. How could a girl make money making movies? That was for guys who had connections. But he had to give her some credit. She was surviving in New York, although it seemed like she was living hand to mouth. "Heh, I don't know. She cause a lot of trouble, no?"

"Well, that's what daughters are for," laughed Lil as Tug barreled into the living room once again, a screwdriver in his hand. A few pieces of old paint were stuck in his white beard and hair.

"Almost, old man, almost. Just got to make some adjustments." The pungent scent of cherry tobacco filled the room. "By the way," said Tug, adjusting his pipe. "I hear congratulations are in order. It's certainly about time."

There was an awkward silence, and Mas glanced over to Lil—whose lips were uncharacteristically drawn in a line.

"I thought he knew." One of Tug's large palms was outstretched toward his wife. His left forefinger was extended out like a Tootsie Roll. "Well, he does know, right?"

Lil adjusted the hem on her dress so it covered the top of her knees.

Tug pulled out his pipe from his lips. "Well, he should know. After all, it's his only daughter."

It took two long minutes before Mas put it together. Mari must be getting married. Who? The tall, pale *hakujin* boy called Lloyd from New York? Mas remembered the time she brought him over one Thanksgiving when Chizuko was still alive. Mari said he was a poet; what Mas wanted to know was what this boy did for money.

"Can't eat words," he had told Mari.

Mari had broken the news a few weeks later. Turned out this boy was in Mas's line of work. A gardener hired by the city of New York.

Mas couldn't speak, and Chizuko broke down and cried right then and there. Mas secretly thought that had led to Chizuko's demise, and he resented Mari for having burst his wife's one last hope—that the future generations would never have any signs of the Arai lawn-mowing legacy.

He looked Lil square in the face. *"Itsu?"* he asked simply. "When?"

Lil blinked hard, and Tug retreated to the porch with his screwdriver. "Last week," she said. "They're on their honeymoon in Mexico now."

Mexico? Mas's throat felt dry.

"I'm sure she was going to tell you, Mas. I just heard it through Joy, and she said she would kill me if I mentioned it to anyone. You know kids these days. It's someone she knew from college. I think his name was Lloyd. A *hakujin* boy."

"Last week." Mas sat still, thinking. No matter how bad their relationship had become, Mari would have told him before the wedding. There was only one reason that . . . "When?" he repeated.

Lil cleared her throat. "They wanted it simple. You know, just at City Hall and then Chinese food later." She stared at Mas through her pink-framed bifocals and blinked hard. Come on, Mas said silently. You're not the kind of lady to twist the truth when you're caught in a corner.

It was as if Lil had heard Mas's silent message. "All

right, Mas. I guess you'll find out soon enough. I haven't even told Tug. The baby's due in December."

Mas swallowed, and remained frozen in his chair. How could she do this and bring shame on the family? thought Mas. The family. What family? There really was no one here in the States. They were like masterless samurai, wandering nomads with no blood ties to anyone here. But precisely because they had no relatives, no prior reputation, the family name was so important. Here, Masao Arai was a blank white sheet of paper. Unknown. Pure. Anything was possible. But once something was written on the paper, it would be irreversible. It was up to just them to create their honor for their friends like Tug and Lil. Somehow, some way, the word would get out that Mas Arai's daughter had had to get married. There would be disapproving nods of heads and smirks behind closed doors, while face-to-face there would be those sickening, false smiles. For once, Mas was happy that Chizuko was dead.

He had some dreams for Mari. That he would walk her down the aisle in a proper wedding ceremony, followed by a reception of thick steaks and large glasses of liquor. That she would produce healthy children, their hair jet-black and their faces pale and formless like potatoes. They would visit the house, yelling in high-pitched voices, "*Ji-chan, Ji-chan,* Grandpa, Grandpa." He would teach them how to safely drive nails into wood, how to place bait on a hook, and, when they got older, the best strategy for blackjack.

Now he had to contend with an unplanned grandchild whose father was a poet and, even worse, a good-for-nothing gardener. And what if the baby came out— But Mas stopped himself before he went too far. He felt like popping out of his easy chair, yelling and screaming, but instead he quietly listened to Lil go on—speaking faster and faster—about children and their universal insensitivity, how things were different with young people today. But Mas knew this wasn't about any kind of generation gap. It was about Mas and Mari plain and simple. Mas was tired of surprises and disappointment, and wanted instead to crawl back underneath his crumbled bedspread on his soft mattress.

He was relieved when Tug finally called out from the wire mesh, "Mas, old man."

Mas rose slowly but eagerly, seeing a polite closure to his conversation with Lil, and limped over to the screen door, which was now firmly back on its hinges.

The silver hair and beard of the tall man glowed underneath the hundred-watt bulb hanging from the porch. The moths circled his head, creating a haphazard halo. "I think I got it." Tug grinned as his thick index finger pressed down on the smooth round doorbell.

✣ ✣ ✣

It was pitch dark by the time Lil and Tug finally left Mas at the door. Mas stumbled into the kitchen and opened the refrigerator for a Budweiser. After taking a gulp, he paused by the sink and looked out the window. For a moment, he imagined two pairs of dark eyes—ones he had seen before—peering at him. Son of a— Mas gasped, and he quickly pulled the curtains together. What, you losin' your mind? he thought as he caught his breath. Just nerves, he told himself, but he went from room to room, clicking on the lights and checking every closet, until he finally returned to the bedroom and lay down on his side.

From his position, he could still see the stack of old magazines by the bed. He knew that it was the third one down, under the February Triple A magazine and the Japanese go book. He knew practically every page by heart—the brunette in the royal blue panties, the blond with the swollen basketball *chichi*. Hell, he could even recall the design of every liquor ad in between the different centerfolds, and then felt an uneasiness in his jeans. He lowered his hand toward the magazines and then stopped. He licked his lips.

It's no good, he muttered. Damn you, old woman, where are you? His heart ached for those sagging, empty breasts and stomach lined with scars from surgery after surgery. He should have done it to her during her last days. Ignored the smell of sickness, and held her.

He heard a crash outside—was it the local alley cat overturning the trash cans again? Mas stood up quickly, spilling his beer onto the green carpet.

Once he reached the back door, there was only a strange and eerie silence. Mas felt the presence of at least another human being. "Hal-lo," Mas called out, but no one replied. He then went to the front to check.

Mas opened the screen door Tug had fixed. There was that smell again. Menthol. Salon Pas. The same as in the mistress's apartment. His neighbors, mostly black and Mexicans, didn't carry this smell. It could be only one person. Mas was sure of it. This visit was a practice for something bigger, like when Mas went to the stables to check out the horses for the next race. You looked for the ones with energy, kick, and bet against the ones who had no fight.

Mas stepped out on the cement porch. The neighborhood was quiet for once. No police helicopters flying overhead, and the teenagers seemed to be away, probably causing havoc in a place with more life. The moon was almost full, and Mas caught a rectangular shape amid the glass and other trash in the old rock garden below. Mas knelt down and fished out the new addition to his garden. It was the black-and-white photograph of the three boys on the bridge. Nakane must have dropped it when the broken screen door had fallen down on him.

"Whyzu you followin' me?" Mas muttered out loud. He felt like destroying that photograph, but thought better of it. He had seen Joji Haneda burn once before. Mas couldn't do it to his friend a second time.

CHAPTER FIVE

Mas didn't like people changing their minds. Chizuko did it at times, first saying that she wanted to see the Grand Canyon, then requesting Yellowstone. Turned out they spent most vacations either on the dunes of Pismo Beach or at the Dunes of Las Vegas, where Mas stayed glued to the poker tables of the Four Queens. Closest thing Chizuko ever got to the Canyon was watching a large-screen presentation at Disneyland one year. "See, just like you go," Mas said as Chizuko clutched her handbag tight at her elbow in front of the giant screen.

So when Mas told Haruo that he would accompany him to the medical exams, Haruo almost fell off the kitchen chair. Now they stood on the sixth floor of a new building, tall and silver like a streamlined rocket.

"Mas, I betcha glad you changed your mind," said

Haruo, his face looking especially oily, so that the fluorescent lights bounced colors of green and blue off his scar.

"I just needed to get outta the house. Neva said that I'd see a docta."

The doors of the medical office were still closed. The rug, a gray rat color, smelled new and factory-made. The hallways were lined with a bunch of *urusai* folks like Haruo. Mas recognized a few of them; a pretty woman with all-white hair belonged to the same Japanese school group as Chizuko. A dark man, formerly from Terminal Island, who always seemed to reel in the biggest fishes at the Mammoth Lake derbies. They nodded to one another, not remembering names but knowing that at one time they had worked or played side by side.

"When are they going to open?" a heavy woman in front of him huffed.

"Yah, already ten-ten," said a man next to her, probably the husband.

Mas steadied himself against the slippery wall. His back was still sore but now hurt only when he sat down in a car. The gardeners' association had sent over substitutes this week, so Mrs. Parsons, the Indian couple, and the doctor were taken care of, at least the bare necessities.

He knew that it was unwise for him to be there for everybody to see. But Mas couldn't hide now, not with the threat hanging over his head. One thing Mas was good at, that was reading people's faces. If he came across the thief today, he would know immediately. Better for me to find him first, thought Mas, than for him to find me again.

He studied the line of people again. Amid all the bald heads and gray hair, Mas spotted a patch of red, like the fur of a wild badger. The badger went from one person to another. It was a young man, dressed in army pants and a black T-shirt. His face was dark, as if he were a gardener himself. Bright eyes and a long nose. Girls like Mari would probably think this guy good-looking, Mas said to himself. That's what was wrong with these young people nowadays, thought Mas. No pride.

The badger had a notebook in his hands and scribbled something in there from time to time. When he came to speak to the heavy woman in front of them, Mas looked away and sank as far as he could against the hallway wall. It didn't work. In a few minutes, the badger stood right in front of Haruo and Mas.

"*Sumimasen,* my name is Yuki. I'm a reporter with *Shine* magazine back in Hiroshima."

"You such a young guy to be a reporter," Haruo replied in Japanese.

Shine? thought Mas. Never heard of it. *Yomiuri, Asahi, Mainichi.* Those were the three kings of Japanese newspapers. And, of course, *Chugoku Shimbun* in Hiroshima. But *Shine*? Kid stuff. Mas was sure of it. Only such a rag would hire a boy with a horrible dye job.

"I'm doing a story on a *hibakusha*. I've been asking around if anyone may know him—Kimura Riki."

Mas felt his head go woozy. Had he heard right?

"I dunno a Riki Kimura," Haruo said. "You, Mas?"

Mas's mouth was paper dry. He merely shook his head. He hadn't heard that name for fifty years.

"He was working at the Hiroshima train station when the *pikadon* fell. Went to Hiroshima Koryo. Hung around *Kibei*, American-born."

"Well, Mas went to Koryo. What class?"

"He was born in 1929."

"Well, thatsu about your age," Haruo said to Mas, and, after meeting his dagger eyes, slightly lowered his head.

"I have something here that might help." The badger brought out a manila folder from his bag and handed the contents to Haruo and Mas. It was a crude illustration done in colored pencil. A body, something like worms crawling out of his guts. Missing a leg, burnt black except for a white square on the chest. Whoever had drawn the illustration also had included a circle by the right side of the body.

"For the fiftieth anniversary of the bombing, our national TV station, NHK, asked people to submit paintings and illustrations from survivors. This was one that was turned in."

Mas felt his hands shake. He couldn't help but take in the power of the simple drawing. How the man must have suffered there alone.

"The woman who found the body was looking for her husband. She drew her discovery on her clothing with a piece of charcoal. She figured somehow his family would gain some peace to know how he died. When she returned home to the countryside, she even redrew the body on this piece of paper with colored pencil. She put it away and forgot about it for fifty years, until the NHK solicitation came up."

"Whatsu that?" Haruo pointed to a crooked circle beside the body.

"We think it's some message that the man had tried to leave before he died. I've tried to decipher it. But nothing."

"So what about this Riki Kimura?" asked Haruo. "Important guy?"

The reporter shook his head. "No, no. He was my grandfather."

"Grandfather?" Mas couldn't help blurting out. "Whatsu your name again?"

"Yuki. Kimura Yuki."

How could that be? They had all been fifteen, sixteen years old. Just teenagers. Too busy with work at the train station to even think about girls.

The boy continued his story. "They never found his body. . . . Eventually, my grandmother was called in and given a large bone, supposed to be my grandfather's remains. It wasn't, of course. Probably a horse bone."

Haruo nodded. "Somehow that made people feel betta."

"We were able to meet last year with the woman who drew this picture," the reporter explained. "She also kept this all these years." He took an envelope from his wallet and carefully lifted a square piece of cloth. *Kimura,* it read. *Riki.* And the letter *A*.

Seeing the cloth name tag, Mas felt dizzy. A weight seemed to drop to the pit of his stomach. He could still hear Haruo and the boy talk, but he could barely make out the words.

"I rememba these," said Haruo. "We all had to wear them. IDs. His blood type, A, *ne.*"

"She kept this for us. But look—flawless, not burnt at all. Strange, we thought. Why would Grandfather be so charred in this drawing, but this so perfect?"

Mas leaned against the wall. His legs seemed almost to buckle under him.

"Hey, you *orai?*" asked Haruo, taking hold of Mas's elbow.

"Back," Mas said, pounding his spine with a closed fist. He hit himself so hard that even his chest seemed to rattle.

"Can I help—" Yuki folded up the cloth square and placed it in his wallet.

"No," Mas said, a little too loudly and a little too quickly. But the boy ignored him and, together with Haruo, guided him to the front of the line.

Yuki pounded on the locked door. "This *ojisan*

needs to sit down. He needs some medical attention," he called out.

The crowd murmured, and within a few minutes the door opened.

✣ ✣ ✣

Mas refused to be seen by any doctor but did agree to rest in one of the hard folding chairs lined up against the wall near a coffee machine.

Haruo was soon directed into one of the examination rooms. "You sure you don't want to—"

"I wait, Haruo." Mas spoke so sternly that Haruo merely nodded and disappeared through a curtain divider. If Mas had his truck, he would have left, that minute, that second. How had that ID, so perfect, appeared on the dead man's chest? Had it all been planned, calculated, from the very beginning?

The red badger returned to Mas's side, this time with a Styrofoam cup filled with water.

Mas accepted the cup. His lips were parched as if he hadn't had a drink in days. "Your grandmother," he finally said. "Is your grandmother still alive?"

Yuki nodded. "Oh, yes," he said. "Her name is Akemi. Actually, we're looking for her brother, who may be over here. Haneda is his name. Haneda Joji."

✣ ✣ ✣

Akemi Haneda was a couple of years older than Mas. A strange girl with an awkward American accent, she had a round face, round eyes, and deep dimples like someone had poked her cheeks with a pointed stick. She and her younger brother, Joji, had moved into the neighborhood around 1939. Mas spoke to her for the first time when she was burning something in her backyard in the middle of the night during the war.

"Do you have any coal you can spare?" Her long hair had been recently chopped to her earlobes, and she wore a thick, padded jacket and loose pantaloons. Mas at one time had thought she was pretty, but now she looked more like a boy.

He grudgingly gave her some dead coals from their table heater and watched as she threw one book after another into the tiny fire. The books were all thick, and written in English. Mas sat with her all morning until the last book fell apart into flat pieces like dried seaweed. "Thank you," she said, her fingers black with charcoal. "I wouldn't want to do that alone." She gathered Mas's face into her hands and kissed him hard, her teeth sharp against his gums.

When Mas went back into the house, his second-oldest brother was lacing up his boots on his way to the naval station. "Where have you been?" the brother asked. "And what's that black stuff on your face?"

All this time in America, Mas had thought Akemi was dead. He, in fact, had not seen or heard anything about her since August of 1945. But now everything was off balance. Akemi and Riki, together? Impossible.

Riki had mercilessly teased Akemi—calling her white-radish legs, even though they couldn't see her legs in *monpe* pants. He even followed her around with a dirty sweet potato, holding it below his waist and making obscene noises. Through all of this, Joji remained silent. Mas himself had four sisters who seemed only trouble, but even he would have put an end to such torment.

And now, why had Shuji Nakane and this red-badger boy descended upon Los Angeles at the same time? It was as if goblins had been released from tightly secured boxes. Who had let them loose? Mas had a sneaking suspicion that it had been Joji Haneda, seeking a final *bachi* that would send them into hell.

"Oh, I'm tired." The reporter sank into the plastic chair next to Mas with a steaming cup of coffee. "Got in last night. Jet lag."

Mas could get a better look at the boy. Why hadn't it hit him before? The physical similarity was there. He was tall and lean. High cheekbones. And those eyes, sharp enough to see a lie fifty meters away. On the boy's arm was a tattoo, barely visible because of his dark tan.

Mas must have stared too long at the tattoo, because the boy responded. "It's a wild boar. Ugly, huh?" he said proudly. The creature was squat and hairy, like a mountain yam with tusks. "I was born in the Year of *Inoshishi*. Like my grandmother."

"So . . ." Mas said without thinking. He remembered. Akemi had told him once that she was as stubborn as a warthog.

The reporter placed his cup on the floor. "How come you're not in there?" He gestured toward the different rooms in which doctors measured blood pressure and heart rates.

Mas shrugged. "What for? What can they tell me that I dunno already?"

"It's for the future, *desho*? For my kids and their kids."

"You got kids?"

"No." The reporter laughed, and Mas noticed that his lower front tooth was pushed in. "I'm not even married. But I'm speaking generally."

Mas pulled at some callused skin around his thumbnail. "Everyone knows the Bomb is bad. All the tests in the world don't change anytin'."

"A lot of people don't know. They don't even care anymore. Most of the *hibakusha* have died—" The reporter then blushed a little. *"Gomen,"* he apologized. "I didn't mean—"

"Don't worry," said Mas. "I am dead. Just look alive."

The reporter looked puzzled for a minute.

"I'm kidding," Mas said. "Itsu a joke." What was wrong with young people these days? he thought. No sense of humor.

"Oh," the reporter said. "Well, I even go in for exams. Back in Hiroshima."

Mas pinched his dead skin into a tiny ball. "You not there fifty years ago."

"They want to test the second generation, and even the third, like me. See if there are some latent effects."

"And . . . ?"

"And nothing conclusive."

"Ah—"

"But my first test results came back with an abnormal number of white blood cells."

Mas shifted in his seat. "You get it checked out?"

"They couldn't figure out why. The doctors check now, once a year."

"You look plenty healthy," said Mas.

"I just look alive," the boy said, picking up his cup from the floor. He then looked squarely at Mas. "Joke," he said.

"Oh." Mas pursed his lips. The boy was smart; there was no getting around that. They sat in silence as doctors in white coats passed by with clipboards and long white strips of paper. "So, your grandmother have many kids?"

"No, she just had one son, my father. His name was Hikari—"

"Hikari?"

"I know, a strange name. Not Buddhist or Christian. He was named after the light of the bomb.

I guess *Obaachan* felt that *hikari* could stand for something good. 'My child of light,' she called him. While the others came out with big heads, he was perfect—that is, until he hit fifty." The boy scratched his arm, near his tattoo. "He died last year. Lung cancer. Never smoked a cigarette in his life."

Mas wanted to say that those things happen; you can't blame the Bomb. Accept it, go on, and forget.

"Growing up, I hated America. I figured they were heartless. Barbarians. Then *Obaachan* sat me down. She said, 'If you hate America, you hate me.' I didn't understand. Then she brought out a passport, hers, stamped U.S.A. She kept her dual citizenship the whole time. But she never came back to America."

Mas's secret question had been answered. Akemi had not set foot back in California and, most likely, would not in the future.

"She's the one who told me to accompany the medical tour this year. She's hoping that I go back to school and become a decent salaryman, I think. But I don't think that's going to happen." The boy turned a new page in his notebook. "I'd like to interview you, when you have the time."

"No time for interview."

"It'll just take an hour or so."

An hour? An eternity. Mas shook his head more vigorously.

"There's about one thousand of you here in America. Those who survived the Bomb. Every year, fewer and fewer. Don't you think that you have a responsibility to tell your story?"

Mas's ears began to grow warm. Responsibility? I have no responsibility to you, red-haired boy. "Plenty of folks ready to talk. They all ova dis place. Betta catch them before they leave." Mas shook his finger over his head as Yuki finally rose.

"You don't have to tell it to me. But at least your children and your grandchildren. They deserve to know. The *pikadon* is still inside of them, after all."

Yeah, yeah. Mas wished the boy away, and in a matter of minutes he got his wish when Yuki disappeared down the hall. Mas continued waiting in the folding chair. His eyes felt as though they were covered in a sticky film. He rubbed them with his fists until they were dry again.

❖ ❖ ❖

They say that they can fix my face," Haruo said as they left the medical building. "*Tada*. Only thing is, I gotta go to Hiroshima. In a airplane."

"You had that face for fifty years. Why do you have to change now?"

"Think, Mas. I can go to my grave with a beautiful face."

A waste, thought Mas. Such a surgery should be reserved for young girls looking for a future husband. Not an old man close to seventy who might not even last another five years.

"You can go with me, Mas."

"Ha." Mas took out a fresh cigarette. "I don't think so."

"But I don't wanna go by myself."

"If you do such a foolish thing, you deserve to be by yourself."

"So, I saw you talking to that boy. Whatsu his name, Yuzo?"

"Yuki."

"Yah, Yuki Kimura. Nice boy, huh?"

"Heezu *orai*. Gotsu too many questions."

"Well, heezu a reporter. Thatsu his job. You can't get to the truth without asking questions."

Mas grunted and stared out the dirty passenger window.

Haruo rattled on and on about the people, new and old, he encountered at the medical exams. Mas, on the other hand, was disturbed by his meeting with the boy. Even when he closed his eyes, he could only think of that terrifying illustration drawn in muted colors. It was even more frightening than a real photograph. It held secrets—the crooked circle, the cloth ID—that became magnified in the artist's hand. Had he gone quickly, he wondered, or was he alive when the maggots began to eat his body?

Mas remembered when the military police paid a visit to the Haneda household during the war. On the day Mas was to report for work at the Hiroshima train station, he noticed a couple of old women gathered outside the Hanedas' home.

"The MPs were here," hissed one gnarled woman, a bamboo basket filled with sweet potatoes tied on her curved back. "Took away the girl. She's a strange one, all right."

Akemi did not return for several days. Mas heard stories of the military police seeking out *inu*, those who aligned themselves with the barbarians. Radios were confiscated, English-language letters and cards burned. The old women whispered rumors of the MPs forcing girls into corners, slipping their hands into shirts, the rolling of loose buttons.

Akemi finally returned home. She sat on the stone steps of her house. Her head was now completely shaven.

"Masao-*kun*," she called out as Mas walked past the Hanedas' gate. "Masao-*kun*." But Mas kept walking as if he had not heard.

CHAPTER SIX

After Mas returned home from the exams, he didn't leave the house for three days straight. He darkened all the windows and didn't even start up any fans. The whole of the house became as hot as a barbecue, but Mas didn't care. Let me be roasted alive, he thought. For three days and three nights, Mas left the phone off the hook. Nobody, not even Haruo, bothered to come around.

The television was on the whole time, the volume at low. Mas watched some of the sports broadcasts, but he wasn't a baseball fan. It was too slow, too methodical. Mas liked old-time basketball, when UCLA and coach John Wooden ruled the courts. Even Chizuko watched the games with vigor, cheering and yelling at every guy in blue who missed a basket. While Mas closely followed the point guards, Chizuko loved the tall man, Lew Alcindor. He was as awkward-looking as a giant praying mantis, but when he released that ball in a hook, it was more beautiful than any prima ballerina. When he announced that he had converted to Islam and was changing his name to Kareem Abdul-Jabbar, Chizuko thought he was plain crazy. "How can you just change your name like that?" she said. "Your name is everything."

"How 'bout you? You changed your name to Arai."

"That's different." Chizuko frowned. "Women are used to that."

"And back in Japan, they have *yoshi*, *desho*? People adopt grown men all the time to carry on the name."

Chizuko didn't like to lose a fight. "People will get confuse. He's a big-time basketball star."

Mas shook his head. "Pretty soon, you won't even rememba Lew Alcindor," he told her. "His past all gone."

Turns out that Mas was right. All the fans, even Chizuko, eventually adjusted to the name Kareem. Lew Alcindor was gone, and nobody seemed that sad about it.

✣ ✣ ✣

On Tuesday morning, Mas finally dragged himself off his mattress to scramble up some old eggs, soy sauce, and rice. He heard someone rapping at his screen door. The neighbor's dog again? Now the doorbell, ringing clearly after Tug's handiwork. Mas stood on tiptoe to look through the peephole in his front door.

Red hair and a dark face. How had the boy figured out where he lived?

"I know you're home, *Ojisan*," Yuki called out.

Mas cursed silently and finally cleared his throat after not having talked for more than seventy-two hours. "I tole you that I had nutin' to say."

"That's not what I heard." Yuki was almost yelling. "That's not what my grandmother said."

Mas turned the key that he had stuck in the deadbolt lock. No sense in having the whole neighborhood hear about his business. He opened the front door to reveal Yuki behind the beat-up screen door.

Yuki was in all black, like a midnight thief. "I spoke to her a couple of nights ago." His voice now was lower but intense. "She told me that she lived next door to a Masao Arai back in 1945."

Mas swallowed a fistful of air.

"Well? You going to let me in?"

Mas held out the loose screen door, and the boy went to the living room and sat on Mari's old piano bench. "Why didn't you mention that you knew her?"

"I forget. My mind not workin' too good."

Yuki stared at Mas's face long and hard. Mas stared back, trying not to blink. Young people always thought old people were losing their minds. Maybe this kind of thinking would help Mas today.

"She said that she even went around with you at one time."

Went around? Mas almost spit out his dentures. Nobody dated back then. Besides, it had been only one kiss, and she had been the one to go after Mas. "Itsu war. No time for girlsu. She a lot older than me, anyhowsu."

"Older? I thought that you didn't remember her."

Mas cursed himself. He usually didn't slip up like that, especially concerning made-up stories. He tried to cover himself. "Your age. Izu not old enough to be your grandpa."

"Is that so?" Yuki rolled his eyes and snorted. "You must be at least seventy years old."

"Sixty-nine."

"Close enough."

Yuki took a fresh cigarette out of his day pack and tapped it against his knee. I hope you not thinking of smoking in my house, Mas thought. It was one thing for his own Marlboros to pollute his rooms—quite another for this young Japanese boy to light up his funny cigarettes inside without permission.

"So who tole youzu where I live?"

"Asked around."

Asking questions about me? Mas was both annoyed and worried. Why would this boy go to all this trouble to find a rotting house in Altadena? Mas made it a point to get a look at the boy's shoes. Black high-top sneakers, old-style, with white circles on the sides.

"Look, you betta go now. I dunno nutin' from fifty

years ago. Izu still sick, anyhowsu. No feelin' too good, rememba?"

Yuki stuck the cigarette in back of his ear. He looked like he wanted to ask Mas more questions, but the old-fashioned, Japanese side of him prevailed. Honor your elders, right? thought Mas.

"This isn't over, *Ojisan*," Yuki said on his way out.

No, Mas had to agree, not by a long shot.

✣ ✣ ✣

By this time, Mas had lost his appetite. He returned to his bedroom, where his sheets were damp with sweat. After balling them up at the foot of his bed, he lay down on the bare mattress. There was an intensity to the heat; it coated his body, the entire bedroom. It had become a furnace, orange flames everywhere.

"Water, Daddy, water." It was Mari, her hair tied back like an old lady's. There was a package in her hands, wrapped in a blanket.

Mas rushed over to the sink and turned the faucet. Bone dry. The tub. Dry. Shower. Dry. Mari was crying now; she needed his help. He could see her eyes—dark and filled with fear. "Help, Daddy, help." Everything was burning hot; the palms of his hands burned as he touched doorknobs and appliances. There was a glass door now, separating him from his daughter. "Mari-*chan*, Mari-*chan*," he bellowed. Mari seemed to be getting smaller and smaller, although her head remained the same size. No, it couldn't be, but— The realization hit Mas hard. Mari was melting. He pounded the glass door. Kicked it with his foot. Then it disappeared, and Mas rushed over to his daughter, whose head was barely visible in the sticky ooze of her body. "Take care, Daddy, take care," she called. Mas realized she was talking about the bundle wrapped in a blanket. As Mas lifted the package, the blanket opened to reveal the charred remains of a baby. He felt vomit rise to his throat, and before he knew it, he was screaming.

✣ ✣ ✣

Mas, Mas, old man. You were having a bad dream." Someone was pulling at his sleeve. Pure white hair and beard—it was Tug Yamada.

Mas focused on the peeling paint on his ceiling. His hands brushed against the mattress. Warm but not burning. The light was dim through his dusty window blinds.

"Didn't mean to scare you. The door was open, and I thought that you were in trouble."

Mas blinked. There was no daughter, no baby; at least not now.

"Whatsu the time?"

"About seven-thirty."

Seven-thirty. Mas couldn't believe that he had slept all day after Yuki's visit that morning.

"Are you okay, Mas? You were really yelling a few minutes ago."

"Yah, yah." Mas tried to get up, but his muscles had become as soft as pounded rice cakes.

Tug went to the door and picked up a grocery bag and his red tool kit that he had left in the hallway. "Sent here by Lil, fresh peaches from Fresno," he said, gesturing to the paper bag. "And I came to fix your water problem, once and for all."

"Water?" Mas's head felt as though it were stuffed with cotton balls.

"Your toilet. Last time I was here, I noticed that it was leaking." Tug walked down the hall, probably to leave the peaches in the kitchen.

Damn. Mas was finally awake enough to drag himself out of the bedroom. "No, no, you don't hafta." Mas followed Tug from the kitchen to the bathroom. "*Honto*, really, Tug."

Tug had just retired from the County Health Department as a senior inspector at age seventy-two, and Mas knew he had keen eyes to spot the gathering place of bacteria and other deadly organisms. He would note the streaks of week-old toothpaste, sticky pools of hair and scum.

Tug had already made himself at home in the bathroom. His large body sagged on the edge of the bathtub as he opened his toolbox on Mas's worn blue bath mat. He took out a large, grooved rubber ball, a new float ball for the toilet. "Remember when we did this during the drought? I bet you still have the same equipment from back then."

Tug pulled off the ceramic lid to the tank and jangled the chain to the flush valve. "Yep, sure looks like it. When we were here last week, I heard some water running. You don't want to be wasting any of that stuff; they say another drought's coming. Plus you don't want your bill to be sky-high—not with our set incomes."

"Not retired yet, Tug." Mas still felt dizzy, and leaned his elbow on the edge of the sink. He watched as Tug tinkered with the toilet bowl tank and then struggled to untangle a chain attached to a new flapper flush valve. The stub of his amputated forefinger stuck out like a frightened sea creature.

Finally Tug seemed to give up. "Here, Mas, old man. Maybe you'd have a better crack at this," he said, holding out the valve.

"A lot of trouble, huh?" The words came out before Mas could swallow them in his throat. He had never made mention to Tug's face of his war injury.

"Well, after almost fifty years, you kind of get used to something that's missing. I can even type with it—can even beat my grandson at computer games."

Tug spread out his huge left hand, accentuating the silhouette of his forefinger cut off at the knuckle. "At work, if some restaurant was giving us some trouble, I would just make sure they saw my finger and make some reference to 'the gang.' Bingo—*yakuza,* they'd start thinking. That would keep them quiet. But little did they know that Japanese gangsters have the pinky cut off."

Tug wiggled his little finger, which was whole and complete with all its joints. "But figurin' I just lost half of a finger, and other guys lost much more than that, well, I guess I can't complain. I've received a lot of blessings."

Tug and Lil attended the Sunrise Baptist Church in Boyle Heights, just east of Little Tokyo. Every summer, the Yamadas would bring over yellow tickets for their chicken teriyaki fund-raising dinner. Mas complained the church's chicken wasn't salty enough, but Chizuko would berate him, saying his *monku* was just another sign of his own moral failure.

"The 442nd's having another reunion next year in Hawaii. I'm not into all these veterans' shindigs, but I guess it would be a nice trip for Lil. I wouldn't mind seeing the guys again, especially the ones on the Islands.

"We missed the Biffontaine tour. I guess it was a big to-do. Lil wanted to make it over to Europe, but I don't know—there's a lot of things I could just as well forget."

Tug took back the untangled chain from Mas. "You must have seen hell, too, huh, Mas?"

Mas pulled a screwdriver out of Tug's red toolbox and began loosening connections to the toilet's old float ball. What was it with the Nisei and their desire to memorialize the past? Camp, the war front, they wanted to remember now that their families and wood-framed houses were secure. They had their Purple Hearts and Silver Stars, and could die with their souls at rest. But Mas filled his days with numbers and odds, his only hope to change his history. And now the young red badger was in town, tugging at remains that were never meant to be unearthed.

Tug tried again. "I get bad dreams, too." But Mas didn't bite. The image of melting Mari crept back into his mind. It didn't matter that she was thousands of miles away. No parent could forget a child's cry for help, even if it was in a dream.

They continued to work in silence; Mas unscrewed the lift wires while Tug handed over the new parts from his paper bag. In the end, they fastened the black float ball on the new flush arm.

"Listen, Mas," Tug said. "Sorry I blew it by spilling the beans about Mari. I caught hell at home. I guess I was never that good about keeping things to myself."

Mari and Tug's daughter, Joy—soon to be Dr. Yamada—had played together in this very house, attended each other's birthday parties, and posed in the same class pictures. What had happened to take them in such different paths?

Tug stood over the empty toilet tank. "You know, they never quite come out the way you expect it. I guess that's just the risks of parenthood."

The phone rang, and Mas paused for a moment.

Tug must have placed the receiver back on the cradle. Mas left Tug to contend with the toilet bowl and answered the phone.

It was Wishbone Tanaka with some nonsense about a poker game.

"Don't play no cards no more. You know that."

"Yeah, I heard about that." Wishbone didn't sound convinced. "Hey, I wouldn't be calling, but I'm all jammed up right now. Bunch of guys are going to this Heart Mountain reunion. I need more guys to fill the table."

Mas wanted to slam down the phone. Why was Wishbone bothering him about this? Should've kept the phone disconnected, he thought.

"Hello, hello." Wishbone sounded like his mouth was too close to the handset.

"Yah."

"You know any guys?"

"There's Whitey Tsukamoto. Shy Amano," Mas offered impatiently.

"Them two are going to the camp thing. Look, I promised my friend that I could get a game going tonight. He owns one of those storefronts in Little Tokyo and knows someone who wants to run regular card games up on his second floor."

Not my problem, thought Mas. "Can't help you," he said.

"There's another thing." Wishbone took a breath.

"Gonna sell my shop, Mas. Everyone's dying, or gettin' out of the business; no fun anymore."

Mas sucked his metal dental plate. No Tanaka's Lawn-mower. Hard to believe. It would be strange to enter that shedlike store and not see Wishbone's pockmarked face behind the counter.

"Look, Mas, you owe me; you know you do. Gave you a break every time things didn't work out so good. Remember when your back went out real bad, fifteen years ago? Prac-tically gave you that gas blower."

Sonafugun. He *would* bring that up. Even though Wishbone was Nisei, there was a big part of him that was Japanese, and it was coming up now.

"Hey, what about Haruo Mukai? He's your buddy, right? Heard he sold his house. He's, what, somewhere in Crenshaw?"

"No, bad idea. He don't do cards." Mas tightened his grip on the telephone receiver.

"Well, he sure did back in the old days. Crazy bettor, that skinny man was."

"Hotteoke," Mas said. Leave him the hell alone. Although Wishbone didn't speak much Japanese, he would understand that much.

"Okay, okay, no need to get so touchy—"

Something clattered onto the tile on the bathroom floor. "Wishbone, I gotsu someone here."

"Listen, I'll call you in ten minutes. Game's starting at eight."

Mas wanted to tell him not to bother, but Wishbone had already clicked off. What trouble. Mas tried to clear his eyes of the film that had accumulated during the past three days, but it was no use.

Mas and Tug completed the work on the toilet bowl tank and then sat at the kitchen and talked over 7-UP and rice crackers. It was about eight o'clock when the phone rang again.

"Hey, Mas, it's me, Wishbone."

"Yah." Mas could hear the clicking of poker chips and men's voices in the background.

"Don't worry, you don't need to come. Got plenty of guys."

"*Orai*. What, Whitey and Shy help you out?"

"No, Haneda found them all. We're covered."

"Haneda? What Haneda?" Mas could barely speak.

"You know, Joji Haneda, from Ventura. He's back in town. That's my friend's connection." Laughter in the background. "And hey, your old buddy Haruo is even here. Seems like he plays cards now."

Before Mas could interrupt, the line cut off. "Wishbone, Wishbone." Mas jiggled the receiver. It was no use. Wishbone was probably back absorbed in his game, and Mas had no idea where they were.

"Everything okay?" Tug called out.

Little Tokyo, wasn't that what Wishbone had said? Second floor. It all sounded familiar, a faint echo of something recent. Mas went into the bedroom and rummaged through the pockets of his old jeans.

There, in the pair torn from the accident, in the front pocket, was the map, folded in half.

Even after looking at the photo of Haneda at the mistress's place, Mas couldn't remember his face. It seemed blurry, hazy, like a photo of a moving man. He tried to recall the photo of the bridge, how he had looked as a teenager. He could remember certain features, the prominent nose, high cheekbones, pointy chin. But they were separate parts that didn't quite match together, like those police composites of suspected rapists shown over the television. Those drawings were all similar. The faces were devoid of any racial distinction, could be either black, Mexican, or *hakujin*. When the guy was finally caught—say, like the Night Stalker in East Los Angeles—Mas was always amazed how different he seemed from the early drawings. Perhaps the victims couldn't clearly describe their assailant; the darkness of the crime pulled a film over their eyes, blinding them to the softness of a mouth, the liveliness of the eyes, or the curve of an ear.

He sat in the passenger seat of the Yamadas' old Buick, in front of their fabric dashboard cover. A line of decorative pins had been attached to the right side, above the glove compartment—a swirling American flag, the words 442ND REGIMENTAL COMBAT UNIT—GO FOR BROKE; a church and a cross outlined by an orange sun, SUNRISE BAPTIST CHURCH—CENTENNIAL; and the rings of the 1984 Olympics.

It was eight-thirty at night and the sun was just starting to set, casting an orange hue over the hills north of Little Tokyo. Barely visible, they were dried out and brown. Tiny homes crowded the base of the slopes like globs of salmon eggs.

Mas grasped the shoulder strap of the seat belt. "You know, when we get there, betta if you just drop me off. I can get a ride home."

"I can hold my own, Mas. Don't be worried about me."

There was plenty to worry about, though. There was Haneda, and then Haruo, the sickest gambler alive. Mas remembered the time when Haruo had disappeared for some days after his divorce.

"Probably turn up dead," Stinky Yoshimoto had said at the lawn mower shop. "You know—pah." He pointed a finger toward his head like a gun.

Mas kept his mouth shut. Stinky and the others knew nothing. Death was easy, but Mas and Haruo had been cursed with surviving. To take your own life was an insult to the dead—like stealing a medal and wearing it proudly over your shirt pocket. No matter how bad things got, you had to just wait and hope that someone or something else would cut you down, cleanly and swiftly, like pulling weeds out from the ground.

Haruo had eventually turned up in Laughlin, feeding his last nickels into a hungry slot machine. Stinky seemed a little disappointed; gossip at the lawn mower shop had reached a lull, and news of a suicide would have sure sparked things up.

Little Tokyo had not been a part of town that you went to at night. That's when the *manju* makers brushed rice flour from their hands and darkened their sweet shops, the bankers went home to the suburbs, and *bento* lunch shops closed their doors. To the south, the beggars dragged out their cardboard homes, while City Hall remained lit but deserted. Mas had heard of a friend whose car had been broken into, and a ten-pound bowling ball had been stolen. In another case, a thief had taken a radiator out of a car and was on his way to a local dive with his prize when he was apprehended.

That was before they began cleaning it up—building new, fancy structures and sending out a troop of citizen patrolmen. But Mas was still not going to take any chances.

"That parking lot best place," Mas said, pointing to a place with a security guard, and Tug nodded. No sense in Tug's having his car stolen, too.

A few bars were open, as well as all-night noodle shops catering to carousing young people and red-faced Japanese businessmen. Mas glanced at the map and figured out that it was on the second floor of a brick building painted white. On the first floor was a video store, still open with paper hearts twirling from the ceiling.

"This way." Tug opened a glass door, which led to a dark, narrow staircase.

"Wait, Tug, maybe—" Mas was having second thoughts. Tug was a family man, after all, with a wife and grandchildren.

"C'mon." Tug slapped Mas's back with his huge palm, practically pushing him up the stairs.

At the top was a door. Mas turned the knob. Locked. The staircase was pitch-black.

Mas turned, bumping into Tug's stomach. "I guess no one's there."

"Try knocking."

But Mas was having second thoughts. "Let's just get outta here."

"Who's that?" A muffled male voice sounded from the other side.

"Mas. Itsu Mas Arai."

The door opened, and there was Wishbone. In the shadow of the room, the pockmarks on his face looked like the surface of a peach pit, all bumpy and dark. Out of the context of Tanaka's Lawnmower shop, Wishbone didn't seem like himself. He wasn't smiling, and his usual mischievous grin was replaced with a cold stare. "Thought you weren't coming." He held a strange-looking skinny cigarette in his wrinkled hand.

"Change my mind," said Mas. While Tug was introducing himself to Wishbone, Mas examined the room, which was cloudy with smoke. A light hung from the ceiling over a card table. Mas didn't recognize most of the faces, young ones with shaven heads and tattoos, some even with zigzag scars. There were paler Japanese with meticulously oiled hair and expensive suits. A few *hakujin* men—one with a pitiful wisp of a mustache—looked like they hadn't bathed for at least two days. This crowd was a rough one. Mas could smell the scent of jail time and illicit activity. This wasn't what Wishbone was bargaining for, Mas knew.

"Where is he?" Mas asked.

"I'll get him."

Mas meant Haruo, but Wishbone was speaking to another man in a corner. The man turned, and Mas felt like his heart had stopped. It was the same man in the photos in the North Hollywood apartment, but this one had been reduced to skin and bones. His cheeks, even his eyes, seemed sunken into his skull. His hair was cropped short, and age spots marked his bare skin like raindrops.

The man was walking toward Mas, coming closer and closer, and then the face, once a composite, now was real flesh and bones. The reality now hit Mas squarely. He could no longer think of this man as other than who he really was.

"Riki," Mas whispered.

"Haneda," the man said. His voice was gravelly, the sound of work boots crushing pebbles and sand. "You call me Haneda."

✣ ✣ ✣

Somehow thinking of Riki Kimura as Joji Haneda all these years had slowly erased the painful memory of the real Joji. But having Riki Kimura standing in front of him changed everything. Time had not been kind to him, that was for sure. Mas didn't know if it was because of the decades of hard living. Or maybe the decay of Riki's insides had finally grown to reach his outsides. Whatever it was, Mas didn't want to be anywhere near Riki, but he had to, at least for this night.

Tug, who had been surveying the room, approached Mas and Riki. "Tug Yamada," he said, sticking out his hand.

"Joji Haneda," Riki said easily, slipping a fresh cigarette in the side of his mouth. "You a friend of Arai's?"

Mas stepped in front of the two men, his back toward Riki. "Haruo," he said to Tug. "Check table."

Tug nodded, looking a little confused. Here good manners don't count for anything, Mas said to himself. You may be bigger than most of the men here, Tug, but you're way out of your league. Watching Tug's white head disappear in the crowd, Mas turned his attention to Riki. "People are comin' 'round, askin' about Joji Haneda."

"So I heard." Riki lit his cigarette with a match and grinned, fifty years falling from his face. Other than the stained brown teeth, it was the same man. He took a drag of his cigarette, and Mas could see him in the middle of that Hiroshima boulevard, teenagers and children crowded around barrels of fire.

"You betta leave, go back to Ventura."

"Oh, yah?" Riki extinguished the match with his fingers.

"They gonna find out."

"What? That thousands of people die in Hiroshima? Thatsu no secret, Masao-*san*."

"You make him die."

"America, heezu country, your country, killsu him. You say I killsu him—where's the evidence?"

"They gotsu a drawing, a picture."

"A picture?" Riki laughed. Brown tobacco stains had darkened his teeth like an ancient Japanese harlot. "Whatsu that suppose to prove?"

"Itsu Haneda, wiz your name on him." Mas remembered the crudely drawn jumble of maggots, the strange circle by the body.

"Oh, yah?" Riki smirked. "What the harm? Whole family's dead. He was almost dead when we found him."

"Well, Akemi's not dead. Alive."

Riki took another drag from his cigarette, but Mas noticed that his spotted fingers trembled.

"Gonna come out."

"You gon' tell them?" Riki sneered. "Someone should warn you about that." An image of tasseled loafers flashed in Mas's brain.

Before Mas could mention the grandson, someone called out, "Haneda, a spot opened up. You in or you out?"

Riki raised his hand, the ash falling down like dust. "Izu in."

✣ ✣ ✣

Mas pushed his way through the crowd, past two blackjack tables and one pai gow. Here, above this brick, low-level storefront, was a gambling operation that rivaled that of any Indian casino. After Riki slipped into a chair at a green felt table, a dark mustached man on his left began dealing cards. A flat leather pouch with a tiki design hung from a string around the dealer's neck. To his side was a metal cash box. On the other side of the cash box sat Wishbone, plastic poker chips piled up in front of him like a skyline. To the right of Riki was Haruo, his chin down in his chest and his head shaking back and forth. Mas first thought Haruo was petrified to be found out, but he must have been this way for a while.

Mas noticed that only five chips lay scattered on

the table near Haruo. "How much gone?" he hissed in Haruo's ear.

Haruo continued shaking but didn't respond.

"How much?" Mas said—this time louder.

Haruo lifted his face, the bump of a keloid scar showing beneath his hair. "Almost five hundred."

Mas cursed. "Dis guyzu out," he said as the man with the pouch dealt the last card to Wishbone.

Riki spread his cards in his hand like a peacock raising its feathers. "Too late, Mas. Already started."

"Howzyu get five hundred, Haruo?" Mas remembered that Haruo had proudly shown him his personal monthly budget, figures from his social security, all six hundred dollars, written in one column, with his expenditures in another—seventy-five cents for the Laundromat, eighty dollars for gas, a hundred dollars for groceries, three hundred thirty for rent, and so on. It left only six dollars and thirty cents for the column "Savings."

The seated dark man patted the metal cash box. "He borrowed it from the bank. His car is the collateral." His voice was staccato, reminding Mas of his occasional helper Eduardo.

"It's probably only worth that much," muttered Wishbone.

"I tole you don't call him. Heezu sick. Heezu a sick man." Mas bent down so close to Wishbone that he could smell his sour breath.

"I'm no social worker. Besides, I wasn't the one who called him."

"You were always one to jump to conclusions." Plastic poker chips clicked in Riki's hands. "*I* called Haruo."

"Itsu my choice, Mas." Haruo pulled at the green felt. "I needsu to take *sekinin* for my actions."

"Thatsu what good-for-nutin' counselor saysu? Whatta 'bout your kids? You gonna go ova there in some bus?"

"Maybe. If I hafta."

Mas felt heat rise to his ears. That damn Haruo. No pride.

The dark man, called Luis, patted the metal cash box. "There's the five hundred dollars."

"I match it." Mas shifted his weight from one foot to another. "Okay, two hundred, but I get fifty dolla in chips. He's got about that much left, anyhowsu."

Luis brushed down the overgrown whiskers above his lip. "Sounds good to me."

"Mas, howzu you gonna get four hundred?" Haruo whispered, remaining in his folding chair.

"Let's see it right now," said Riki.

"I gotsu it," Mas said, thinking about the IRA Chizuko had opened for them years ago.

Riki lifted a cigarette from an ashtray to his dry lips. A line of ash an inch long bent down from his fingers as he inhaled. "Cash," he repeated.

Mas opened his wallet and dumped wadded-up

bills and change onto the table. Luis flattened the bills and organized them in neat stacks. "A hundred thirty-five and nineteen cents," he said.

Haruo shook his head and shoved his hair behind his ears. "No, Mas. I needsu to take *sekinin*." The scar on the left side of his face was clearly visible now. A web of puffed skin and deep recesses, gnarled like the bark of a diseased tree, stretched from his mid-forehead to his cheek. With his left eyebrow and eyelashes missing, Haruo's fake pupil looked undressed, naked, startled, while the right side of his face held his true nature—soft and lightly freckled, thin eyebrow, gentle double-lidded eye.

Tug, who had been silent, stepped forward with a rectangular blue checkbook. "How about I pay for the rest?"

The men stared at Tug and began laughing. Riki almost spilled his drink on the table. "Check?"

"This not your business," Mas said to Tug. Tug and Lil were careful with their money, going to senior citizen early-bird specials at coffee shops, and even trading flattened aluminum cans for mere nickels at the local recycling center.

"He can just pay me back. In monthly installments, right? That would be the responsible thing to do."

Haruo bit his lip, folded his arms, and rocked in the folding chair. "I dunno."

Luis's dark brown eyes seemed to take stock of Tug's clean golf shirt, his pressed khaki pants, his neat loafers, a pipe sticking out of his shirt pocket. "He's good for it, Joji."

"No." Riki smashed his cigarette stub in the ashtray. "We're not a pawnshop."

"Now, Joji—" interjected Wishbone.

"No." Riki clamped his jaws together, and his eyes seemed to burn like coals in their sockets. Mas felt something charge in his brain. It was dread, like the time his car overheated right there on the Pasadena Freeway. The whole car had rattled as if it were going to explode.

Luis arranged Mas's bills in various compartments in the metal cash box. "Look, I'll cover him." He counted out five blue chips while Tug asked for the spelling of his name for the check. "Luis Saito," he said. "L-U-I-S, the Spanish way."

Riki, looking a bit defeated, got up and poured himself a beer by the makeshift bar in the corner. On his way back to his seat, he muttered in Mas's ear, "You betta watch your friend. You don't want nutin' to happen to him."

As if his body were reacting to Riki's poison, Mas felt a jolt go up his back. Then he saw another familiar face among the other good-for-nothings standing around the table. Yuki Kimura.

"You," Mas could only manage to spit out. The boy must have followed him and Tug to Little Tokyo.

Yuki pulled at a long chain that was attached to his belt loop and grinned. "Second time today," he said.

Mas said nothing. He didn't have time for the boy right now. He needed to concentrate all his energy on the card game and getting Haruo out of his jam.

Riki must have noticed Mas's reaction to Yuki, because he invited the boy to sit down. "Might learn sumptin'." Riki smiled, pulling a flimsy wooden chair beside him.

Yuki sauntered to the chair and sat down, his brown arms folded at his chest. Mas felt queasy just thinking that grandfather and grandson were unknowingly right next to each other. There was definitely a physical resemblance around the eyes, the high bridge of the nose.

"It's your call, Mas," Wishbone said. "What you going to do?"

Mas settled in the chair and picked up his hand. Seven of diamonds, ten of diamonds, jack of spades, three of hearts, three of spades. A pitiful hand worth nothing. "We drop."

"But, Mas—" Haruo muttered behind him.

Mas bit down. That's what Haruo's problem was: He didn't know when to quit.

"Okay, I call." Luis proudly displayed a full house—two eights and three kings.

"Damn." Wishbone tossed his cards in the center pile.

"Chotto matte." Riki grinned, exposing his black, rotting teeth. "Got me a straight flush." He had a line

of clubs—all in ascending order: seven, eight, nine, ten, and jack.

Luis's mustache went flat.

"Too bad, Saito." Wishbone laughed as Riki pulled in the blue, yellow, and green chips.

"New hand, new chance," Luis said, lifting his beer glass.

Wishbone was the dealer. His arthritic, bent fingers shuffled the cards into a red spray of cascading curves and straight-flowing rivers. Everyone tossed in a blue chip, worth ten bucks. The cards were dealt, and both Tug and Haruo sat in back of Mas like trainers in a boxing match. The young reporter, on the other hand, remained next to his secret grandfather. The whole scene was enough to make Mas sick.

It had been years since Mas played with Wishbone, and even longer with Riki. This other man, Luis, turned out to be a Japanese from Peru.

Wishbone threw two cards toward Luis. "If we got a few more guys, we could start another game. But that dang Heart Mountain reunion. Seems like every guy wants to see their old buddies and dance partners from camp."

Yuki, who had long been quiet, finally spoke up. "Heart Mountain? What is Heart Mountain?"

"It's a camp. You know, internment camp during World War Two." Wishbone wrinkled his nose at Yuki. "You not from around here, are you?"

"Heezu Japanese, from Hiroshima," said Haruo. "Really smart boy."

"Not that smart," mumbled Wishbone.

Mas, trying to drown out their conversation, studied his cards. A ten of spades, jack of spades, jack of diamonds, king of spades, and seven of hearts. Strong possibilities. Now, was he going to go for an entire set of spades, or maybe a royal flush? Or maybe just stick to the two jacks. Two jacks were decent enough, and he could hang on to the king for another match. But then, Riki asked for just one card. Meant that he had something big going on in that hand.

Mas's instincts told him to play it safe. He could faintly hear Haruo in back of him, breathing loudly through his mouth.

"Decision, decision." Riki raised another cigarette to his mouth. "Pretty soon, the moon will be out."

Mas tried to ignore Riki. Do something rash in cards, and you pay for it later. He put the seven of hearts and ten of spades facedown. "Two," he said.

"Hey, that's it." Wishbone sent two cards Mas's way. A four of spades and a king of diamonds. Two pair, face cards. Good, but was it good enough?

Wishbone turned his attention to Tug. "That's where I know that name, Yamada. From Heart Mountain. You got a sister, right? She was a member of one of those girlie clubs, the Divines. Softball player, if I remember correctly. Catcher."

"Yep, won the camp championship." Tug removed

his pipe from his pocket and began stuffing it with cherry tobacco.

Luis put down one of his cards.

"Big girl," Wishbone said. "What's she up to now?" A new card was dealt back to Luis.

"She's an assistant principal in the valley. Married to an insurance man. Got three kids and a grandkid. He's playing football over in Ohio."

"Wow, imagine that." Wishbone fanned out his own cards. "A Buddhahead playing football. And he's pure Japanese, right? None of these mixes. Yessiree, one of these days we'll see one of our boys in the NFL."

Luis thumped down his empty glass on the table. "Wishbone, play." The scent of cherry tobacco pervaded the room.

"Ah, you're just sore because you've been salty all night. Ah, hell." Wishbone looked at his cards. "I'm gonna get me four." He counted out four cards from the deck and added it to his single remaining card.

It was back to Riki. "Izu in." He threw in another blue chip. He exhaled smoke in a steady stream, a snake inching forward and then disappearing.

Mas hesitated. Could two pair of kings and jacks beat whatever Riki had? Even three deuces could do it. But then again, Riki was the champion bluffer.

"You all knowsu that me and Mas were friends back in Hiroshima?" Riki spoke up. "Yah, weezu known each other a real long time."

Yuki seemed mesmerized by Riki and even took out his notebook from his backpack. Mas, meanwhile, steadied himself. He knew that losing his head would only quicken his ruin.

Riki continued. "Youzu think friends help each other. Watch each other's back. Not always the case."

Mas felt his face grow hot. He was thankful for the liquor that flowed freely throughout the room. Maybe everyone figured that Riki was drunk, or maybe the listeners themselves couldn't grasp the conversation. He finally threw in a blue chip. Only about fifteen left. He could barely hear Haruo murmuring something in the back.

It was Luis's turn next. His elbow on the cash box, he remained still. He rearranged his cards, poking one from the side into the middle and then repeating it again.

"Move it around; don't change anything, Saito." Wishbone crinkled his nose and let out a dry laugh. He scratched his scrawny chest and then returned his attention to Tug. "So, were you in Wyoming, too?"

"Just in the beginning." The spicy sweetness of the cherry pipe tobacco pervaded the room.

"Oh, you were a 'No-No'?"

"I enlisted and was shipped out to Camp Shelby."

"Oh, I see." Wishbone's face lost its gleam. "Hurry up, Saito. We don't have all day. *Ándale, ándale,*" he added in Spanish.

Luis moved a blue chip to the center pile.

Wishbone tossed his cards. "I'm out."

"In, and raise another ten." Riki flipped in a yellow chip. "Your turn, my friend."

Mas sucked on the insides of his loose cheeks. That probably was some hand Riki had. Still, he couldn't give in now. He pushed two blue chips toward the center pile.

A line of sweat rolled from Luis's thick black hair down his forehead. He stared at the litter of chips in the middle and at his steadily decreasing stack. He tried to twirl a yellow chip like a top, but it merely bounced awkwardly on the green felt. "I'm in," he said finally. The yellow chip clicked against the blue ones.

"No more waiting." Riki set out his hand. "Two pair." He flashed two queens and two tens. Mas felt the top of his head tingle.

"Can you believe this? I have some kind of curse." Luis shook his head over his pair of aces, and then a single king, queen, and jack.

Wishbone began collecting the discarded cards. "Some kind of *bachi*. Maybe you didn't treat your wife so good last night."

"Wait." Mas carefully put down his pair of kings and jacks. Their stoic faces were beautiful against the green felt.

"Hey!" Wishbone clapped his hands. "We got a poker game going here. Pot goes to Mas. Two pair—king beats out queen."

"Yatta!" Haruo made two bony fists and threw punches in the air. Settle down, thought Mas, counting the blue and yellow chips. One hundred, counting the thirty dollars he put in. They were only seventy bucks ahead. More than three hundred to go.

Tug puffed on his pipe and patted Mas's back. "Good job. I would have gone for the straight, and come up with nothing."

Riki doused his smashed cigarette in his glass. "More beer," he called out to no one in particular.

"Next time you make sure you shuffle those cards good, Wishbone," said Luis, wiping his forehead with a napkin.

"You got complaints, you deal, then." Wishbone dropped the deck of cards in front of Luis.

"No, it's Joji's turn." Luis passed the deck to Riki and then rummaged in a blue airline bag at his feet. He brought out a wrinkled paper bag, and from that he pulled out a short black bottle. It had the face of a tiki warrior, geometric eyes, nostrils, and mouth, much like the design on Luis's pouch. "Pisco," he said.

Wishbone batted his hand as if he were shooing away a fly. "Not that Peruvian poison. That'll kill us for sure."

"Hey, my brother brought this back from Lima. Best quality. Can't buy this here." Luis pulled out the cork and took a big sniff. He began pouring a small amount of the clear liquid into each glass. "Back home, we drink with lemon and egg. Today, try it straight."

Riki put his hand over his glass. "Pass."

"No, just try. I insist."

"I said pass," Riki rasped. He began coughing, first a few times, and then more furiously, until he hacked up some spittle and aimed it into a metal trash can next to him. Mas puckered his lips and moved a few inches to his left. There was something wrong with Riki. He was like a snake shedding its skin—only this one wasn't generating anything new.

"You need to do something about that cough. Go see a doctor or something," Wishbone said.

Riki ignored him and poured himself some beer.

Luis passed out the glasses. Tug demurred, explaining that he didn't drink, and instead got some 7-UP from the corner vending machine.

Yuki poured a generous amount in his glass to the point that Luis even commented, "Hey, this kind of pisco is kind of expensive, son."

Mas rearranged his chips in short, neat stacks and accepted a glass of pisco. He was ready to take a sip when Luis stopped him. "We must make a toast."

"A toast to what?" Wishbone's left eyebrow arched upward.

"To life, to our families, to happiness." Luis's voice was almost musical.

"To ole friends." Riki lifted his beer glass before letting out another cough and spitting into the waste-paper basket. Mas himself almost choked on the powerful liquor, which bit like whiskey but went down like the finest tequila.

They were in the middle of their next hand when Tug excused himself to go to the rest room. When he had left the table, Wishbone leaned over toward Mas. "So, why the hell you bring Mr. Straight over here, Mas?"

"Whatchu talkin' about?"

"That guy, Yamada. Writes checks, doesn't drink. Betcha he's one of those religious types, huh?"

Mas remembered the Yamadas' affiliation with the Sunrise Baptist Church. "That don't mean nutin'."

"That kind of guy can really put a damper on things." Wishbone's pockmarked face was red; even the tips of his pointy ears were flushed.

"He the type to get us in trouble," Riki added. "How do we knowsu heezu not callin' police right now?"

"Heezu not doing that," Mas said without conviction.

Riki cut the deck of cards with one hand. "Heezu *inu*, I betcha."

Inu. Dog. Snitch. The lowest thing one man could call another.

"He's a Go for Broke guy," Wishbone said. "If he figures out who I am, probably knock my head off. Or maybe I should knock his first."

Yuki was scribbling in his notebook again. "What's 'Go for Broke'?"

"Army man. That's their motto—you know, 'Go for Broke.' " Wishbone seemed wary of having to explain everything to Yuki.

Mas felt his chest tighten. "Whatchu have against him?"

"I'm a 'No-No' boy; my brother's a draft resister. We on the other sides of the line from guys like him."

"Dunno what you talkin' about," said Mas.

"My brother went to Leavenworth, okay? The federal penitentiary, for not fighting."

Mas remained quiet. The Nisei who were in California during the war all seemed to be thrown into some kind of jail—whether they were trying to prove a point or minding their own business.

"Never heard of it, I betcha. Yeah, just lately, the young people are making a big deal about it. My brother's a hero to them. And rightly so. Nobody else had the guts to say no to the government. Instead, those others were patsies, sacrificing their lives, for what? They say 'yes, yes' to the loyalty oath. 'Yes,' they were willing to serve in combat; 'yes,' they wouldn't bow down to the emperor. Like any of us would."

Wishbone's bloodshot eyes grew large and still. "So I checked 'No-No.' What the hell. They were gonna keep me behind barbed wire; I wasn't gonna promise anything. My brother did one better—he said he would serve, if we were restored our constitutional rights. So they were sent to hard-time prison, eighteen months. I had to go to Tule Lake. We all were the black sheep of the community."

"So the U.S. government imprisoned your brother for not fighting?" Yuki seemed confused by Wishbone's personal history lesson. It was confusing. First the Nisei were placed in camps because they lived near the Pacific Ocean; then they were put in jail if they didn't agree to fight on behalf of the government that had put them in camps in the first place. Didn't make much sense, Mas had to agree.

"Yes, yes," Wishbone said impatiently. "But my brother would have killed you son of a guns back in Japan if we were left free."

Mas tried to shield the boy from Wishbone's wholesale anger toward the Japanese and American wartime leaders. "That's fifty years ago. So what?"

"Mas, you weren't over here. You don't understand," said Wishbone. "Your friend and his people are the ones making a big deal about being veterans, making monuments. They're the ones talking bad about us, even now. All running scared about dying."

"Tug's not like that. He minds his own business." Thinks more about fixing toilets and doorbells than anything else, thought Mas.

"That's what you think." Wishbone picked his teeth with the fold of a matchbook cover, while Luis had his own stories about being kidnapped in Peru by the U.S. government, to be used as a pawn in a possible prisoner-of-war exchange. Yuki was scribbling even more furiously in his notebook. Soon he'd have enough for a full-out book.

Mas traced his front dental plate with his tongue and then noticed Riki staring right at him. He hadn't said much during the past few minutes, and Mas took that as a bad sign. When Riki wasn't talking, it meant that he was thinking. And Mas knew that that didn't lead to anywhere good.

From the very beginning, Riki didn't have anything nice to say to Mas. "You're a *chibi*, and nobody notices you," Riki said after school. Mas didn't let anyone call him runt, and got ready to box the new boy's ears. But then Riki held up his hands. "No, no, I'm saying that's good." Halfway good-looking people, according to Riki, blended into the crowd. They never left any kind of strong impression. They were bland and anonymous. Ugly people, on the other hand, with fleshy noses or thin lips, always attracted attention.

Mas, who was smack in the middle of seven brothers and sisters, never really accepted Riki's theory. But there was something intriguing about this new boy. So when Riki invited him to his house in the city one day, Mas went along with it. Even though it was in the middle of downtown, Riki's house was still large, almost as big as Mas's in the countryside. They left their shoes in the *genkan* and entered the two-story building. An old man, his face squeezed with wrinkles, nodded from his seat on the floor. He sat underneath a *kotatsu*, even though the room was already oppressively hot. A piano coated with dust sat on the left side of the room, while a Buddhist altar was placed on the right. A framed photo of a man wearing round-framed glasses was displayed next to a stick of lighted incense masking the scent of rotting tangerine.

"Who's the man in there?" Mas asked as they sat outside on a wooden deck. Next to Riki were a newspaper, matches, and something wrapped in a purple *furoshiki*, the kind that women knotted over a box of fresh rice balls.

"My grandfather." Riki creased the corner of the newspaper. "He doesn't even know when it's morning or night. He even does *unchi* in bed. It's disgusting. Mother has to drag him in the neighborhood bomb shelter every time she hears a siren. Two blocks away. I tell her just leave him. It would be better if he were blown away.

"She slapped me when I said that," he continued, and grinned. "Pretty hard. Right here on the *hoppeta*." Riki tapped the side of his cheek—smooth, aside from a few stray hairs. "Felt good."

"No," said Mas. "I mean the man in the picture, by the *Butsudan*."

"My father." Riki carefully tore out a square from the newspaper.

"Is he dead?"

"No. At least I don't think so. Mother thought it would be easier on us if he were." Riki took a package from his shirt pocket and sprinkled some dried-out grass into the newspaper square. He rolled it, twisting the sides. "Here," he said.

Mas was going to refuse. Smoking these makeshift cigarettes sometimes made his head spin. But he thanked Riki and struck a wooden match against the wooden deck. "So, what did you want to tell me?"

"I didn't say I was going to tell you anything." Riki had folded himself a cigarette and tipped a flame against the end.

"Yes you did. On our way home." Mas coughed.

"No good?" Riki blew out some gray smoke. "Here, take mine."

"No, I'm fine." Mas's head pounded, and his stomach was starting to feel queasy.

"I just said I was going to share something with you." Riki untied the *furoshiki*. "Look what I have." It was a bottle of sake, manufactured by a local distillery before it closed due to lack of rice. The label was still intact, with cursive Chinese characters glimmering in silver.

Mas licked his lips. "Where did you get that?"

"Connection." Riki twisted the top of the bottle

and poured the clear liquid into a chipped rice bowl. "Here," he said, handing Mas the sake. "You first."

Mas balanced the cigarette on the side of the deck and received the bowl with both hands. "Why me?" he asked. "Why do you want to share this with me?"

"Why not? We're friends, right?"

Mas nodded, gazing greedily at the rice wine. He raised the bowl in thanks and slurped it down, feeling it warm the back of his throat and bite into his nasal passages.

Riki poured himself a bowlful of the sake and tipped it into his mouth. He then traced the lip of the bowl with his finger and licked it, not to waste a single drop.

"How about a game of *hanafuda*?" Riki returned to the deck with a stack of small cards.

Mas grunted and folded his arms around his bent knee. The sun was at the same level as the low mountains, but there was still plenty of light. The cicadas droned, and Mas and Riki played, taking swigs of the sake and puffs of their cigarettes in between hands. As they flipped over cards of maple leaves, cherry blossoms, banners of purple, an orange warthog with raised hairs, Mas could almost forget that while his two brothers were in the navy, he was hungry, fifteen, and worthless.

"So, you close to the Hanedas, huh?"

Mas was surprised that Riki would even notice. "Neighbors," he merely stated.

"Heard the MPs were at their house yesterday."

Mas shrugged. His parents had told him to stay away from Joji, but Mas hadn't listened.

As they kept playing, Riki kept pushing. Where was Mas from? Didn't he want to fight in the navy, too? Mas began to feel weak. The sake didn't even seem to have the same bite, the cigarettes tasted even worse, and a grayness covered the yard. Mas laid out his last hand, the set of maple leaves. His favorite card was the one with the deer, its rear, plump legs tapered, and short tail taut. The deer was looking back, waiting to see what was beyond the autumn leaves of the maple trees.

✣ ✣ ✣

After Tug returned to his seat, the table grew quiet. The only sound was the flipping and shuffling of cards. Even Yuki had stopped asking his questions. Mas watched the motion of tiny red diamonds in Riki's hands, which were arched in the shape of two Cs. Finally he folded his hands over the cards and produced a flat, neat deck.

"Cut." Riki stretched out his palm toward Haruo.

"Wait a minute," Mas interrupted. "He not playin'."

"Cut," Riki repeated louder.

Haruo lifted half of the stack and then bent toward the table. The cards were being edged onto the green felt when they began to tip and then fell onto the spotted linoleum like blown dead leaves.

"Baka." Riki spat into the trash can again. Haruo and Tug knelt down to pick up the scattered spades, hearts, diamonds, and clubs, but Riki stood over them, the metal tips of his boots shiny and pointed. "Leave it. You'd probably end up bendin' some card anyhows."

Riki gathered the cards and placed all except one on the table. He turned over that one card, a king of spades, and held it toward the window. The scar on Riki's neck bulged like a row of deadly crabs. "Wishbone, come here."

"What?" Wishbone stumbled out of his chair, his face bright red.

"What do you see here?"

Wishbone struggled with a pair of reading glasses extracted from his shirt pocket. "Well, yeah—"

"Sometin' wrong?" Mas felt his stomach churn.

The scarred neck twisted around, and then, in one swoop, the card was slapped onto the green felt. "This card's marked." Riki traced his chipped fingernail alongside a thin pen mark. Faint, but distinct. Looked blue, dark blue.

Luis, his elbow on the cash box, propped himself up. "Yes, that's a marked card." He blinked, his heavy eyelashes batting together. "Who—"

"King of spades. Part of the winning hand." The chipped fingernail tapped against the fine line. "Mas's hand."

Mas almost started laughing. So that's how Riki

was going to play it. But Mas wasn't interested in silly games anymore. "No sense cheatin'. Not with *shiroto* like you."

"Shiroto?" The linoleum squeaked under Riki's boots. Calling Riki an amateur had apparently hurt. "You fools are the ones ova your heads. Cheatin' is your way of life, Mas—you knowsu that."

Tug extended his right hand, the one with the shortened finger. "Look, I'm sure there's a perfectly logical explanation for all of this. Maybe there was some ink on the floor; maybe it was marked from before."

Riki grinned, his sagging cheeks tightening into creases. "You trust this man," he said to Tug. "You know him?"

"Known him since our daughters were in preschool. At least thirty years."

"Knowsu how he thinks?" Riki now tapped the side of his head. "Just thinks about his own self, I tellsu you."

And you don't? Mas said to himself.

"You all think heezu your friend. But watch out. He'll cut your throat. I know. I saved his life, and look what he did to me. Sold me out. Escape to America with my money."

Everyone was looking down at the green felt poker table, scared to look at Mas eye to eye. Mas remembered sitting in that makeshift police station, a former tofu factory. He was only eighteen. You better not hang around that *chinpira,* they said. Tell us his name and where we can find him, and we'll let you go.

Haruo picked up a stray card and laid it on the table. "Sad things happen to all of us." His long hair was again behind his ears, and his *Ron-Pari* eyes seemed to be focused on Riki and Mas simultaneously. "Can't change the past. Just can look ahead."

"You shut up, you old fool." Riki twisted a card in his hands. "You have no sense. I know; I've heard. Stealin' other people's money. There's only one thing worse than a *dorobo*—an *inu.*"

"Now, there's no need to call names—" The linoleum creaked underneath Tug.

Riki gripped a half-empty beer bottle. "Stay away." Tug seemed unafraid. Mas had seen Tug in action a few times before. In one incident, when Mari was still small, their families had been waiting in a restaurant in San Diego after going to a wild animal park. For five minutes, nobody seated them. Ten minutes later, still no one came around. Mas told himself that it wasn't any big deal; he was used to it, anyhow. But Tug made a fuss—demanding to see the manager, and kicking the door open when they left without eating. Mas had turned to Chizuko, expecting her face to be like his, withdrawn and tight with embarrassment. Instead, her eyes behind her glasses practically gleamed, so genuinely was she in awe of Tug's power and righteous anger.

It was as if that passion were being transferred from Tug to Mas. "Youzu betta go now," he told Riki. "I not gonna keep quiet. I warnin' you. And I knowsu you behind my truck gettin' stolen."

"What? Your stinkin' Ford? You still have that old relic? Why wouldsu anyone want that piece of trash?"

By this time, all the pai gow and blackjack tables were silent and everyone in the room seemed to focus on Mas and Riki. Even Yuki, his notebook limp in his right hand, wasn't able to write anything down.

"I not scared of youzu." As the words left his mouth, Mas was surprised that they were indeed true.

Riki edged closer to Mas. "But you should be, Mas. This your summer of the big *bachi*."

"Anytin' youzu do won't hurt me."

"Yah, maybe not youzu, but how about people around you?"

Before Mas could fully understand the weight of his nemesis's threat, Riki swung his beer bottle, aiming for Tug's white head as if it were a piñata. The glass broke, and the beer sloshed onto the green felt and then the linoleum. Tug dropped to the ground.

"You—" Mas lunged at Riki, his hands pulling at his knit shirt and then wrapping around his neck. The scar felt rubbery, the worn tread of a tire. Riki wheezed and then laughed. The whole room seemed to shake and moan. In a matter of seconds, the table was overturned, poker chips of red, blue, and yellow cascading onto the linoleum. Fists pounded faces; chairs burst against walls. Mas lost his grip on Riki and was shoved to and fro, and then, from the edge of his eye, saw a shadow descending. As he turned to face it, he saw a line of stained teeth before he was finally thrown to the floor.

CHAPTER SEVEN

A few seconds later, Mas was shaking himself off the floor. His whole body smarted bad, but he was able to make out a familiar voice yelling, "Police, police." It was Haruo at his finest.

The room magically cleared. The door flung open, and men were streaming down the stairs. Mas looked across the linoleum floor, past poker chips and flattened cigarette butts, to see Tug's sprawled body. He was out cold.

Later, in the hospital waiting room, Mas got the rest of the story from Wishbone, who seemed especially despondent. Mas didn't know if it was because the police were now investigating the card game or because Wishbone had lost a small fortune in the scuffle. "I didn't see much blood," Wishbone said. "Actually, I think if it weren't for some quick thinking from that Japanese kid, Tug would really be in trouble."

"Japanese kid?"

"You know, that reporter. Right after Tug went down, the kid dumped the poker table on its side. Shielded Tug from those SOBs. They were drunk out of their mind, anyhows. Got tired of pounding the table." Wishbone pulled at a whisker on his pock-marked face and then took a look at Mas's head. "You okay?"

"Yah," Mas lied. He didn't mention Riki, but Wishbone must have read his mind.

"And Haneda—" Wishbone shook his head. "Well, nobody can find him. He disappeared, along with a big chunk of change. Never should have gotten involved with him. Never should have."

❖ ❖ ❖

Mas felt like he was stuck in that emergency waiting room for hours. It smelled bad and sour, like *shikko,* but something else, too. It was familiar, almost like burnt rubber. Within the next couple of hours, he pieced together that there had been a fire over in a factory near the garment district. A bunch of women had been rolled in on stretchers from a string of ambulances. As they were wheeled through the emergency room, Mas could see only their dark hair matted together like scouring pads Chizuko used on dirty dishes.

Tug was still behind the metal doors, and so was Haruo. Wishbone told Mas that he should get checked out, too, but what for? Getting pushed around was no big deal for a gardener like Mas. One time, when he was trimming an overgrown oak tree, he accidentally disturbed a wasp nest. He was off of that ladder in five seconds flat, traveling headfirst. Chizuko said that it was good that he was *ganko,* that his head was as hard as a bowling ball.

This time Mas felt a little woozy, he had to admit. The various languages spoken around him seemed to merge into one endless prattle. He sank deeper into the black padded chair. He ached for a cigarette but remembered that he had left his last carton of Marlboros in the truck, now gone.

What was taking so long? Haruo had a simple cut on the cheek that could be remedied with a couple of Band-Aids. But Tug. That beer bottle had hit him hard. Mas should have known better and kept him safe at home with Lil and his red tool kit.

"Can't stand dis no more." Mas finally got up, leaving the melted ice bag on the chair. He couldn't wait for Wishbone, who had gone to ask the nurse for an update. Mas needed to find out for himself what was going on.

Mas went through the double doors, which swished open when he stepped onto the rubber mat. There were cloth curtains dividing the wide room like horse stalls. Nurses and doctors in green, white, and pink gowns walked back and forth with IV bottles and charts. On one side, two police officers in black passed by, their leather holsters and belts squeaking with each step.

The smell coated the entire room. Mas felt sick to his stomach, but continued to look through the curtains for either Tug or Haruo. He tried to breathe out of his mouth, but the stink was still there, soaking into his pores.

Then there were the moans. They were at first soft, like dry whispers, and then began to grow louder and deeper. They were coming from a curtain on the left side. Mas tried to look away, but wasn't fast enough. The woman was one of the factory fire victims. Her whole body was raw and blistered like boiled shrimp, while her eyes were sucked into her swollen face.

Mas took a few steps back, banging into a metal tray of syringes and bandages. The policemen with the squeaky holsters turned around and stared.

"Mas." It was a familiar voice. Haruo was sitting on one of the beds, a piece of blue string hanging from his cheek. Standing next to him was the boy, the red badger.

"Mas," Haruo repeated. "You *orai*?"

Mas tried to say something, but his mouth was raw.

"Crazy, huh, Mas? I'm glad you *orai*. Tug's still gettin' checked out. Dis young guy saved his life."

Mas grunted. Against the white curtain, Yuki seemed taller and thinner than at the poker game. He was in his black T-shirt, with only a white swatch, a hospital guest sticker, over his heart.

Leaving Haruo in the emergency room, Mas and Yuki went outside for a smoke. In the hospital, Mas had lost track of time. It was four in the morning, and a reassuring hush lay over the small bungalows and palm trees in the distance. Yuki took a package of cigarettes from his backpack and offered one to Mas.

Mas was ready to refuse, especially anything coming from a package named Mild Seven. But a Japanese cigarette was still a cigarette. "You turn up everywhere," Mas said, accepting the offer.

Yuki lit his cigarette with a silver lighter, while Mas had his Bic.

"You follow me," Mas stated more than asked.

"Actually, it was luck," Yuki said after inhaling.

"Whatsu that?"

"Luck," Yuki repeated. "I did follow you and Yamada-*san*, but I had already heard about the card game from people at the Empress Hotel."

"Empress?" It was a fleabag hotel on the second floor of the chop suey house that had since closed down. "Whatchu doin' at Empress?"

"Stayin' there."

Mas was surprised. "I thought you Japanese guys stay in fancy places."

"Maybe I'm not just an average Japanese guy."

Mas had to agree with that. They smoked silently for a few minutes, until Yuki finally spoke up. "I lied to you."

Yes, that much was for sure, Mas thought to himself.

"Back at the exams. I said I was looking for Riki Kimura."

Mas stood still, listening to some sparrows chirp in a nearby bush.

"It's not him. Not really. I'm actually investigating someone else. Joji Haneda."

Mas blew out a stream of smoke.

"What's your connection?" Yuki asked. "Why is he so mad at you?"

"What's yours?" Mas replied. He wasn't going to offer anything, at least not without getting more. An alley cat poked its nose into the bush, sending the sparrows away to rest on some telephone lines.

"It's related to a piece of land," Yuki explained, "where my grandmother lives."

So, thought Mas, this all has to do with land, which meant money.

"It's not my property but my grandmother's," Yuki clarified. "It's where her family house is—just on the outskirts of town. My grandmother inherited it because her older brother, Joji, was dead. Or at least we all thought that he had died. It's not a big piece of land or anything, but it's the location. There's a new set of mansions they're developing. Sort of retirement mansions."

Mas hadn't been back to Japan in forty years, but he had watched enough Japanese soap operas to know their version of mansions was like those two-bedroom condominiums sprouting all around Pasadena.

"So this developer's been after us for the past five years," Yuki said. "But then NHK compiled this report from America, about *hibakusha* in California. Who should we see on television, but this man named Joji Haneda."

Damn Riki. Mas remembered the CBS interview last year. Why did he have to be an *ochoshimono* and go after attention? Like bugs to light.

"Joji Haneda in California, we think. What a coincidence. There's another Joji Haneda over there. But then the developer starts getting ideas. What if this Haneda is the same Haneda? Then the land would automatically revert to him—you know, son over daughter. Calls are made to various governmental agencies. Faxes are sent to the consulate's office. Turns out this Joji Haneda is born in the exact same year, exact same village. And his parents have the exact same names. Then all of us start wondering, Is this the same Joji Haneda? My grandmother gets excited.

'Is this Joji Haneda my brother?' She can't tell on the television screen. It's been fifty years, right? She wants to call him up, but I tell her not to. I need to find out for myself."

"How much dis land worth?"

"Well, I guess, in American dollars . . . three million."

Mas nearly choked on his cigarette. Everyone has an angle, he thought. And this boy has a three-million-dollar one.

"It's not about the money." Yuki furrowed his eyebrows, and his skin looked darker than ever.

Yah, right, thought Mas. It's always about money. With Akemi's son dead, the grandson would be set to inherit it all.

"Do I look like a person who cares about money?"

"I see all kinds in my job," said Mas. "Looks don't mean nutin'."

Yuki's jaw tightened. "I would never sell the land. That's one thing my father told me before he died: 'Hang on to it. Keep it in the family. Don't let it go.' "

"Thatsu all your business. Has nutin' to do with me."

Yuki rubbed his head, the tips of his hair bristling forward. "You know him well. That man who calls himself Joji Haneda."

The ash of Mas's cigarette had burnt down to his knuckles. Mas now had no doubt that Yuki had been pursuing him ever since the medical exams. He knew that he had to be careful—who knew what the boy was up to?

Yuki continued his interrogation. "What was he talking about? Why was he so upset?"

"I talk to lots of sonafuguns at a poker game, big deal. Dis free country. Why didn't you go ova, ask him face-to-face?"

"And tell him about this property that may be in his name? I don't think so. I don't know this man. He could pretend that he's somebody he's not."

Mas tapped his cigarette and watched the ash blow onto the sidewalk.

"So you tell me, Arai-*san*. Don't you know anything that can help me?"

Mas swallowed. It was so early he wasn't thinking straight. Or maybe he had known all along what was going to happen to Yuki Kimura. "Give me some paper and a pen."

The boy retrieved a mechanical pencil from his backpack and tore off a piece of notebook paper. Mas wrote down the information as best he could. "Her name is Junko Kakita," he said. "She ova there in North Hollywood. You ask her whatsu goin' on."

✣ ✣ ✣

Just when Mas thought he had gotten rid of one kind of trouble, another kind came along. This time it was in the form of a seventy-something Nisei woman in jeans, T-shirt, tennis shoes, and bifocals. Lil Yamada. Mas didn't know how she'd gotten to the hospital, but she was there, outside, by the pay phones.

She was inserting quarter after quarter into the public phone like it was a video poker machine. She stopped for a moment and fumbled through her purse, most likely for more change.

"Whatcha need?" Mas said, pulling a fistful of dimes and nickels from his pocket.

Lil looked up, flustered. When she saw that it was Mas, her faced colored and hardened just enough for him to know that she was mad as hell. She hesitated, and then picked up some of the coins. "Thank you," she said. "Calling Joe."

Mas let Lil alone for a while. He overheard her talking to her son, saying words like "concussion" and "tests." But mostly she kept her voice and head down as if she were trying to keep dry in a rainstorm.

✣ ✣ ✣

As Mas snuck glances at Lil from the hospital driveway, the pain in his head and back slipped away. Instead, he felt a sharpness in his gut, one that Chizuko used to trigger.

Chizuko had been the daughter of a small-business man, and smart. She was wearing glasses when Mas met her for the first time, at a meeting arranged by her grandparents and his parents. She wasn't beautiful, but she didn't seem to care. Mas was impressed with the way she sat. Her back was rail straight, her thin legs folded underneath her body. Her blouse was striped and neatly tucked into her skirt. Her shiny glasses were perfectly balanced above her tiny nose.

This woman was a woman of principles, Mas had thought. And his hunch was right. Chizuko had the cleanest *kokoro*, character and soul, of any person he had ever met. She was the personification of *chanto*, of doing things just right. She read instructions to everything, from the Bisquick baking mix to tax forms to Dr. Spock to car manuals.

And she followed each instruction with every power in her being. "Shift the car to D2 on the freeway above 40 miles per hour. You must do it. It says so in the manual," she said as Mas was driving their new Datsun to San Francisco.

She valued her female friends, and often gathered flowers in her garden, wrapped them up in newspaper, and presented bouquets on a regular basis. Sometimes she baked cookies or rolled sushi—strips of avocado and imitation crab stuffed into sweetened vinegar rice and covered with black seaweed. Always the rejects, the cookies with burnt bottoms, or crooked slices of sushi, were left for Mas and Mari.

"Always the *kuzu*." Mas munched on a piece of

sushi in which the avocado and crab were coming loose from the rice.

Mari fingered a cracked oatmeal cookie. "Yeah, how come we get the messed-up ones?"

"Because you give the best away. Tastes the same, anyway, right?"

Mas complained too, but he secretly agreed with Chizuko. Friends should be given the best of everything. But now, without Chizuko, look what he had served up for Tug and Lil. He had mixed them up in a world that they had no business in. He needed to separate them again, but deep down inside he knew it was too late.

✣ ✣ ✣

After Lil finally got off the phone, Mas mustered up all the courage he could. "Tug *orai*?" he asked.

"Well, you know how he is. The doctor wants to keep him overnight for tests, but Tug doesn't want to listen. Says he's fine."

"Umm." Mas kept his hands awkwardly at his sides.

"Didn't even want to make a police report."

"Police?" Mas didn't know how far they were going to get involved with this.

"Well, this is a crime, Mas. Assault and battery. That man could have killed Tug."

Mas gritted down on his dentures.

"To see him all banged up like that—" Lil shook her head. "Mas, how could you take him to a place like that?" Her eyes, magnified by her bifocals, were steely black. The sun was starting to rise, and Mas could see the strong lines around her mouth and chin. He wanted to run and escape, but he couldn't. This was his punishment. His responsibility. He had to hear Lil out.

"He's an old man, Mas. I know he still thinks he can do anything, but we only have a few good years left to enjoy. Go places we've never been before together. Hawaii. Even Europe."

"Sorry," said Mas. "Very sorry."

"I was worried sick. When he didn't come home by eleven, I even went by your house."

"Very sorry," Mas repeated.

Tug and Lil were inseparable, especially as they grew older. They had met during the war. She was in a camp in Arkansas; he was in Camp Shelby, Mississippi. She and some other girls had formed a group to cheer up the Nisei soldiers. They made chicken teriyaki and rice; Tug was the only one who bothered to help. When he was sent overseas to Europe, they wrote each other every day until he was wounded. They got married a few months later in an army chapel.

Lil paused and looked at her watch. "You must be tired now. Why don't you go home?"

"No, I fine."

"No, please, we'll be all right."

As Mas stared at Lil's face, he realized that she

wasn't trying to be polite. She wanted him to leave because she couldn't stand looking at his face.

✣ ✣ ✣

By the time Haruo was released, it was already nine o'clock. It was way past breakfast, and Mas was hungry. "I'm stoppin' ova at the store," he told Haruo, who was resting in the passenger's seat of his car.

Mas was driving, and sped to the old Honda's limit, causing the car to tremble and cough like Mari's dog in its last days.

Mas parked in front of Frank's, a plain, one-story concrete building with barred windows. Haruo was sleeping now, so Mas entered the liquor store alone.

"Hey, Mas, haven't seen you around in a while." A black man with grizzled hair stood behind a counter surrounded by rows of potato chip bags and shiny bottles of distilled spirits. He wore a short-sleeved cotton shirt over a white undershirt curved at the neck.

Mas carried a couple of six-packs of beer from the refrigerated cases to the cash register and placed them on the counter beside a fishbowl filled with wrapped bubble gum.

"Starting early, Mas." Frank punched buttons on his old-fashioned cash register. "So, what, pack of Marlboros?"

"Nah. Not today." Mas pulled down a large bag of tortilla chips from a rack next to the counter.

"Don't tell me you quittin'. Heck, I should start selling those patches and nicotine gum. Can make a bundle, I think."

The cash register rang, spitting out the bottom drawer. "Nine-ninety," Frank said, collecting Mas's twenty-dollar bill. As he made change, he asked, "Hey, by the way, you see Yano's kids anymore?"

Mas shook his head. The Yanos had owned an old, rickety store next door full of pickled plums and dried seaweed. Mr. Yano had been tall for a Japanese. Most of his teeth were rotten, but that hadn't stopped him from smiling all the time.

"Yeah, I've been thinkin' about 'em. That was a shame, I tell you. Now, why would anybody go and shoot the ole man—for fifty dollars, no less. That Mr. Yano, he wouldn't hurt a fly. 'Hey, Frank-*san*,' he'd call out to me anytime I'd come through the door. He had some nasty stuff in there—long pickles in this mean brown stinkin' stuff. What do you call it?"

"Tsukemono."

"Yeah, *su-KI-mo-no.* Ooh-whee. He'd always pick that stuff up and shake it in my face." Frank lifted the six-packs into a brown paper bag. "And remember how Yano liked your daughter. He would call something every time he saw her. What was it again?"

Mas hugged the bag of six-packs, feeling the coldness against his chest.

"It was that word, you know, for 'daughter.' Huh, Mas, 'daughter'?"

As Mas pulled the door open, Frank spoke again, this time louder. "Oh, now I remember. *Mu-SU-me*, wasn't it?"

✣ ✣ ✣

Haruo awoke when Mas climbed into the car with the beer and chips. After they got back on the road, Mas scowled. "That ole man talk too much. Now he goin' on and on 'bout Yano-*san*."

"Yano, Yano. Oh, yah, Yano." Haruo patted down his strip of hair. "That was so *kawaiso*. Was gonna retire, huh? Rememba we all went down to Huntington to give blood for Yano-*san*. You got all dizzy, almost gotsu sick."

Mas had agreed to do it only because Chizuko had pushed him. Then later he found out that his blood type—AB—was not even compatible with Yano's. "Yah, all for nutin'."

"Not for nutin'. I mean, Yano didn't make it, but maybe you helped some other fella."

Mas cringed to think that his blood was now pulsing in a stranger's veins and heart.

"Even me, I plan to give my body to doctas after I die." Haruo opened up the bag of tortilla chips and shoved some into his mouth.

"They gonna take it?"

"Oh, yah. Who wouldn't? Everyone wants to know whatsamatta. Some people ask right out. You know those *hakujins*—'What happened to your face?' I used to say, 'Bomb, World War Two.' Then the people got real quiet; didn't wanna talk no more. Then I start changin' my story. 'Car crash.' 'Wife got mad.' 'Fire.' People start noddin' their head, tellin' me about same kind of accident their brother, sister, in-law, was in."

Mas didn't know how Haruo was going to help anybody by giving his body to science, but there was no use asking more questions. The ride back home was quiet, aside for Haruo's licking his fingers, one finger at a time.

"You're lucky, Mas," Haruo said finally.

"Huh?"

"You got no mark on you." Haruo folded over the top edge of the plastic bag. "Itsu like it neva happened."

✣ ✣ ✣

Once he got home, Mas could not rest. He wandered from the refrigerator to the living room easy chair to the bedroom to the kitchen table. No matter where he wandered, he heard the ticking of the clock on his bowling trophy. He had grown used to the quiet, but now it felt so heavy that he couldn't breathe.

He remembered, years ago, whenever he returned from work, the house was full of smells and sounds.

His daughter, Mari, was usually in the kitchen, her books sprawled out on the table, her strange-looking shoes called wallabies abandoned by the doorway. Chizuko, a full-length apron tied around her neck and waist, would be putting a tamale pie in the oven, or frying potato and ground beef croquettes over the stove. The whole kitchen would smell like freshly steamed rice, short-grain and sticky.

But one winter day, no remnants of Mari were seen or heard. "What happened? Is Mari home?" Mas asked after closing the screen on the kitchen door.

"Masao-*san,* take off your work boots. I just mopped. She's somewhere. Maybe in her room." Chizuko continued chopping her carrots.

Mas left his lunch cooler on the kitchen counter and flung open Mari's door.

"Dad!" Mari looked up from her pink desk, her dark eyebrows pinched together. Her hair, long and frizzy, dominated her tiny body. On her teeth were metal braces, which cost Mas at least a grand. "Knock, I keep telling you. This is my room. Private." A textbook was open on her desk, and someone had drawn fierce lines and circles through one of the photographs.

"Whatchu doin'?"

"My homework, Dad. Leave me alone." A large framed corkboard, which Mas had assembled and painted, was hung over her desk. Magazine clippings of young, pale *hakujin* boys with long hair were displayed on the board with thumbtacks.

"Orai, orai." Mas left, pulling the door closed until he heard the click of the latch.

As they ate their curry rice that night, Mas knew that something was wrong. Mari didn't fight to see her television program, and let Chizuko view the nightly news with Walter Cronkite. She went straight to her room afterward, and Mas could hear the static from her portable AM-FM radio behind the closed door. When Mari went to the bathroom, Mas snuck into her bedroom and took a closer look at her textbook. It had maps of Hawaii and Asia, photographs of *hakujin* men in helmets and uniforms. He flipped to the page that was defaced. A newsstand full of papers that read JAPS BOMB PEARL HARBOR.

The next day, Mari seemed in a better mood. Even her bedroom door was open, and she had a large poster board on the shag rug.

"Whatchu doin'?"

"Homework." Mari bent over the board. She wore striped kneesocks, which were worn at the heels.

"Don't bother her." Chizuko was standing behind Mas, wiping her damp hands on the sides of the apron. "She has an oral project on Friday. World War Two. She's doing it on Hiroshima."

Mari turned, her teeth glittering with metal. "Yeah, I'm going to interview you, Dad. Because you were there, right? That's what Mom told me."

Mas went into the hall closet and took out a fresh T-shirt and jeans. In the bathroom, he stripped off his green-stained clothes and stuffed them in the hamper. He washed his hands with soap and hot water, trying to remove the dirt from his fingernails with a brush. But no matter how hard he scrubbed, he couldn't get rid of those lines of dirt.

Mari had Mas sit on his fake leather easy chair, while she settled on the couch. Her hair was pushed back with a headband, exposing her high cheekbones. She held a pen and notebook. She even crossed her bony legs, her striped socks cuffed at the knees. "Okay, tell me your full name and birth date."

"You know my name."

"Your full name. Like a middle name."

Chizuko appeared from the kitchen. "Japanese don't have middle names."

"Mom, I'm interviewing Dad."

"Masao Arai. Octoba eighteenth, 1929."

"Okay, so that means you were sixteen—no, fifteen—at the time of the bombing."

Mas nodded.

"So, where were you on that day?"

"Huh?"

"When the *pikadon* fell," Chizuko hissed from the dining room table, a thread and needle in her hands.

"Mom!"

"Okay, I'm just helping. Dad gets confused sometimes."

"At train station. In the basement." Mas swallowed. It seemed as if something were stuck in his throat, but it wouldn't budge.

"Okay, so were you by yourself?"

Mas looked at the lamp. Dim. He would have to check the lightbulbs, he noted.

"Dad, was anyone else with you?"

"I have no time for dis." Mas got up from his easy chair.

Chizuko stopped sewing. "What?"

"But, Dad, I have to interview you. I told my teacher and everything."

"I have two sprinkler systems to work on."

"Masao-*san*, they say it's going to rain this week."

"Talk to *her*." Mas gestured toward Chizuko. "She likes talkin'."

"We were in the *inaka*. I didn't see anything until afterward." Chizuko stuck the needle straight into the pants she was mending. "She's counting on you to get a good grade."

Mas stumbled in the hall, leaving his daughter on the couch. Her face was expressionless, aside from her small nostrils, which flared out ever so slightly.

Later, Chizuko made arrangements for Mari to speak to Haruo. He came, sat in the easy chair, and put his stockinged feet up on a padded rest. He spoke of standing outside that morning with his older brother, cupping his hands, and staring at the plane and then white light. The next moment, he was covered in debris, surrounded by fire. He felt something roll from his face. It was his eye. He told Mari how his brother, less wounded, carefully took the bloody mass and placed it in shreds of cloth. Together they found their parents and other brothers and sisters. All alive. A miracle. Except for the eye, which medical workers eventually tossed into a bonfire.

Late at night, Mas saw light coming from Mari's room. He placed his face in the slim crack from the half-open door and watched Mari fold origami cranes, a pile of red, green, yellow, and purple growing on her desk. Chizuko pushed him from behind, her rolled-up hair covered in a pink cap. "Don't bother her," she said. "You could have helped, but she doesn't need you anymore."

On Friday morning, before she left for school, Mari proudly displayed her poster board to Chizuko in the kitchen. "I'm the only one who interviewed someone firsthand. Well, aside from Leroy Johnson, who talked to his uncle who was in the horse cavalry."

"I think you will get an A for sure." Chizuko pulled some plastic bags from a drawer. "Just make sure it doesn't get wet in the rain."

"Hi, Dad."

"Hullo."

Mari held up the poster, the top of it touching her chin. Multicolored cranes were pasted on the sides of the board, while the center was taken up with black-and-white photographs from newsmagazines. Mas had seen the images before. The woman with a thatched pattern burnt into her face. The boy with the melted ear. The shadow of a man permanently recorded in the stone steps of Sumitomo Bank.

In a corner, Mari had written in stenciled letters, HARUO MUKAI. Underneath it were his birth date, birthplace—Fresno, California—and other information. Mari had even drawn a bloody eye with colored pencil.

"What do you think, Dad?"

"Um. You finished. Don't have to worry about it no more." Mas reached for his Sears nylon jacket from the closet.

"Where you going?" Chizuko pointed to the raindrops hitting the window. "Can't work; it's raining."

"Just have *yoji*."

"*Yoji?* More like horse business, right?"

"I saysu *yoji*, I mean *yoji*." Mas turned the double lock on the door.

"What time you coming home?" Chizuko asked from the doorway.

"Don't know." Mas released the screen door and walked down the porch steps. He pushed his horse racing crib sheets further in his jeans pocket and felt the rain wet his head.

As he backed out the Ford truck from the long driveway, he noticed that Mari was still standing behind the screen door, holding the poster board, smudges of red and yellow held captive with Elmer's glue.

Now, thinking back, Mas wished that he had agreed to the interview, or maybe at least told Mari what he thought of her poster. "Nice job, beautiful." But he was jealous, mad that Haruo could do what he could not.

✣ ✣ ✣

It was past noon when the phone rang. It was Haruo again—this time panting like one of the those wild dogs on the run in Mas's neighborhood.

"Whatsamatta?" Mas said. Haruo was the last person he wanted to talk to.

"Itsu bad." Haruo wheezed. "Itsu badder than bad."

"What?" Mas's heart began pumping hard. It couldn't be about Tug. He had to be in good condition.

"The boy. The Kimura boy. Mas, heezu in jail."

"Jail?" Probably driving, thought Mas. Those young kids were crazy these days.

"Itsu so bad."

Mas pushed some air out of his lungs in disgust. Haruo was always the one to make a big thing out of nothing. "He a Japanese citizen. I sure the government back him up."

"Me heezu only phone call. You believe that? Before I left the hospital, I tell him, 'You needsu help, just call me.' And look whatsu happen."

"Haruo, stop actin' like a fool and tell me."

Haruo's breathing, which sounded wet and sticky, slowed. "That girl all beat up, Mas. Haneda's mistress. Ova in Kaiser on Sunset. Hangin' by a thread."

Mas's heart sank. He pictured the woman with her eyes darkened like a raccoon's. She was no prize, but why would anyone want to hurt her?

"Yah, someone smash her head. You believe that?"

"When?" Mas wound the excess telephone cord around his left hand.

"Dis morning, I guess." Wheeze, wheeze. "The police found him at her place and arrested him on the spot."

"Police." Mas pulled at the cord.

"Yah, somebody call it in. Left no name." Haruo swallowed noisily. "Thatsu not all, Mas. The boy blames you."

"Me?"

"He says you the one send him ova there. He say you set him up."

Mas felt his fingers turn cold and numb. He released the telephone cord and let it drop to the floor.

"I tell him he wrong, but he don't listen. I tole him to say nutin', then he have to hang up. I tell him I help him, Mas, but what can I do?"

A man who knew the rules, that's what the boy needed. With Tug laid up, they needed the next best alternative. "Call Wishbone," Mas said. "Tell him to get a lawyer. And then come ova here and pick me up."

"Whatsu we gonna do?"

Mas wasn't sure. But this time, he couldn't just wait.

CHAPTER EIGHT

It turned out that Yuki hadn't really been arrested, just held for questioning. Twenty-four hours. He had been found at the scene of the crime, the mistress's apartment, around eight in the morning. The mistress was still alive, just barely. Wishbone was working on finding a lawyer, while Mas insisted that Haruo come over and pick him up.

"What he say, exactly?" Mas asked after getting into the car.

"Didn't have much time to say nutin'. Just that he found a lady on the floor, her head bashed in and bloody. He got scared, and was going to run when the police found him."

Mas began to think hard.

"So, whatcha gonna do, Mas?"

"Letsu go."

"Where?"

"North Hollywood."

✣ ✣ ✣

The cul-de-sac was quiet. The police must have done their work and left. A little boy was riding a tricycle on the sidewalk. A stray dog crossed the street. Mas and Haruo walked past the mailboxes and went up to the second floor. The door of the apartment was closed, but the drapes were open. Yellow plastic tape with the message DO NOT CROSS limply hung from the door frame.

They looked as far as they could from the window. Blood, looking like dark paint, was on the wall and also splattered on the floor. The living room looked in disarray, not like the time Mas had visited a few days before.

"Hey." The Latino manager appeared from the end unit. "You better stay away from there—"

Mas was ready to leave, but then the manager stopped him. "Hey, you Junko's friend, huh?"

Mas merely nodded. Well, she had once offered him yam wine. That was as friendly as he got.

The man looked around like he was planning some kind of heist. "Come on," he whispered. "You want to take a look?" He selected a key from a knot of keys on a chain and unlocked the apartment. "Just don't touch nothing," he warned.

Haruo was plain afraid, so only Mas followed. Both

he and the manager stepped over the police tape into the mistress's apartment. Cushions and a broken lamp were on the living room floor. The row of bonsai trees had been overturned. It was obvious there had been a fight.

"She has a lot of visitors. Men visitors. You know what I mean?" The manager obviously liked to spread stories. "That's what I told the police."

"You see anybody?"

"You mean this morning? Just that boy with the red hair. Younger than the other ones. And then there was the other one coming around. But I forgot to mention that one to the police."

"What he look like?"

"Hair slicked back. Glasses. Looked kind of rich."

Shuji Nakane, thought Mas. He circled the apartment and noticed Nakane's business card on the mistress's table. The trash hadn't been taken out, so it smelled bad, like rotting chicken. He glanced into the bedroom. The sheets were all in disarray. The black Casio watch that had been on the jewelry box was gone. Other than that, everything seemed in its former place. As Mas walked through the hallway, something didn't seem the same. There were the photos of Junko with her girlfriends in exotic places, but then, on one side of the wall, just a piece of masking tape. What had been there? Then it hit Mas. That was the photo of the girl with the man who called himself Joji Haneda.

✣ ✣ ✣

So you see anytin'?" Haruo asked when they got back into the Honda.

Mas remained quiet. His mind whirled. "What did Haneda want with you? The truth," he said straight out.

Haruo slumped in the driver's seat. "He said we were gonna make some money at the poker game. That he had set sumptin' up."

Fixing a game among friends was unforgivable. Even Riki wouldn't stoop that low unless things hit rock bottom.

"I tole him that I would have nutin' to do with it."

"Whyzu then—" How come Haruo ended up at the card game?

"I just went to play, fair and square."

"Then why you here when my truck getsu stolen?"

"No, no. I come nowhere near dis place," Haruo maintained.

Mas ignored this. "How come he needsu money? Heezu doin' good with the nursery, huh?"

"I dunno. I guess times are tougher. All those big chain hardware stores selling plants. Hard to compete, I guess."

Mas sucked in his loose cheeks.

"What, you think sumbody beat up Junko for money?"

She had said Riki had owed her money, big money.

Mas wasn't sure, but he knew that someone close by would have some more information.

❖ ❖ ❖

The ramen house was crowded today. There were families with babies, teenagers dressed in black, and young Japanese men puffing on cigarettes, even though everyone knew smoking in restaurants was illegal in L.A. Keiko was sweating up a storm, her tray full of cold drinks with melted ice and a dirty dishrag. *"Ara—"* she said when she noticed Mas and Haruo at the door.

She pulled them in a corner, beside the bookcase with the fat Japanese comic books. "You hear about Junko?"

Mas nodded.

"*Hidoi, ne?* I can't believe it. Why would anyone do that to Junko?"

"How you find out?" Mas didn't think word would have gotten out so quickly in North Hollywood.

"My girlfriend Rumi came by my house. Her whole body shaking and wet. They had been close, like sisters. She must have gone by Junko's and seen the police. Poor thing. It's so scary these days. How could someone do that to Junko?"

"You got some ideas?"

Keiko frowned. "Me? You think I would know those types of people?"

"No, just wonder if Junko say sumptin'. Maybe about Haneda?"

"Well, she had enough of that guy. That's what she told me last time I saw her. Two nights ago, in fact. She was so *kusai* drunk. I made her stay for ramen and tea before she went home. She even mentioned that she was thinking of going back to Japan. That craziness again."

"Whyzu crazy?" asked Haruo. He spoke in a voice lower than usual, and Mas knew that he was already sweet on the ramen lady.

"Listen, when a Japanese woman comes to America, you can never go back. You didn't know that? It's a curse." With the way Keiko was talking to Haruo, Mas knew she was the type of woman who unwisely dumped her insides at a stranger's front door. "I've been here twenty years. Can you believe it? Seems like yesterday."

Haruo deftly covered the edge of his scars with the back of his palm. "Where you from? Tokyo, I betsu."

Shut up, Haruo, Mas thought silently. We're not here for this lady. But there was no turning back.

"Yokohama." Keiko's face brightened for a few seconds. "My family owns a ramen house there. For *champon ryori*, Yokohama is the best."

Haruo nodded. "Oh, yah?"

"Lot of Chinese restaurants, all crowded around. It's really cleaned up now."

Haruo seemed mesmerized by Keiko's sharp red lips. The fool, thought Mas.

"Many Chinee in Yokohama, huh?" Haruo said. "Didn't know."

Keiko looked at Haruo a bit oddly, and Mas held back a laugh. Silly Haruo. He really didn't know much about the underbelly of Japan—the part filled with outsiders and rebels. He was instead one of those mama's boys who had just hung around the house in Hiroshima. Mas, on the other hand, was like a stray dog, wandering from his seven brothers and sisters into all parts of the city. He ran for a while with two Korean boys, and visited their home by some factories. It was a shantytown, with makeshift stoves and lights hanging from bare wire. Japan was like America. There were plenty of people pushed down that the mama's boys and girls never saw.

Keiko continued, "We don't fit in here; don't fit in there. If you don't go back by the time you're thirty, it's too late. America's fully corrupted you. Like me and Junko. But this time around, she sounds like she's serious. Like she has a sackful of money now. That she could finally retire in style in Tokyo, and show up all her family and friends."

Mas bit down on his dentures. Go back to Japan, huh? What kind of money had she stumbled across? "Was she gonna go back with Haneda?"

"That old fool? Are you crazy?" Keiko's voice came out like a slap on the face. Mas was surprised. This was a different picture than she had presented during his last visit. "She finally had enough of that man. Do you know that guy was dying? *Gan* in the lungs, I think. Said that he was going to divorce his wife and leave everything to Junko."

"Cancer," Haruo muttered, echoing Mas's thoughts. Riki had looked bad, and now it seemed for good reason.

"Now she may never be able to see Tokyo again." Keiko's huge eyes watered, and Mas saw Haruo soften like a piece of cheese in the sun too long.

"We all knew it was a dream," Keiko said, sniffing loudly. "But then, we all need dreams, *desho*?"

✣ ✣ ✣

After they left the ramen restaurant, Haruo took all the change from his empty ashtray and headed for a pay phone next to a 7-Eleven. Mas stayed in the car, squeezing and rubbing his forehead in an effort to figure it all out. Shuji Nakane, the man with the clean white business card, must have offered the lady money, and big money, too. It must have been way over the measly thousand dollars in the envelope Mas had left on the mistress's kitchen table. What had she told him—that this Joji Haneda was a fake, like a piece of cheap metal covered with gold paint? If Nakane was going to buy her silence with dollar bills, there was no reason for him to kill her. So it must have been Riki Kimura who had done away with his mistress. Mas could picture him, his terrible brown teeth bared, knocking the lady's head against the wall until her head split open. Mas had seen it before, more than fifty years ago. "You're an *inu*, just like them," one of their classmates, a star shortshop, had taunted Riki.

"Shut up, shut up," Riki cried. Even back then, his fingers had been long and bony. Striking as quickly as a serpent, Riki wrapped his hands around the taunting boy's throat, pressing down, closing the air passages.

"Stop, Riki-*kun*." It had been Joji who had thrown Riki off the boy. They both were tall and thin, but the similarities ended there. Riki ran off at the mouth, talked big, but usually changed his mind when things looked bad. Joji, on the other hand, was quiet, but when he took a stand, there was no moving him. "No sense in getting in more trouble," Joji told Riki. "It's bad as it is."

✣ ✣ ✣

Haruo returned to the car with a sloppy grin on his face. "Heezu out," he said. "Wishbone gotsu dis Sansei attorney. The one who helped him get redress."

Leave it to Wishbone to hire a lawyer—particularly a third-generation Japanese American—who specialized in getting money from the government for its past sins. But crimes like murder? "Sounds like the wrong type of lawyer."

"Well, heezu out, isn't he?" Haruo shrugged. "I'm gonna go by Tanaka's and get the whole story. You wanna come?"

Mas drummed his fingers against the seat's torn upholstery. "I gotsu to borrow your car, Haruo. I can drop you off at Tanaka's. I sure Stinky or somebody give you a lift home."

Haruo's good eye focused on Mas's face. "You not gonna get yourself in trouble?"

"Ah—" Mas spit out some air, but inside he knew that new trouble was always waiting around the corner.

CHAPTER NINE

Mas didn't know quite why he was heading to Ventura. He didn't think that it had to do with either his or Riki's confessing. Confessing didn't change anything. Couldn't make the past right. But Mas knew that he had to travel back—not to the beginning but to where he once saw hope and possibilities.

✣ ✣ ✣

Mas had discovered the spot in Ventura during one of his fishing trips in Oxnard. He preferred ocean fishing—casting over the rough foam of the waves—to the idyllic quietness of lakes. Ocean perch, lake trout, they were pretty much the same—white meat and lots of fine bones—but at the beach you could grill your catch with the grit of sand, the hush of the sunset over the sea, and the never-ending crash of the tide, a sound that lulled and prodded Mas into getting out of his sleeping bag and unzipping his tent.

Ventura was sprawling, a city ready for something big. Mas felt it. Along the coastline were the gigantic summer homes, two-story and freshly constructed. These beaches were much cleaner than the ones down south—it was a surprise to see even a single beer can abandoned in the sand. And farther inland were the new housing developments, quaint shopping malls, all in need of plants and landscaping.

Farther north of Ventura, past Santa Barbara, was Pismo Beach. Every summer from the time Mari was six, Mas had taken the family out to the dunes for a week. Holding a sharp, long shovel, he sloshed in the surf in his rubber boots and overalls. Chizuko squatted by the yellow bucket and poked her index finger at each clam and counted quietly, while Mari created a maze of footprint patterns. Mas called her over, handed her a shovel, and pointed to the delicate air bubbles emanating from the perfect round holes in the sand.

"Inside there," Mas said, forcing Mari's hand and shovel in the sand. They scooped quickly until the tip of the shovel hit a clunk, and then Mas revealed a sandy striped clam, its siphon extended a couple of inches. Mas placed the clam against a metal measure attached to the worn wooden handle, jiggled it back and forth, and shook his head. "Too small," he said, his lit cigarette tipping out of the side of his mouth.

"Not that small." Mari's thumb could barely fit in the space between the clamshell and the metal measure.

"Too small." Mas bit into his cigarette and chucked the clam out toward the diluted gray sun. "No good, you know." He looked at Mari. "Can't take it too soon."

One summer day in 1972, he saw the nursery on the corner of a large intersection in Ventura. The metal sign read BUD'S TREES AND PLANTS, next to a symbol of a fish. There were rows of yellow and purple pansies in plastic squares, African daisies, and clematis vines tied to wooden stakes. Arranged in the back were ficus trees and succulents. A few bonsai trees were placed by the cash register.

A *hakujin* man who could have been as young as fifty or as old as seventy turned from arranging packages of seeds. "Well, hello."

"Hallo," said Mas.

"What can I help you with?"

"Lookin'."

"Well, look away. That's what I'm here for. My name's Bud Ryan." The man had a soft chin, which dipped down toward his chest. "You're a professional man, I bet."

"Excuse?"

"A man of the vine, I call them. As precious as the good book itself."

Mas checked some buckets of cymbidium.

"You know our Maker was a gardener, and I consider it one of the holiest professions around. He knows when to prune, how to produce good fruit. But the thing is, He does it through us."

Mas grunted. The cymbidium was healthy, with taut stems and waxy flowers.

"I would've been a gardener myself, but I don't have the patience for it. I leave it for all of you to contend with. I just sell the stuff. But can't complain; would have been in business for twenty-five years next year. Too bad we're not going to be open for that."

Mas glanced at the row of gardening tools. "You close?"

"Well, I'll be outta here. What can I say, affairs of the heart. Lost the wife two years ago. Thirty years we were together. But the Lord provided. Met this one at a church retreat for singles. But yes, Shirley had to be from Florida. Just couldn't bear to leave her kids, even though they're all grown. So here I am, lookin' around for potential buyers."

For Mas, this was his window of opportunity. He didn't understand Mr. Bud Ryan's talk about Maker and producing good fruit, but he could smell "potential."

He located a Motel 6 down the street and went back and forth from Altadena to Ventura at different times of the week, monitoring the flow of customers, their ages, making note of their cars. At night he drove in different areas of town, stopping at each new construction site and logging it on a piece of paper he kept in his wallet.

Once he decided for sure, he told Chizuko. He thought she would be happy about the lower crime rate, the clean air. The schools were even better, he figured.

"Mari's education. Just think. Lots betta ova there," he said, crumpling the bedsheets in his palms. It was five o'clock in the morning, the best time for talking about the future.

"Don't include her. You just thinking about yourself. Never mind how we feel. *Kattenahito.*"

"But this means future. This place just gettin' worse and worse. Just look around." Last week someone had painted obscenities on every mailbox on the east side of the street. Dogs ran wild. Naked toddlers splashed in the dirty water in the gutters. A few homes had even been boarded up by the government.

"Drag me around from place to place. No relatives. I have to make friends all over again."

"My father, mother, not here when I came the second time."

"But you hated them. That's different. It was your choice. It's always about you." Chizuko, slight bean-shaped marks by the sides of her nose, sank her head in her pillow. "And don't think you're going to use my parents' money to pay for any of it."

Later at breakfast, Mari clattered her spoon against the half-empty cereal bowl. A marshmallow green clover floated in the thin milk. "We're not going away, are we, Dad? My friends just started a new club. They voted me secretary. I've always wanted to be secretary."

Mas even went by Wishbone's place to discuss the pros and cons.

Wishbone leaned against a lawn mower motor he was repairing. "Think it's good. There's fresh land up there, not like L.A. More opportunity."

"But the family—"

"So they're upset. They're women. They're supposed to be upset. If you had sons, it would be a whole different story. They'd shut up, and so would the wife. A lot easier that way, I tell you."

Mas picked up a loose spring from the counter and pressed it in and out like a mini-accordion.

"They'll get over it. But hell, don't back down. If you do, they're always going to have the upper hand, here on out. You better not wait any longer. You know what they say: 'Snooze, you lose.' "

Mas nodded, soaking the information in.

"By the way," Wishbone added, as if he just remembered something, "we got a new card player over here. He says that he knows you."

Mas just grunted in reply. He had little use for either friends or acquaintances now. His mind was focused entirely on his business deal and the opinions in his household. If he had just paid more attention, everything would have been different. He had been too distracted to tell Wishbone that the deal was confidential, that no one else, especially new gamblers, should be told of Bud's Trees and Plants on the corner of PCH and Second.

Mas collected the cash he had hidden in his tool chest and went to Ventura to seal the deal. A CLOSED sign hung from the front window, but Mr. Bud Ryan was in, packing circles of hoses in large boxes.

Mas rapped on the glass window and waited for Mr. Ryan to open the dead bolt. "What's goin' on?" Mas asked.

"Mas, been trying to call you. Had to make a quick sale. Wanted to wait for you to get back to me, but it has been two weeks. Shirley's been calling. She can have any guy she wants. Can't let her have second thoughts."

"Who buy?" I'll offer him a better deal, thought Mas. "I can give you more."

"No, Mas, it's all signed, sealed, and notarized. It's official." Mr. Ryan went into a drawer and lifted a document stapled onto light-blue paper.

Mas felt his knees buckle a little and the tips of fingers tremble. This was his way to make good. A deal like this came your way maybe once in a lifetime. "But you knowsu I wanna buy—"

"Mas, this guy had the cash. In fact, he's here, in the back." Mr. Ryan gestured toward a stack of boxes down a narrow hall, and Mas noticed the shadow of a slight man with a hooked nose.

"Hallo, Mas," the man said.

Mas felt the wind whoosh out of his gut. He knew the voice—older, thinner, yet still hard as nails.

"Welcome to my nursery," said the man who called himself Joji Haneda. "Now get the hell out."

❖ ❖ ❖

Mas could've blamed Wishbone for not keeping his big mouth shut, or yelled at Mr. Ryan for being ruled by a woman and not honoring a promise between two men. He could have berated Chizuko and Mari for their sniveling, which made him delay a decision on a good deal. But when you came right down to it, it had everything to do with *bachi* and Joji Haneda.

❖ ❖ ❖

Mas had not been back to that intersection for more than twenty-five years. Now he stood on the gravel parking lot, facing the large metal sign, HANEDA'S NURSERY.

Riki had remodeled and added a new greenhouse and showroom of propane-powered mowers. Mas walked to the building and pressed his face against the glass. There were lines of gardening products: pruning knives, pesticides, parrot-beak shears, saws, leather gloves, sprinkler heads, and hose attachments. Large bags of fertilizer were stacked against the wall.

Mr. Bud Ryan's old cash register had been replaced by a computer.

It didn't surprise Mas that Riki had so dramatically improved the nursery. He had been good with money from the beginning. Even during the war, he had figured out, through paying some servants a few yen coins, where a closed-down sake manufacturer had stored its old inventory. Soon Riki had his own inventory in his backyard, which he sold to soldiers passing through Hiroshima. Mas never asked any questions, but took those few sips while playing *hana* cards with Riki. Just that had been enough to seal his mouth shut.

Mas edged toward the front of the nursery. A statue of a white good luck cat, its paw beckoning customers to come in, had been placed at the foot of the glass door. Just above it was a handwritten sign, CLOSED DUE TO ILLNESS. Letters, bunched together with a rubber band, were stuffed through the mail slot in the glass door. What the hell. Mas pulled out the letters and glanced at the return addresses—banks, gas company, pizza delivery companies. Bingo—the last one read OXNARD CITY HOSPITAL.

Mas got back on the freeway and headed south. Lines of eucalyptus trees shielded freshly plowed fields and tiny farmhouses. Bushes along the freeway swayed from the wind, and the fog brought white mist over the skyline.

Mas steered Haruo's Honda into a parking lot and followed the arrow for visitors. He parked between two white lines and stopped the engine. Leaning against the Honda, Mas drew out a new package of Marlboros, tore open the plastic wrap, and slid out a cigarette.

He looked at the three-story building. The hospital must have been built recently, over the past five years. There were baby palms planted outside the building and boxwood shrubs in grass islands in the parking lot.

A Mexican woman parked her car in the employee parking area on the other side of Haruo's Honda. She was dressed in a white uniform, with a light-blue sweatshirt that opened in the front, and carried a plastic bottle topped with a jumbo straw, the ones people purchased at gas station mini-marts. She was heavy; her uniform top bulged. She didn't seem happy about going to work, almost indifferent.

Maybe she would be the nurse on the next shift to take care of Riki, thought Mas. What would she say to him? "Hello, Mr. Haneda? How are you doing, Mr. Haneda?" Would she be the one to prick his skin, give him a sponge bath, take his temperature, give him painkillers?

Mas exhaled and felt cold. The sun was still out, but a breeze, smelling salty, rustled through the boxwood leaves. The shrub in the island closest to the Honda was only three feet tall, but then boxwoods always tended to be small.

Mas zipped up his windbreaker and shoved his hands in his pockets. Last thing he wanted to do was to meet up with Riki again. But then, he remembered what the ramen lady had said about dreams. It wasn't fair that Riki had offered them with no intention of following through.

✣ ✣ ✣

The sliding glass doors automatically opened as Mas stepped on the rubber mat. Families with Mylar balloons sat quietly in the waiting room. The gift store was neatly stocked with magazines and a cooler full of flower arrangements. Rows of different-shaped bottles lined the brightly lit pharmacy.

Mas wandered around the gift store and pharmacy, stopped at the information desk, and then found himself taking the elevator to the third floor. He got off and stared at an erasable plastic board matching doctor with patient.

"Are you here for Joji Haneda?" asked a young woman in a pink cotton top and pants, a stethoscope hanging from her neck. She was Asian, her skin dark. Filipino, thought Mas. "The rest of the family went down to the cafeteria. It closes at six. He's over there, in three twenty-six. But don't stay too long."

The door of room 326 was wide-open. After waiting for a cart full of meals in plastic trays to pass by, Mas could clearly see a figure wrapped in a sheet and blanket. Riki had an oxygen mask over his nose and mouth. Tubes connected holes in his arms to machines and bags to his side.

There was the steady beeping of a morphine dispenser. Mas knew it well from Chizuko's final days in the hospital. One press of a button, and a shot of clear liquid entered one's veins.

The curtain to the window was drawn shut. A fluorescent panel of light poured a yellow hue over Riki's body, a withered plant, shrunken and dim. He has aged so much in just a matter of days, thought Mas.

He wanted Riki to rise and sneer, as Mas always remembered him. Here the oxygen mask covered his hooked nose and sharp mouth below his chestnut eyes.

Riki didn't seem surprised to see Mas, and greeted him with the press of his morphine machine. He gestured Mas to remove his mask so Riki could talk.

"Pretty good, huh, to die this way." Riki's voice was raspy, as if these were the first words he had uttered. "No pain." Riki looked old, as if he were eighty, even ninety. His voice was thin, like the buzz of an electrical wire.

Mas studied the squares of white and gray linoleum on the floor. He wanted to hear the din of a television set, anything to fill the silence. Finally, he cleared his throat. "Sheezu still alive," he said. "But barely. They give her fifty-fifty."

Water seeped from the edge of Riki's eye. "I thought so. She look pretty bad."

"So itsu you." The killer had struck again, fifty years later.

More water ran down the side of Riki's face. Then his eyes, like bullet holes, focused on Mas. "No, you gotsu it wrong. Why would I try to kill her? I care for her."

Mas shuddered. He couldn't imagine Riki showing affection for anyone.

"Gonna leave my wife for her. She didn't believe. Then I tole her. All about me and Haneda."

So the mistress did know. Mas wasn't surprised. After all, it had taken only a few glasses of yam wine for her to reveal half of her life story.

"I just needsu money. Money to take her back to Japan. Some comin' out of card game in Little Tokyo."

"Da nursery—"

"What? You think I'm makin' money off of that place? Youzu have last laugh, Masao-*san*. Big chain stores runnin' me down to the ground. A gardener a betta living."

Mas didn't know how to react to Riki's revelation. Maybe Riki was just trying to get on his good side. It would be just like him to try to pull a fast one on his deathbed.

"I didn't hurt her," Riki insisted again. "Was outside her place. Five in the mornin'."

"What, you just go?" Like I abandoned them, thought Mas. *"Water, water,"* Joji had murmured. *"Just a little longer,"* Mas had told him. *"A little longer."*

"I was scared," said Riki. "Police was already there. Even watched the ambulance take her away."

"Well, the police gotsu a suspect. A young guy, heezu name Kimura. Yuki Kimura."

Riki's face looked as blank as rice porridge.

"You knowsu," Mas said, "your grandson. Akemi's, too."

Riki's wrinkled face contorted and finally broke out into a black grin. "What kind of stories you been hearin', Mas? I gotsu no grandchildren back in Japan."

Mas found himself enjoying this, even at the foot of Riki's deathbed. It was what he deserved. *Bachi* during his last days on earth. "I knowsu, Riki, what you did with Akemi. I knowsu it all."

"Well, you knowsu sumptin' I don't, because I didn't do anytin' with that Akemi Haneda."

"Thatsu not what I heard."

"What, some woman saysu sheezu Akemi. Some kind of liar. I hear she die in the *pikadon.*"

Mas stuffed his hands in his jeans pockets. "She had a son," he finally said. "Hikari."

"Hikari?" Riki snorted. "What kind of crazy name is that? If you think I had anytin' to do with him, your mind gone completely *pa*, Mas."

Was Riki telling the truth? Then what about the boy's story? What did he even know about the boy? Maybe he didn't even work for a magazine. Maybe he was up to no good. Maybe he really had done something to that Junko Kakita.

"Whatsu they tellin' you, Mas, that I was a daddy back in Japan?"

"Whysu not? You always sweet on the girls."

"Mas, get serious. No time for anytin' like that. Besides, you around all the time. You knowsu where I'm sleepin', eatin'."

"Everytin' you didsu, a secret," Mas maintained. "Like Joji."

The morphine machine buzzed again. "You know what I did. He was practically dead. Like all of them."

Most of them were dead. Charred black like burnt food. Skin peeling away, ripe fruit bursting open, leaving only a pool of stickiness. Arms webbed together like a kangaroo's.

Mas stared at Riki, now the one close to death. "What didsu you do with Joji?"

Riki's chest heaved.

"Whatcha do to him afterward?"

"You had your family, Mas. I had nutin'. They all gone."

"But Joji—"

Riki pressed the button for the morphine machine again. "He was like you left him, barely alive. His papers were in his boot, I knowsu. I tore it off, and his whole foot came off with it. I just took that boot, foot and everytin', and ran."

Mas recalled the illustration that Yuki had shown him at the medical exams. The man without a foot.

"America won. I knew it. Those other people, those *bakayaros*, crying about hearing the emperor surrender. But I knew before I heard. I knew when I saw miles and miles of nutin' after the Bomb. I knew when I see the black rain. I knew that Japan had no chance." Riki swallowed slowly and continued. "Youzu and some of the others, you had a way out. You American citizens. You could just forget about us and go away.

"So I stole Joji's foot. I found a piece of metal and tore open the boot. The papers were right there. His birth certificate, everytin'."

"And then youzu put your name on his." Cold-blooded murder, that's what it was, thought Mas.

"He gonna die anyhowsu. You saw him, Mas." Riki swallowed. "I buried the foot, Mas. I'm not without *kokoro*. In the mountains, by the bamboo grove we played by. I even said a prayer."

Mas felt wetness at the edges of his eyes. He imagined Joji there alone, still breathing, with one foot. Did he think that Mas had abandoned him there, too? Was his last thought on the betrayal of his friends?

"Lies. Thatsu all you tole me." Mas felt the words wretching out of his throat like vomit. "You tell me that you take care of Joji."

"You just believe what you want to believe, Mas."

"You sonafubitchi," Mas finally muttered.

"Mas, you no betta," Riki said. "You take my money to go to America. You leave me, just like I leave Joji."

"I nutin' like you," Mas was only able to gasp as he walked out of the hospital room, past the open doors to the elevator, back to the car, and back to the purple hills of Altadena.

CHAPTER TEN

When Mas was upset, he usually retreated to his garage. It was musty with the smells of grease, oil, and rusty metal. While surgeons had their operating tables, Mas had his own version, crowded with glass jars of nails, screws, and even fishhooks. A greasy clamp was fastened to one end of the table. Beside it were small metal parts, a pair of pliers, wrenches, and a can of WD-40. Here Mas performed miracles on his Trimmer and Ford engine (rebuilt two times). The problem today was that there was no lawn mower, and there was no truck.

It was in this same garage that Mas had prayed for the first and last time, when Chizuko had had another relapse of stomach cancer. There, in between his broken-down lawn mower and his oily pliers, he had prayed: "God, *Kamisama,* I know that I'm a good-for-nutin'. But save my wife. Not for me. She needsu to enjoy. Enjoy life. Neva gotsu the chance." But God didn't answer his prayers. And from that point on, Mas swore that he would never make a fool of himself again. His heart would be closed to both religion and doctors.

Mas pulled the chain to the bald lightbulb above his workbench. No broken gears, just a bunch of one-and-a-quarter-inch wire nails scattered like dried-out pine needles. Dropping them into a Gerber's baby food jar, Mas felt like smashing something good and hard with his hammer. But there was nothing to build and nobody to build for. Mas felt anger move from his gut into his throat. Why had Riki had to come and disturb him? Why had Riki told him about the foot that he had stolen from Joji Haneda? Why couldn't those secrets have just died, been buried or burnt away?

Mas knew that he couldn't lose those images of the ravaged bodies as easily as before. Before, there were card games and horses and mouths to feed. Now his mind was like a good-for-nothing videotape player, the same thing showing over and over.

✣ ✣ ✣

Mas never regretted marrying Chizuko, but he often suffered for it. Mostly because she was smarter than Mas—at least with language and books—and reminded him of it every day of her life.

"You fill out the form. It's *your* contractor's license,

not mine," Chizuko said, her lips pursed over her slight overbite.

Mas struggled with the terms, the exceptions, which seemed to rise and float from the white sheets of the renewal form for his landscape contractor's license. He then silently and secretively went to the side of his junior high school daughter, who was reading at her desk.

Mari sucked on the end of a pen. "Have you taken California Pesticide Test 105 in the past five years? You know—pests, bugs, *mushi*?"

"Yah, yah, I knowsu. Took it last year."

"Then we'll check yes." Mari drew a crooked X in a box.

So they went down all twenty questions on the form, and then Mari turned the bottom toward Mas. "Here, sign here, Dad." Her fingernail, old pink polish chipped away and now shaped like fish food flakes, tapped a long line.

Mas took the pen from Mari, held tight, and signed his name carefully, with a magnificently large M and A. He felt another presence and noticed Chizuko's dagger eyes staring at them from the doorway. "Pitiful," she said. "Pitiful man."

It was hard to explain why he couldn't write English, or even Japanese, well. He'd never taken to school—spent more time teasing classmates and terrorizing teachers, like the rest of the boys. *Asobi*, play, took up all of their creative energy—that is, before the war.

There was *shogi*, in which they advanced white Japanese chess pieces, uniformly shaped and pointed, on a square board. They waxed cards of their favorite sumo wrestlers and devised various games. Throw it down; faceup was the winner. Throw it down; the one touching the most cards was the winner.

They went into the countryside, tore off vines, and braided rope, which they used to whip bamboo tops into cyclonic circles. They dug small holes in dirt to simulate a baseball diamond, and took turns trying to launch marbles into the holes and get to home plate. In the wintertime, they helped the village men assemble a large bamboo frame in the shape of a triangular cone, covered it with hay, and set it on fire. While some people sang, Mas and his friends poked *mochi* speared atop long sticks into the flames. Once the rice cake puffed up, they dipped it in soy sauce and sugar and stuffed the stickiness into their mouths.

Joji moved next door in 1939, and the first time he saw him, Mas could tell he was different. First of all, Joji combed his hair back with some kind of grease and always seemed to have a smile on his lips. He usually chewed on a sliver of bamboo, and Mas always wondered if it was the same piece day after day. Joji liked football, not baseball or judo, and his Japanese sounded strange, as if he cut the words in pieces that didn't fit together so well. Before the war, all the boys in their class respected Joji, much like they would an exotic lizard. They kept their distance, but then, they didn't try to anger him, either. But when the war with America began, the boys became bolder, chanting *"inu, inu,"* as he approached, throwing dirt and blows whenever convenient.

Mas, on the other hand, feared Joji, thinking that he was like a magnet, bringing trouble to all who were close. There were plenty of other *Kibei*, American-born, at Koryo High School, and many of them blended in. But Mas didn't want to take any chances. As soon as he turned fifteen, he went by the family registry office to see if he could join the navy like his two older brothers.

The office was a simple shack with a metal roof. The clerk, his neck as droopy as old chicken skin, wet his fingers in a dish of water and leafed quickly through the registry. "Arai—yes, eight children."

"Masao; I am the middle one."

"So . . . Arai Masao." The clerk held a straightedge to the pages of the registry. "Fifteen years of age. Too young. October."

"But I want to go. They take old men. I'm just four months away."

The man paused and then moved the straightedge up and down several times. He glared at Mas and pulled on the loose skin under his chin. "It says here that you only have American citizenship."

"What? That can't be."

"No," said the clerk. "It is very strange. The record shows that you are the only one in your family to have solely U.S. citizenship."

"But my two older brothers have dual. There must be some kind of mistake. I was just born over there, but all I really know is Japan." Mas didn't remember much about California, other than the rows of lettuce that he had grasped like a giant ball. The leaves were crisp, with white veins; he could even tear the first layer off, then—smack—a slap on his dimpled hands, and then back on a scratchy blanket, alone in an empty field.

"There might be a foul-up, but it's not our office." The clerk slammed the registry shut. "Check with your parents, and find out why they didn't change your status. As far as we are concerned, you are legally a full-blooded American."

Mas felt sick to his stomach. To be one of the enemy—a hundred percent. How could his parents have forgotten to make sure he was properly registered? The family registry was everything. It didn't take much to make sure an American-born child also had Japanese citizenship status. But it did require the parents to care enough to follow through with it.

Mas's stomach churned, like when he was lost on the train when he was a child. He was desperate for the familiar, the indigo butterflies of his mother's kimono, the pokes and teasing of his older brothers and sisters. But the train was only full of strangers, grim faces, and musty clothing. Finally the stationmaster pulled him out of the car at the last stop.

His mother came two hours later. She usually walked like a man, steady and wide, but the butterfly cloth constricted her large gait. "You have to be alert, Masao-*chan*," she said on their way home. Her hands were callused and dry. "You can't expect me to always be looking for you."

Those words haunted Mas as he left the registry office. His vision was so blurred he couldn't see straight. When he arrived at his front gate, he began throwing rocks at his house, first pebbles, and then round stones near their fish pond. With the impact of each rock, the wood frame shook and rattled. In spite of the noise, no one came out. Everyone was probably in the rice fields without him.

Joji Haneda had come out of his house. "Arai-*kun*, what are you doing?" he said.

Mas threw more stones toward his parents' bedroom.

"What are you doing?" Joji repeated. He was still wearing his work uniform with his name tag sewn on the left-hand side.

"It's none of your business. Stay out of it." The last thing Mas wanted was to be associated with Joji Haneda.

He raised another rock, and Joji held back Mas's

arm. Mas then swung the other side of his body into Joji's chest, easily flipping him over.

Joji seemed stunned for several minutes as he lay beside the koi pond. "For a little guy, you sure are tough," he finally said.

After that point, the two began walking together to work at the train station in the middle of Hiroshima. Joji would tell him about life in Los Angeles, the tall buildings, the steaks as thick as concrete slabs, and the women—their legs as long as gazelles'.

"I'm going back," he told Mas. "My papa's there."

"You can't go to America."

"When America wins."

Mas was thankful that no one was around. "But Japan is going to win."

Joji laughed. "You don't know, Masao-*kun*. You don't know all they have over there. Land, manpower. The streets are full of cars. How is Japan going to beat that?"

Mas pondered the image of a large boulevard crowded with shiny American automobiles.

"You can come with me."

"No," Mas said. Hiroshima was his home.

"You will," Joji said. "We can even live together. Eat steaks and play football all day. You can get a job designing cars, and we can get married to some beautiful girls. Even the Japanese ones look different over there."

Mas stopped putting up a fight. Joji's imagination was the only thing that was making him happy, and Mas wasn't going to rob him of that.

✣ ✣ ✣

Mas sat in the garage for what seemed like hours, until a car pulled into the driveway.

This was first time Mas had seen Tug since the poker game. Tug looked a bit haggard, puffy bags underneath his eyes. He hadn't trimmed his beard; the white hair seemed scraggly, rough. Some hair had started to grow over his wound, like white fuzz on an Elberta peach.

"You lookin' good," Mas lied.

Avoiding a large oil spot on the floor, Mas pulled out an old metal Coleman cooler. "Sit down," he said, offering Tug an Orange Crush from the old refrigerator in the corner.

Tug tipped his head back and took two large gulps of the soda before wiping his beard with the edge of his sleeve. "You got anything stronger, Mas?"

Mas frowned. There hadn't been a time when he'd seen Tug drink liquor. Even at Tug and Lil's son's wedding, waiters in black tuxedos poured fizzy apple juice into plastic champagne glasses, much to Mas's disappointment. "No wine, even," Mas had mumbled, and received a sharp jab from Chizuko's elbow. And now here was Tug, begging for alcohol.

The timing was fitting, so Mas reopened the

Frigidaire without so much as one word. He tore off two cans of Budweiser from the plastic six-pack holder, and together they drank in silence in front of the oil stain.

Tug got up from the Coleman cooler, placed his drink on the top, and went over to the workbench. He spun the end of the clamp. "Thought about picking up woodworking since my retirement. There's a class at Pasadena City College."

"Class? You got to pay money?"

"Yeah, I think fifty, sixty dollars, something like that."

"Forget it. You come here; I teach you all you need to know. I even teach Mari, *honto yo*. She pretty good. Made a little car." The wheels had been nailed in somewhat unevenly, but it still was able to roll forward.

"Didn't do much with Joy, although I did take her to work a couple of times," said Tug.

"You kiddin'? You mean to those dirty restaurants?"

Tug smiled and brushed down his beard. "It wasn't company policy, but when Lil was sick, I snuck her in one of my jobs. Actually, she seemed to enjoy it a lot more than her brother did. Checking out grime, looking for rodent infestation. Who would have thought a little girl would take to it?"

"Maybe that's why she's a docta."

"Not yet."

"But soon." Mas dropped a small bolt into a jar that had once held creamed corn.

"You ever take Mari on your route?" Tug asked.

"Yah, one time. In the summertime." It had been Mari's idea, actually. Chizuko and Mas both tried to dissuade her, for different reasons, but finally Mas relented.

"How did she like it?"

"She liked lunch; I can tell you that much. She eat sandwiches Chizuko packed, then wanted to get some fast-food hamburgers. I gave her easy work—raking leaves, that kinda stuff. Oh, she make a mess. I tole Chizuko when I getsu home. No more. Dis work, not play. Now she killsu every plant. No joke."

"Black thumb, huh. That's kind of funny." Tug returned to the Coleman cooler and gulped down his second beer.

Mas returned to his workbench. He jiggled one of the baby food jars and watched the nails settle.

"Do you think he did it?" asked Tug.

A cool breeze tickled Mas's neck. "Huh?"

"Did that boy hurt that woman?"

Mas waited a moment until he understood. "Oh, that Kimura boy," he said finally. "Could've. I dunno. Dunno either way."

"But why? What would he have to do with that woman?"

"Well, women, you knowsu how that goes," Mas

said, who then quickly realized that Tug had little idea. "Money. Maybe money."

"Money?"

"Tug, itsu always about money," said Mas, before reopening the Frigidaire to make sure he had a second six-pack.

"But this isn't a rich woman. She lives by herself in a one-bedroom apartment. They even aren't too sure what she does for a living."

"But maybe she knowsu sumptin' thatsu worth a lot of money."

"Like?"

"What did that boy tell you? Whyzu he here, anyhowsu, and don't tell me itsu because of a stupid magazine article."

Tug sat quietly on the Coleman cooler.

"Heezu gotsu an angle, Tug. We all gotsu one."

"I know all about angles. I worked for the government for fifty years. I know more than you think." Tug frowned. While most Japanese would be flushed red from the alcohol, Tug's face was stone white. "I've had people offer me kickbacks. Lakers tickets, even cash."

Mas's hand grew slippery around his beer can.

"Every time, I told them 'No, no.' "

Well, of course, thought Mas. You're that kind of sonafugun.

"Except once." Tug sighed. "Once, I didn't say no. They were Dodgers tickets. The pennant race in seventy-eight. Seats right behind home plate."

"Oh—" Mas pushed out a breath. He knew how much Tug loved the Dodgers.

"I tried to fool myself, Mas. Told myself they weren't a bribe. That it was a gift, between friends. But I had known that restaurant owner for only six months, and he wasn't a friend. I didn't even like him." Tug took another sip of his beer. "So I went. Even took Joe. The thing was, the seats were so good that we landed up on TV. Every time someone went up to bat, you could see me and Joe there, eating peanuts and drinking Coke. The next day at work, people told me that they saw me and my son. Didn't say much of anything else. But I know what they were thinking. That I was just like them.

"I felt sick to my stomach, Mas. I wanted to take those tickets back. But I couldn't. Then I went back to that restaurant. Rat droppings everywhere. I told the owner that I would have to close them down."

"Howsu he take it?"

"Not good. He said we had an agreement. I told him I'd pay for the tickets. He said that wasn't good enough. He was going to go to my boss and report me."

"Whatcha do?"

"The only thing I could do. I beat him to it. I confessed everything."

Mas blinked hard. He could only imagine how difficult that had been for Tug.

"I was ready to be fired. Even warned Lil. She was

plenty furious. Even said I had tainted Joe by taking him to the game.

"So anyhows, I revealed everything. Afterward, my boss looks at me. 'I'm going to forget everything you just told me,' he said. He fixed it all. Gave the restaurant a temporary reprieve. Was assigned to another inspector. I got a second chance, Mas. And I never blew it again."

"Lucky, Tug," Mas said.

"Lucky nothing," said Tug, ash white. "It was a curse. He held that over my head my whole career."

✣ ✣ ✣

They had not yet completed the second six-pack when Mas sent Tug home. There was no use getting Lil even madder than she had been that day at the hospital. Before Tug left, Mas made him suck down two cups of freeze-dried instant coffee and even stuffed some old coffee candies in his pocket for the five-minute drive home.

From what Mas could figure out from the last hour with Tug, the boy was still in trouble. The police had wanted him around for questioning. "Don't leave L.A.," they told him. Mas knew what that meant. They were waiting for the mistress to die. Once the death certificate was issued, they would work like hell to send the boy away.

Tug was convinced of the boy's innocence. Mas wasn't as sure. But he was Joji's flesh and blood, after all. His grandnephew. His only heir. At times at the track, Mas made a bet on a long-shot horse. Yuki Kimura was no horse, but he might as well be one since he was alone in America with only a faint promise of a three-million-dollar prize.

Mas returned to bed for a while, but sleep would not come. Tug had said that the police weren't sure what the mistress did for a living. And then there was the apartment manager, making comments about the men coming by. And Shuji Nakane. Where the hell was he now?

Mas tried to slow his thoughts down. He remembered that when he mislaid something, Chizuko had always told him to travel backward. In his mind he went back, step-by-step, until he landed up in that apartment in North Hollywood for the first time. He pictured the bonsai trees lined up all perfect on those boards, the box of aluminum paper on the counter. The Casio watch. The photos pasted on the wall. One in somewhere like Hawaii, Junko with another girl, wearing leis around their necks. There had been that one with all the girls and men in suits, holding beers and smiling like at a New Year's party. The girls had been all made-up, lipstick and eyelashes. The photo of Riki and the mistress in Vegas.

Mas then tried to remember the mistress. Was there anything about her that could tell him who she was? The Shuji Nakane business card. Hardly any papers. And the envelope with money.

Something then snapped on in Mas's mind. The map in the envelope that had led him to the poker game. It had been written on some kind of blank receipt form. Probably nothing, he thought. But he got up and pulled at the pockets of his discarded clothing again. Sure enough, there it was. The map had been written on back of a receipt for some kind of business named "Chochin's." There was an address in Los Angeles with a zip code and phone number. One look and Mas knew where it was. West L.A. Sawtelle.

Mas used to get together with a Sawtelle gardener who was crazy about the game go. Mas could play go well enough; he even had a set of flat, polished stones stored in covered bowls—one black, the other white. A wooden board, which folded in half with a hinge, completed the set. The board was lined with a grid, hundreds of perfect squares, hundreds of potential moves.

Kids like Mari thought that the winner of go was the one who got five in a row first. It actually had nothing to do with that. Go was all about territory, about closing a solid line around the other guy's markers. The key was to set traps in unexpected places. Then, when the other guy was barely looking, you started on your plan.

Mas drove out west on the Santa Monica Freeway, then down on the dreaded 405. He hated that side of town. Cars were almost piled upon one another. Some were going to the airport; others, who knew where. Traveling on the 405 from the Santa Monica was like risking a bad sunburn. You didn't want to stay out there too long.

Mas got off the short stretch of the 90, went on the Marina Freeway, and then finally drove into the Sawtelle District. It had changed a lot. Instead of sleepy storefronts, there were new mini-malls full of fancy cars. Bookstores and video rental places with neon Japanese signs. Sawtelle had moved up in the world.

Chochin's was on the edge of the business district, between the new and the old. The building itself looked kept up, but it seemed like it was one foot away from tumbling into nothingness. For one thing, there was no sign. Not anywhere. Second of all, there were no windows.

The parking lot was virtually empty, aside from a beat-up Chevrolet with a tarnished hardtop, and a white Acura. Mas opted to park across the street, near a new mini-mall. He cautiously approached the nondescript building, glancing through the glass door. Dark. All he could make out was a stand with a display of fake flowers.

He had heard about these hostess bars but had never gone inside one. They were reserved for big shots from Japan, or the *sukebe* rich ones over here who liked to have a pretty woman with their beer and sake.

Women had never been Mas's weakness, even during his younger years when his hair was black and full. Mas liked a different kind of excitement, which involved dice, money, and cards. Gambling, that's what pulsed through his veins more than any other kind of lust. He couldn't imagine paying money for young girls to sit down and talk to him. A waste of time and a waste of money.

But he knew plenty of other men with different tastes and passions. Riki Kimura, for example, who probably chased everything that he couldn't have. It didn't surprise Mas that Chochin's would be one of his L.A. hangouts.

A mailman, wearing a light-blue shirt and gray shorts, approached the nondescript building. "It's closed until five, I think," he said, pushing some letters through a slot in the door.

Mas grunted and shoved his hands in his pockets. Last thing he wanted to do was make small talk in front of a place like Chochin's.

The mailman was tall, with gray hair everywhere, from the top of his head to his arms and knobby legs. "Hey, you wouldn't happen to know what kind of establishment this is, would you? Recently got this route, and I tell you, I sometimes see some pretty women coming out of this place."

This mailman had too much time on his hands,

Mas figured. Living off the energy of other people's lives, instead of finding it in his own. "Dunno," Mas said, and left for Haruo's Honda. As he passed the parking lot, two girls came out of the back door of the building. One was so thin that she barely filled out one-half of her leather miniskirt. Mas couldn't make out the other girl, only that she kept her head down like a sick animal. As they proceeded to a red Corolla next to the sidewalk, the thin girl stroked the other one's back. It was obvious that the one hunched over was upset, even crying.

Mas slowed his gait and snuck a look, a long one this time. He had seen the sobbing girl before. Her skin was white and smooth as a newborn's, except for two red marks on her cheeks. His mind flipped back in time. Keiko's ramen house, he remembered. It was the girl with the tadpole eyes, except now they were almost swollen shut from despair.

✣ ✣ ✣

Mas got back into the Honda and then traveled east along the Santa Monica Freeway. The downtown skyscrapers were barely visible in the late-afternoon smog, and Mas knew he had one more stop to make. The Empress Hotel, in Little Tokyo.

There was nothing imperial about the Empress Hotel. In fact, they should have called it Hole Hotel or Dirty Inn. Even Mas himself felt apprehensive about entering a place that rented rooms by the week. He had a friend who had once lived in such a place, years ago. One of the hotels was being closed down, and Haruo and Mas had gone down to help him. He had had a stroke, and couldn't walk so good, and the manager had just left him out there on the sidewalk. All the electricity had been turned off, and the remaining residents, all *kuru-kuru-pa*, wandered around the hallways like ghosts. They had little grip on reality, but enough so that they could at least cash their social security checks and buy food in the grocery store. Within weeks they, too, would be loaded into trucks and deposited into the heart of skid row.

He parked the Honda at the meter in front of the boarded-up chop suey restaurant. How many times had he, Chizuko, and Mari eaten off their thick ceramic plates? The entrance to the Empress Hotel was on the side, up a narrow flight of stairs. When Mas got to the top, he saw two men, a black man and what looked like a Chinese, sitting on the second flight of stairs.

Mas moistened his lips. "You knowsu Yuki Kimura? You knowsu where he stays?"

"That young guy with red hair?" asked the black man.

Mas nodded.

"Three doors down."

The lights in the hallway seemed to have been burnt out. So much darkness inside, while sun beat down on the sidewalk below. Finally reaching room 7, Mas rapped at the door softly.

No response.

"Kimura," he said, now knocking harder.

Either the boy wanted to avoid any visitors or he had left the hotel.

"Somebody's in there," the black man reported from the end of the hall.

Mas could wait no longer. He twisted the door open, and saw a body covered with a blanket. "Kimura-*kun*," he said louder.

The body moved and then turned toward him. The hair, instead of red and spiky, was wavy and dark brown. The face, instead of tanned, was round and pale, with freckles. The eyes were familiar. Mas had seen those eyes before.

"Yes," the woman said, sitting up. "What is it?"

Mas blinked hard. She first looked like any Japanese woman in her seventies. But as soon as she spoke, Mas could instantly see the remnants of the past. Akemi Haneda.

CHAPTER ELEVEN

"Are you looking for my grandson?" she said, now in Japanese.

Mas felt like his whole body was shaking, as if his bones were connected only by a skinny string. But when he looked down, his arms, legs, and feet were perfectly still.

Akemi stood up. Her hair was a rich shade of brown, like good soil, instead of speckled gray and white. The face was made-up, even in this hole of a hotel room. The clothing comfortable, yet well made, with fine stitching. She even smelled sweet. It was obvious. Sometime during the past fifty years, Akemi Haneda had become a high-tone woman.

"Ah, mistake. Wrong room." He retreated back into the darkened hallway. He passed the two men, still sitting on the stairs, and then finally stumbled into the street. How could Yuki just leave his grandmother alone in such a place?

Mas bought a Coke from the video store next door to buy some time. He waited thirty minutes and then an hour. Soon he couldn't stand it anymore and went back upstairs. He knocked on Yuki's room, first a couple of times, and then one more round.

"Who is it?"

Mas coughed, and then it came out, clear and loud: "Masao, Masao Arai."

It was quiet for a full minute. The door creaked open enough for Akemi's eyes to study Mas. "I knew a Masao Arai once," she said.

Mas nodded. "Izu that one, Akemi-*san*." After Mas spoke her name, Akemi finally opened the door wider. "Excuse the room," she said, and then gestured toward the bed. "Here, please sit down."

Mas felt his knees grow weak and complied. The bed was mushy like mashed potatoes. The bedspread reeked of something old and unwashed. Why were they staying in such a no-good place?

Akemi eased herself into a rickety chair next to the bed. Her feet dangled; Mas noticed that her stockinged feet were not flattened down with hammer toes and blemished corns. She had obviously not spent her life toiling in fields or other people's homes. Akemi smiled so wide that Mas could see the gold on her molars. "I frightened you, it seems like. I guess you couldn't recognize me like this."

"Your eyes. Your eyes are the same." They were large for a Japanese, double-lidded, and lined with long eyelashes. Only the lashes weren't as full as they used to be, and the eye color seemed a little dull, but it was indeed the eyes of Joji Haneda's older sister.

"Masao Arai, it's really you. Yuki mentioned that he had met you. It's so good to see you."

It was apparent that the boy had said nothing about blaming Mas for sending him to the mistress.

"You look the same, Masao-*san*. Little gray hair, a little more weight. But it's definitely you."

Mas didn't know whether to speak English or Japanese. He couldn't stay with one language, and did what he always did, mixed it all up. "So, *ne*, itsu been long time, Akemi-*san*."

"What happened to you? We left Hiroshima for a couple of years right after the war. I never was clear on where you were."

"America. Came in 1947. Been here ever since."

"And you've never gone back?"

Mas shook his head. "Neva."

"Just like me and America. Until now."

It was strange to be just talking to Akemi, answering normal questions with normal answers, when nothing was normal at all. Akemi should not be alive. But here she was, unblemished, unscarred, perfect.

"So you know my grandson—"

"Yuki, yah, met him at the medical exams."

"Didn't mention anything specific to me. But then,

he hasn't explained much of anything since picking me up from the airport." Akemi pressed down on the side of her eye with her fingers, which were bent like old nails. "Maybe you know—what kind of trouble is Yuki in?"

"Trouble?"

"Well, I know he's supposed to stay in Los Angeles for some reason. He's had trouble with women before. Is it about that?"

Mas pulled at his pockets. So Akemi hadn't heard? Mas didn't know how much to reveal. Riki Kimura. The mistress. Shuji Nakane.

"Yuki didn't tell me much at the airport. He doesn't want me to worry, but I can handle it. You know, Masao-*san*. You know how much I can take."

Mas gritted down on his dentures. Akemi hadn't changed. Even back then she hadn't minced words. Being marooned in Japan for half a century hadn't softened her one bit.

"You know that we Hanedas are a stubborn people. He tries to hide the worst from me, but I won't give up."

Mas remained silent. "We Hanedas," she had said. Nothing about Kimuras.

Mas felt his body go limp. "Itsu a girl," he finally said. "Girl from a hostess bar. Sheezu hurt bad, Akemi-*san*."

Akemi's face fell. Outside the grimy window, Mas

could see a homeless man digging through the trash. "What connection did they have?"

"No connection. Little, at least." Mas failed to mention that he had been the one who had sent the grandson over to North Hollywood. "Just wrong place, wrong time."

"So Yuki's a suspect."

Mas nodded. "I guess so. But no arrest. Yet."

"Yet." Akemi seemed to take in that word like the edge of a razor blade.

"Dis guy I knowsu gotsu him a lawyer. I'm sure heezu gonna be *orai*. The girl gonna wake up and clear him."

Akemi quickly got up from her chair and adjusted her hair in the mirror. She picked up a pocketbook from the corner. "You ready?" she asked.

"Huh?" Mas remained sunken on the mashed-potato bed.

"Take me to the lawyer."

After making a call to Tanaka's, Mas learned that the attorney was based in downtown L.A., in the center of skyscrapers and gridlock. The attorney's name was G. I. Hasuike, which didn't make a good first impression on Akemi. "G. I.—what kind of name is that?" she said, still clutching her pocketbook.

They parked in an underground lot on Wilshire Boulevard. It was one of those that were dark and made of cement yet still charged as much as a hotel room.

G. I. Hasuike, Attorney-at-Law, was on the eleventh floor. The building was not shiny and modern like the other ones on the block. It was blocky and square, with corners that collected dust and dirt. A simple brown door, processed wood, held G. I. Hasuike's shingle. The second T in ATTORNEY was missing, spelling AT ORNEY. At least that's what Akemi pointed out.

The receptionist at the front desk was Sansei, about Mari's age. She was heavy and breathed hard even though she was sitting like a stone Buddha. Her desk was empty, aside from a telephone, memo pad, and a skinny water bottle. "Do you have an appointment?" she asked.

"I'm here from Japan." Akemi spoke like a TV newscaster, and Mas was surprised. Her English was perfect, as if she had never left Los Angeles. "This is regarding my grandson, Yukikazu Kimura. I need to speak to Mr. G. I."

"Well, he's with a client now. And he'll be taking a deposition in an hour."

"I'm sure he can fit us in. We'll wait."

The receptionist looked annoyed but didn't move from her chair. She lifted the phone receiver, pressed a button, and spoke a few sentences before looking up at Akemi. "Have a seat."

After about ten minutes, a man on crutches

emerged from one of the back offices and exited through the front door. The Buddha woman then nodded. "You can go in now."

Mas pictured the lawyer, G. I., as being large, bigger than life. But the man in front of them was reed thin, almost emaciated. He must have been in his late forties, yet there was a fresh crop of pimples around his chin. His hair was thin and he wore thick glasses. Files and papers littered his office. Bright-colored posters with Asians holding rifles and picket signs decorated his humble square space.

G. I. removed a mountain of files from one of the chairs in front of his desk and gestured to both of them. "Please," he said, "sit down. So, what can I do for you?"

Akemi, in her precise, clipped English, explained that she was Yukikazu Kimura's grandmother. She had just arrived from Hiroshima and naturally was concerned about Yuki's case. "I want to know," Akemi said. "What are his chances of going to jail?"

"Little, Mrs.—"

"Kimura."

Mas stayed quiet. He would have to ask Akemi about her last name later.

G. I. twirled the middle of a pencil around his index finger. "He was there. That's been established."

"Otha people there, too," Mas blurted out.

"Yes, we realize that." G. I. seemed surprised to hear from Mas. "Miss Kakita, shall I say, has had an active social life. We are investigating different pieces of evidence in the apartment."

No doubt Nakane's business card, thought Mas.

"If this woman led that kind of life, there would be various suspects, I imagine," Akemi said. "Then why pinpoint Yuki?"

"The blood on his hands. That's the problem. It did check out to be her blood type. I guess they could do a full DNA test, but I don't think they're willing to spend the money."

"Blood?"

"Yeah, I guess he touched the body. Held the woman's hand—yes, that's what he told police."

"Why would he hold her hand?"

"That's the thing. He wouldn't be in the mess he is in now."

"And how about the woman? She's still alive, right? What does she say?"

"She has suffered a lot of head trauma. Goes in and out of consciousness."

Akemi looked at a couple of diplomas on the wall. They hung crookedly between two posters. "Mr. Hasuike—"

"G. I., please."

Akemi pressed her lips together before speaking again. "G. I., where did you go to law school?"

"UC Davis."

"UC Davis—isn't that for agriculture?"

Mas colored. Akemi's tone was a familiar one. In

her voice he heard Mrs. Witt's asking him why the rosebushes near her fishpond were dying.

"I'm not actually a criminal lawyer, Mrs. Kimura. But my partner is. If this case goes any further, you can be assured that my partner will take over. I'm doing this as a favor to Wishbone."

"Wishbone?"

"Wishbone Tanaka. I handled a case for him a couple of years ago. I believe he is a friend of yours."

The attorney turned to Mas.

Akemi pressed her lips together again and sat still, like a computer churning up facts and numbers and coming up with only a bunch of minuses.

* * *

As soon as they left the cavernous parking structure and paid fifteen bucks, Akemi made a declaration. "We need to find Yuki a new lawyer," she said.

"Huh?"

"One with money, clout. Did you see that office?"

Mas clicked on the Honda's turn signal and watched as a river of cars traveled up Flower Street.

"Someone who's gone to the Ivy League. Harvard. Yale. Someone like that."

Mas was concerned, too, but he had little to do with lawyers, aside from a slip-and-fall attorney he hired when someone had crashed into his truck at a red light.

"Money. I just need to get hold of some money." Akemi pressed her pocketbook against her stomach.

"Weezu gotsu Japanese banks in Little Tokyo."

"No, you don't understand. We're having some, well, financial problems. I can't get to our funds right now. That's why Yuki's staying at that awful hotel."

Now, that made sense to Mas. So it had been a lack of money—not any kind of independent spirit—that had taken Yuki to the Empress. "Akemi-*san*," he finally said. "He'll be *orai*."

"Why don't I feel like it will be all right? Her blood was on him, Masao-*san*. Why did he even touch her?"

"Maybe he checkin' if she dead or alive. The lawyer talks like he knowsu whatsu goin' on. No sense in changin' right now. If it getsu bad, we getcha a new lawyer."

"I can't lose him, Masao-*san*."

Mas gripped the steering wheel as they stopped at an intersection.

"He's all I have. My son died. His wife ran off years ago with the money. Said that I was too overbearing. Imagine that."

Mas pressed down on the gas pedal.

Akemi was quiet for a few blocks and then laughed. She sounded like her old self again. "I know what you're thinking, Masao-*san*. I know I say things too clearly at times. But that's my nature, right?"

Mas said nothing. It wouldn't be smart to agree.

"You're just the same. Not the type to run off at

the mouth. I always liked that about you, Masao-*san*. I knew that I could trust you."

Mas felt his face grow hot. He remembered how he had abandoned her during the war. She had sat by the gate of her house and called out to him. But he couldn't help her. He had forsaken her as much as he had forsaken her brother.

Akemi was silent for a while as Mas drove up the Pasadena Freeway. Then she said, "Do you know what hospital that woman is in?"

"Kakita?" Mas thought back to his earlier telephone conversation with Haruo. "Kaiser, I think. The one on Sunset in Hollywood."

Akemi sat on the edge of the passenger seat of the Honda, her hands resting on the warm cracked dashboard. She looked like she was ready to jump out at any moment.

"*Orai, orai,*" Mas finally said. He signaled right, toward the interchange to the Hollywood Freeway.

✣ ✣ ✣

Mas had gone to that Sunset hospital years ago. A longtime customer, a widow in her nineties, had spent her last days there. Although she had two children and half a dozen grandchildren, Mas and Chizuko were her only regular visitors. "How are the peach blossoms doing?" Mrs. Blancher had asked, pressing her cold, papery hands in Mas's tough ones.

"Comin' out, Mrs. Blancher. Looks real nice."

That seemed to comfort the widow more than any other painkiller that the nurses brought in tiny paper cups. Mas even visited her once on his own after working her yard. He brought some daffodils straight from her garden and placed them in water in a drinking glass on her eating tray. She wasn't talking by this time, but Mas thought he saw a tear seep down the side of her nose.

The hospital was a lot different now. As it was apparently being renovated, there was scaffolding everywhere and wooden barriers in front of mounds of dirt. Akemi and Mas wandered from building to building until they located the intensive care wing. As they approached the nurses' station, Mas was surprised to see a beefy black policeman sitting in front of one of the open rooms. Seated, he was about the same height as Mas standing on his tiptoes.

Akemi apparently knew what to do. She went straight to the policeman and nodded toward the hospital bed within the guarded room. "We are friends of the family. The Arais."

Mas was stunned. What had he gotten himself into? The policeman looked over Akemi and then Mas. "I need to see some ID."

Akemi nudged Mas, and he reluctantly pulled out his worn wallet from his jeans pocket and handed over his driver's license. The policeman studied Mas's photo and glanced at Mas's leathery face. "Go on," he said.

Mas walked slowly into the small room. All the walls were of glass, and thick fabric curtains were drawn on both sides. The mistress lay in a small heap in the middle of the hospital bed. Her face was badly swollen, and a large bruise like a ripe plum marked her cheek below her left eye. Her head was now shaven of its wild long hair, and a white gauze bandage was taped over her forehead. Without her heavy makeup, she now looked like a featherless newborn bird, the kind with bulging purple eyelids.

Akemi brushed past Mas's shoulder and didn't seem to care that the mistress's eyes were closed. "Kakita-*san*, Kakita-*san*," she hissed. "This is very important. I need your attention."

Mas could take a lot, but disturbing the rest of a beaten woman was too much. "Akemi-*san*. Dis not a good idea."

"What am I supposed to do? See Yuki get carted off to jail? I'm not going to let that happen."

"Nanda—" The mistress's voice was faint, slightly muffled by the edge of her pillow.

There was no deterring Akemi now. "Kakita-*san*, please listen. A young man's future is at stake. You need to tell us. Who did this to you?"

The mistress's eyes fluttered, her sparse eyelashes like the damaged wings of a butterfly. "Who?"

"I am Yuki Kimura's grandmother. I know that he didn't do this to you. But you have to tell me who did."

"Kimura—" The mistress hesitated, and then looked beyond Akemi to Mas. "You."

Mas looked nervously through the glass wall toward the large seated body of the policeman.

"You," she repeated. The mistress was out of breath, and the electronic monitor began to emanate a high-pitched noise.

"We betta leave, Akemi-*san*." Two nurses, one in a flowered uniform, another in all green, were rushing toward Kakita's room.

Akemi didn't want to leave, but when the policeman rose from his seat, she finally relented. As the nurses entered, Mas and Akemi slipped out, unnoticed as usual.

❖ ❖ ❖

So you know this woman Kakita?"

They were heading east on the Hollywood Freeway, toward downtown Los Angeles.

Mas wasn't sure how much he should reveal to Akemi. It was obvious that she would do anything to protect her grandson.

"Met her one time."

Akemi waited.

"But not the waysu you think. She a friend of a friend."

As Mas exited Los Angeles Street, passing the Federal Building and then the Los Angeles Police Department headquarters, the signal blinked yellow, forcing cars to slow down before they accelerated down the quiet street. It was way after five, and most of the government workers had left for their homes in the suburbs.

"You know, I'm sorry," Akemi finally said. "I should have never forced myself on that poor woman. I crossed the line."

Mas was surprised to hear an apology, much less one from Akemi.

"It's just that I'm so worried. I feel so helpless. I have to do something, for Yuki's sake. I guess this attitude is what gets me in trouble. I should have learned when Hikari's wife left." Akemi's voice cracked. She took out a handkerchief from her pocketbook and pressed it to her eyes.

Mas couldn't stand to see Akemi cry. "He didn't do anytin'," he said. "He be innocent. In a few days, both of youzu be back on a plane to Hiroshima."

Akemi nodded. That much they were agreed upon.

When they returned to the hotel room, Yuki still had not returned. "I wonder where he is," Akemi said.

Mas looked at the shabby furniture and the worn bedspread. Muffled voices could be heard on the other side of the wall. "You can't stay here anymore," he said. "You come to my house."

"But Yuki?"

"Him, too," Mas said before he realized it. "I leave my address."

✣ ✣ ✣

Mas hadn't had a woman stay at the house since Chizuko had died. Now that Akemi was with him, Mas began to see the house with her eyes. The pitiful lawn full of dandelions. The cracked driveway. Dingy windows. Mas was almost afraid when he opened the front door. The smell was the same. The rot of nothingness, like boxes that had been stored away for decades.

"Wait a minute," Mas said, leaving Akemi in the hallway. He approached the room he never entered. He stopped for a moment and then turned the doorknob. Nothing. Then he remembered. The door was always getting stuck. Hadn't Mari always complained that he needed to fix it? After he pressed down and turned the knob, Mas fell back in time. Posters of orange, purple, and blue with *hakujin* and black men holding microphones. High school banners. A record player. Twin bed with the same bedspread. They were all there, all in place. Untouched for twenty years.

Akemi was at the doorway.

"You stay in here," Mas instructed.

Akemi looked around. "Your daughter's?"

Mas nodded. "Long gone. She in New York."

"Really?" Akemi looked genuinely impressed. "I've always wanted to go to New York. How is it?"

"I neva go."

"Married?"

Mas hesitated and only grunted. He went into the linen closet in the hallway and brought in fresh sheets for the bed.

As they stripped the old sheets from the mattress, Akemi asked, "Did you know this man who calls himself Joji Haneda?"

Mas balled up the sheets. "Yah, I knowsu."

"Is he, Mas?"

Mas's heart thumped. Something seemed stuck in the back of his throat. "Heezu not your brotha."

Akemi's face fell.

"But I knowsu him, Akemi-*san*." Both of us do, in fact, he thought.

"Oh." Akemi folded her hands in her lap.

Before Mas could spit out the name Riki Kimura, Akemi stopped him. "Don't say anything more, Masao-*san*. I don't need to hear anything more."

"But I needsu to tell you. Part my *sekinin*, too."

Akemi shook her head.

"Your land. They gonna take away your land."

Akemi seemed surprised that Mas had heard of the property battle. "Land is just that. Dirt. I wanted to leave it to Yuki, but not at the expense of my peace of mind. His peace of mind."

Mas didn't understand. This Joji Haneda had no claim on the property. Mas could testify, go to court if he had to.

"Please, Masao-*san*, I beg of you. My first priority is making sure Yuki is cleared. And then I can take him home." Akemi stared at the yellow shag rug. "We won't speak of this again. Agreed?"

Before Mas could answer, they heard the rumble and screech of a powerful car. Mas looked out through Mari's drapes, caked with dust. Sure enough, it was the grandson in a large Jeep, frowning and looking in need of some explanations.

CHAPTER TWELVE

"I'm taking you to a hotel, *Obaachan*," Yuki said as he barged through Mas's front door. Mas and Akemi emerged from Mari's bedroom into the hallway.

"Empress Hotel—no, thank you," said Mas.

"I wasn't talking to you."

Akemi scolded her grandson, "Yuki-*kun*, don't talk to Arai-*san* like that."

"*Obaachan*, this man is a liar."

"Yuki!"

"He knows a lot more than he lets on."

"He's an old friend." Akemi fingered the top button on her blouse.

"He mentioned none of that. I even mentioned your name straight out."

Mas kept quiet.

"I got a room at a better hotel. I can't permit you to stay here, *Obaachan*."

"You can't permit me?"

The boy's brown cheeks reddened slightly.

"What happened, Yuki-*kun*? Were you with the police?"

Yuki's eyes grew big, and he cursed, using words that Mas was familiar with, and new ones, as well. "You told her, didn't you?"

"It was me," Akemi said. "I forced him to. I needed to know. Now, how much trouble are you in?"

"I can't leave Los Angeles yet. At least until she clears me." Yuki pulled at some limp clumps of his red hair. "She's conscious now, you know."

"So—that's wonderful." Akemi glanced at Mas, who looked down at the worn boards of the hardwood floor.

"The police showed pictures of me to her. She says she can't remember what happened."

"Can't remember," Akemi murmured.

"The consulate may get involved. This may turn into some international incident. Some reporter with *Asahi Shimbun* was even waiting for me beside my rental car."

A reporter from a real newspaper, thought Mas.

"He was asking me if I thought I might be used as an example."

"Example?" Akemi repeated.

"I don't know. I guess a lot of Japanese students are coming here and getting into trouble."

As Yuki spoke, Mas tried to stay quiet and still. But Yuki wasn't fooled, and circled back to him. "Damn old man. You know what's going on. You know who did that to her."

Mas waited for Akemi to defend him, but she seemed lost in her thoughts.

"I dunno. But I gotsu my ideas," Mas finally said.

"It's that mystery man, isn't it? The man who calls himself Joji Haneda."

Mas hesitated. For some reason, Akemi had asked him to keep quiet about Joji Haneda, and he owed her that much. "Shuji Nakane went ova to the mistress's house," he offered instead.

That got Akemi's attention. "Nakane-*san* is here in Los Angeles?"

"Yes, I saw him at the exams," Yuki explained. "I practically spit in his face, and he left." He turned back to Mas. "Why do you think he had something to do with the lady?"

"His *meishi*. It was in her apartment. Kitchen table."

Yuki and Akemi exchanged looks, worried ones, noted Mas. "She knowsu sumptin'." He added, "About your land."

The boy put two and two together. "It's that Joji Haneda. He's the one who's in the middle of this. I know you know him, *Ojisan*. Who is he?"

"Yuki-*kun*," Akemi interrupted, "let's get some sleep. We can talk about it in the morning."

The boy was on the verge of protesting, but his grandmother had already turned toward Mari's room.

Mas gestured toward the couch. "I getsu some blankets."

"Don't worry," Yuki snapped. "I'll sleep in the car."

✣ ✣ ✣

The boy kept his word, and stayed in his car the entire night. "He's fine," said Akemi as Mas looked out the screen door in the morning. "He's been backpacking in Africa. Spent the night on concrete and dirt, sleeping next to crocodiles. A big car like that is a luxury for him."

"Itsu *orai* with you?" Mas always wondered what it would be like to have a grandson. But he never figured that a grandson could be as strange as Yuki Kimura.

"It's a phase; that's what I figure. He'll settle down in a couple of years. Just imagine what he'll be able to do. He'll shake things up. That's what these Japanese companies need, you know."

Mas got some bread out of the freezer. There wasn't much he could offer Akemi. Just some defrosted white Wonder bread and freeze-dried coffee. Oh, and the Fresno peaches that Tug and Lil had brought.

"Whatsu you doin' ova there in Hiroshima?" Mas

finally had the guts to ask after he lit one of the stove burners.

"Worked as a translator for Mazda. Twenty-five years. Know all there is to know about carburetors and cylinders."

Mas was impressed. "Thatsu what I wanted to do. Work on engines."

"I remember."

Mas placed the kettle over the circle of blue flame.

"Actually, I think you told Joji. He mentioned that to me."

Mas pulled a couple of peaches out of the brown grocery bag. They were soft, almost too ripe.

"Sometimes I think of Joji," said Akemi. "Of what he could have become. He was so smart. And not only about numbers. About people. He thought a lot about you, Masao-*san*. Said that you were different than the other boys. Had spunk. Energy."

Mas got a rusty knife from one of the kitchen drawers. He cut into a peach until he hit the hard pit in the middle.

"He wanted to go back to America. Did he ever mention that to you? Said that. Said that he wanted to go back with you. 'Masao-*kun* doesn't know America that well, left too early, but I'll show him around. I'll show him how to play football. He'd be good at it. He's small, but he can tackle.' "

Mas felt his eyes water and kept cutting the peach into uneven pieces.

"Do you ever think about him?"

Mas wished that he could blurt out yes, but the last thing he wanted to ever think about was Joji Haneda.

"Our father died here. Did you know that? Was sent to a camp in New Mexico during the war. Finally buried in a cemetery called Evergreen, in East Los Angeles. You've heard of it?"

Mas threw the peach chunks onto a small dish. Chizuko was buried at Evergreen. He mentioned none of that and merely nodded.

"I'd like to go before I leave. Could you take me there?"

Before Mas could answer, the kettle began to whistle, loud, sharp, and out of tune.

✣ ✣ ✣

The boy eventually came in, just to go to the toilet and take a shower. Ten minutes later, he emerged from the steamy corner bathroom, looking like he was ready to take on something big.

Akemi held her cup of coffee with both hands. "Where are you going?"

"I have to nose around, ask some questions. I can't just sit here, waiting to be used as a damn example."

"I'm sure the woman will remember in a few days. She knows you had nothing to do with her accident."

"Maybe she doesn't want to remember, *Obaachan*. Maybe she's known right along."

Akemi frowned.

"What I'm saying is, she could be protecting someone. And here I come along. Conveniently."

Akemi puckered her cheeks, trying to feign disbelief, but Mas could tell. She was worried.

"And I'm not getting help from you two. So I guess it's up to me." Yuki shoved his car keys in his pants pocket.

"What are you saying? No help? I came from Hiroshima to do whatever I could do."

"Then give me some leads. Tell me who this Joji Haneda is."

Akemi became quiet.

"I help you," Mas finally said.

"Yeah? The way you've been helping me so far?"

"I have idea." Mas left the kitchen to get something from his desk in the bedroom. He returned to the kitchen with a clean white business card. "I'll set up a meeting. And then we find out what he knowsu."

✣ ✣ ✣

In L.A., there were different kinds of gardeners. A few, some of the top guys, looked nothing like gardeners at all. They wore neat slacks and golf shirts with designer labels and carried beepers on their belts. Underneath them were a slew of workers in uniforms who addressed their bosses as Mister and sir.

Mas knew that in going to Chochin's, both he and the boy would have to look the part. It didn't matter that Nakane knew that Mas was a plain kind of gardener, a one-man operation. He still oiled his hair back and even brushed his dentures. He wore an old polo shirt and pants with no holes.

The boy, on the other hand, couldn't seem to shake his image. No matter how he fixed his hair, he still looked like a *yogore* who hung around street corners, looking for excitement or trouble or both. While Mas was waiting in the kitchen, he heard Yuki riffling through Mari's closet. Finally he emerged in a black jacket. Mari's.

She had been wearing that strange, oversized coat when Mas had picked her up from the airport during her first Christmas break from college. He barely recognized her. She had gained some weight, her usually angular face was round, and a fresh crop of pimples dotted her forehead. The coat was from the fifties and apparently purchased at a used-clothing store.

Mas loaded Mari's bag into the trunk of the Datsun. "So, New York, crazy town?"

"I love it. People are alive, interesting. Not all materialistic, like in L.A."

Mas didn't say anything. He had been against Mari's going to Columbia. It sounded like a foreign country, not a school. And so far away. What was wrong with UCLA or USC?

"Gosh, it sure doesn't seem like Christmas around here." The gold-colored holiday banners and plastic holly waved in the breeze next to palm trees. "I didn't even need to bring a coat."

"You did okay in classes?"

"They were pretty hard." Mari rolled down the window a crack. "I think I did all right. So, what's Mom doing? She didn't want to come to the airport?"

"She resting."

"Resting? What's wrong? Is she sick or something?"

"A lot of things happen."

"What are you talking about?" Mari rolled up the window, snuffing out the drone of air.

"She had operation."

"Operation." Mari grew quiet. "Why didn't you guys tell me? It's not serious, is it?"

"You talk to her. She explain."

Mari cupped her hands around her eyes. The coat cuffs were worn, threads coming loose from the fabric.

Mas stopped at a red light at Airport Boulevard and tugged at his wallet.

"Here," he said, pulling out some twenty-dollar bills. "Go to the store and buy yourself a new coat. For school."

Mari wrapped the coat closer to her body, in spite of the seventy-degree weather. "Don't need another one. This one's perfect."

Now, more than ten years later, the redheaded

badger boy was wearing the same coat. "Come on," Mas said. "We don't want to be late."

✣ ✣ ✣

The boy's Jeep was a rental car, but it didn't smell like one. It had a syrupy scent, sweet like cotton candy.

"Nice car," Mas said from the passenger's seat.

Yuki started the engine and began to back out of the driveway. It was close to seven, and the sun was barely starting to set. "Do you know how expensive a car like this would be in Hiroshima? Seventy thousand at least. Got a special deal from a travel agent. My friend. Just have to make sure that nothing's damaged."

Mas continued sniffing and figured out the candy smell was coming from a bottle of blue liquid on the dashboard.

"Car deodorant," Yuki explained.

Mas merely shrugged. There was no telling what they would be inventing next.

"So, what do you want me to do?" Yuki asked. Mari's old coat was tight around his shoulders, but at least it hid the warthog tattoo and gave him a touch of a businessman's look.

"Just look around. Some girls knowsu Junko. Maybe you can ask somebody."

"What about Nakane? You don't think he's just going to give up some information."

"Leave it to me," Mas said, but the truth was that

he was just taking a roll of the dice and seeing how they landed.

✣ ✣ ✣

Other than Mas's grunting out directions, they traveled in silence until they hit the Santa Monica Freeway, a molten river of cars. The sun was right in front of them, bleeding red-orange in the smog. As Yuki changed lanes, a car from the left-hand side swerved into the same lane.

"Sonafubitchi," Mas muttered.

"Chikusho," Yuki shot out. "Crazy driver." He maneuvered the Jeep into the lane behind the car, a beat-up Chevrolet whose back window was blown out and covered with plastic.

"They'd never allow a car like that in Hiroshima. You can't even drive with one scratch on your car. Or you'll get a citation."

"Oh, yah." Mas gripped the side of the Jeep. He remembered when he was last in Hiroshima, and cars literally ran on charcoal and wood. How could he have worked on engines in such a place? And now look—during the oil crisis, when Mas had had to line up for gasoline, Japan had been the king of cars. And Mazda, where Akemi had worked, was right in Hiroshima.

"My friend accidentally hit a car in front of him," Yuki continued. "Just a tap, nothing serious. They took his license away for months."

"No kiddin'."

"That why I like this place. I wouldn't mind living here."

"You crazy. You almost in jail and you want to stay?"

"It's free. It's great that a new Cadillac can drive on the same streets as that broken-down car."

"Huh," Mas grunted. "They push you down."

"That's the old story, *Ojisan*. You got blacks and Japanese doing the TV news. Maybe if I stayed, I could someday write for *The Washington Post, The New York Times*."

Dreams, dreams, thought Mas. The boy was indeed young.

After they drove a couple of miles in silence again, Mas spoke. "I used to think like youzu. Yah, I used to think big. Work at Ford company. Make cars that work good on the road."

"Well, why didn't you? You were young when you came over, right?"

"Yah, I'm young. Eighteen years old. First a houseboy in San Francisco. Got a small room for cleanin' this *hakujin* man's house. Sometimes my friends—no place to stay—snuck in to sleep. We got caught once—kicked me out, and then I decided to go truck farmin'."

Yuki pursed his lips.

"You know nutin' about truck farmin', huh? Goin' town to town, from Watsonville to Texas. Wherever crops were. Tomatoes here, lettuce there. Build a shack from wood to live in—that be our home for temporary. Met a lot of people that way—Filipinos down south and Mexicans." The ashes of his cigarette had burnt down to the edge of his knuckles. "Then I thinkin'. Needsu my own business. Had a relative in Altadena, and that started it all."

"What business?"

Mas stared at the boy, who then quickly added, "Oh, you mean gardening."

"Yah, I'm talkin' about gardenin'." Mas gripped the stub of his cigarette and felt the ash break away. "Built my business from scratch. Gardenin' not too good, you thinkin'. But I'm my own boss. Not too many guys can say that." Mas went on about his customers, present and past. The East Indian who had made a fortune on a chain of teriyaki chicken sandwich shops. The Chinese real estate developer who had real parrots in his backyard. And yes, the divorce attorney who wouldn't agree to give Mas a raise even after ten years of service. "I tore up his check right in front of his nose," Mas said proudly.

He told the boy how it was when he'd traveled on the boat over the Pacific. "Came here on my own. Not one cent from my parents. Wouldn't take one cent, even if they had offered. Had enough. They want me to work on the farm, for *tada*, free. That's crazy. What the hell. Come ova here; take a chance.

"When I first came, I saw people push us down—

'Hey, Jap, get outta here.' But inside I thinksu, I'm an American citizen, after all. I belong here."

✣ ✣ ✣

Once they reached Chochin's, Mas took charge. "I'm suppose to meet him out back. You go in. Talk to the girls. You like girls, right?"

Yuki frowned, but stuffing his hands in Mari's coat, he dutifully walked inside.

Mas felt his heart pound, hard enough so that it seemed to rattle against his ribs. Had Shuji Nakane tried to kill the mistress? Had he wanted to shut her up forever? And now, with Riki on his deathbed, would Mas be the only one standing?

Mas crossed the sidewalk into the small parking lot filled with Mercedes Benzes, Lincoln Continentals, and a few Lexuses. Chochin's was busy this evening; who knew why? Mas checked his Casio watch, the band all worn out and tied together with twine. It was seven forty-five. Fifteen minutes early. Mas always liked to be early. When you were early, you were ready for the unexpected. Accidents, unforeseen events. You always had to be ready for something going wrong. Because it usually did.

Apparently, Shuji Nakane thought the same thing. He emerged from the side of a Dumpster with a black bag stuffed underneath his armpit. He was wearing the same tinted glasses and another turtleneck, this time black. "Arai-*san*. Good evening," he said.

The second Nakane opened his mouth, Mas knew he was up to no good. He knew something; he had a secret winning hand, and Mas was sure to go down in flames. At this point there was no turning back. Mas had to just play along.

"Um," Mas grunted. "Youzu here."

"You said you had something important to tell me. I didn't want to keep you waiting."

Mas shifted his weight from one foot to another. The parking lot was dead quiet. The corner was isolated and away from traffic. "I saw Junko Kakita," Mas finally said. "At the hospital."

Shuji Nakane pressed his palms together and waited.

"She tellsu me all kinds of stories."

"Oh, yes?" Nakane's lenses were lighter in the darkness, but Mas still couldn't see his eyes.

"She say that youzu visit her. Offer her lotsu of money. I figure she not right in the head, *desho*. Because why would you give her money?"

Nakane took the black bag from underneath his arm. "I'm tired of playing games, Arai-*san*," he said, and then opened the bag. A light had turned on above the parking lot, but Mas still couldn't see well. The contents was soon described to him. "Thirty thousand dollars," said Nakane. "You can have it all, if you keep out of this."

Mas almost laughed. He had never been offered so much cash before in his life. He had always wondered what he would have done if he'd hit it big in Vegas or the track, real big. Now would be the chance for him to find out. "Whatchu mean, 'keep out'?"

"Nobody would listen to you, anyway. I'm just making this offer as a gesture. Gesture of kindness. Take it or leave it. I don't care."

Mas felt his stomach flip inside out. Kind of like the time he'd overheard Mari, fifteen years old, complain to Chizuko about not being able to afford ski trips like the other kids. *"Why don't we have money?"* she had said. *"Why can't Dad have a better job, and wear a suit and a tie?"*

"Spoke to his wife and children. Told them that they were in line to inherit a prime piece of property worth ten million dollars." Mas raised his eyebrows. Ten million? Yuki had told him three million.

"The boy lowballed it, didn't he?" Nakane adjusted his glasses. "It's just like him. He's tricky. All he cares about is the money, Arai-*san*. Don't be fooled by his so-called love for his grandmother. He doesn't care about her. He's even tried to replace her name with his on property titles."

Mas tried not to let Nakane's accusations get to him. But he had to admit that he was left with an aftertaste of doubt.

"Riki Kimura's only got a few more weeks, days. He wasn't much of a father, husband. Close to declaring bankruptcy, he is. It's better this way. For his family and for you."

It was completely out in the open now. Nakane knew, and was seeking to erase Riki Kimura for good.

Mas looked down at Nakane's shoes. They didn't have tassels, but they were indeed fancy like the ones he saw when his truck had been stolen. "Where's my Ford?" Mas said. It was a shot in the dark.

Nakane didn't respond to the question. "Here, take it." He pushed the bag into Mas's stomach. He walked toward a Lincoln Continental, got in, and drove away.

✣ ✣ ✣

For a while, Mas knelt by the Dumpster, his hands around the leather bag holding thirty thousand dollars. Twenty-seven years ago, he could have bought the nursery outright, with money to spare. Twenty-seven years ago, he could have bought two houses the size of his Altadena place. Twenty-seven years ago, he could have found a doctor at the top of his field for Chizuko, at the first sign of stomach trouble.

Mas stuck his hand into the bag. They were crisp bills all bundled together like the ones the Las Vegas cashiers would present to those who won big.

He looked down at his watch. Close to eight-thirty. The boy would be coming out to the parking lot anytime now. He pushed up the lid of the Dumpster and pulled out dark trash bags. Half-eaten food spilled out, vegetable peelings, containers. A pink pastry box. Mas grabbed the box and dumped the leftovers. There was no time to waste. He threw the bundles of money into the box and folded in the lid. Ten million dollars, Nakane had said. Not three million. If the boy had his secrets, Mas would have his.

✣ ✣ ✣

Mas waited for a good forty minutes, until nine-ten, when he figured he'd better go get the boy. There was no doubt that he had fallen under the spell of a bar hostess. Clutching his pink box, he opened the heavy door of Chochin's and walked into a small reception area. Behind the reception desk was a glass case full of bottles of the finest liquor, all tagged with names written in Japanese. In the corner behind the door was a mound of salt to ward off the curse of women—and there was good reason to. A Japanese woman in a kimono emerged from a doorway covered by a silky cloth curtain. She was about forty, and her face was covered with white, floury makeup.

"Yes, how can I help you?" she said in Japanese. She didn't seem the slightest bit fazed by Mas's appearance. In the background Mas could hear the beat of music that Mari used to listen to in the 1970s.

"Ah—" Mas tried to compose the words in his mouth.

"*Okyaku-san,* do you have a membership?" she asked in a singsong voice.

"No, just lookin' for a friend. Young one, about twenty or so. Red hair."

"Oh, yes," the hostess replied immediately. She held back the silk curtain so Mas could enter the heart of Chochin's. The room, about the size of Mas's whole house, was awash in blue and loud American music. A ball covered with small mirrored squares hung from the ceiling, covering the guests with dots of blinding white light. Pitiful, Mas thought, looking at the red-faced middle-aged men sitting with young girls of all races about half their age. Finally the kimono-clad woman gestured to a booth in the corner, where Yuki sat. Next to him was the girl with the tadpole eyes. She had something glittery rubbed over her eyes and wore a halter top that revealed the pure whiteness of her arms and shoulders.

"Ojisan," the boy said as Mas approached. He was grinning from ear to ear. On the table was a bottle of Johnnie Walker with a tag, YUKIKAZU KIMURA, hanging from its neck.

Stupid, Mas thought. At least use a fake name. "We needsu to leave," Mas said, ignoring their motions to sit with them.

"You get what you needed?" Yuki's voice took a more serious tone, and Mas could have kicked him. Not here, he thought, not in front of the girl. But the hostess's face was a complete blank; she was apparently well trained to look invisible during conversations between men. Mas could imagine all the business, both legitimate and illegitimate, that occurred within the four walls of Chochin's. The girl didn't even seem to acknowledge that she and Mas had met once before.

Mas tugged on Yuki's T-shirt with his right hand, the pink box firmly in his left. "We needsu to get out of here," he said in the boy's ear. Yuki finally nodded and said his good-byes, slipping a twenty-dollar bill underneath the girl's empty glass.

When they finally got back into the Jeep, Yuki showed Mas a square Polaroid photo. "A souvenir," he said. He had had his picture taken with the hostess. "She was *kawaii*. Kind of quiet, though," he said, throwing the photo in the glove compartment. Then he noticed the box on Mas's lap.

Mas was careful to look away. "Got hungry. Went ova to that place across the street. Got some stuff for your grandma."

That was enough for Yuki. "Where's Nakane?" he asked.

The lies came easily to Mas's lips. He was not ashamed. One after another, they dribbled out like rain. *Nakane didn't seem to know about the mistress. He had given up and was planning to return to Japan. They didn't have to worry about him anymore.*

"He told you all that?" Yuki got back on the Santa Monica Freeway, this time going east.

"Yah."

Yuki then hit the steering wheel and cursed.

"What?"

"Your jacket. I left it at the bar." The boy was in his T-shirt, the tattoo poking out below his right sleeve.

"Don't worry." Mas held on to the pink box. "It was old. Just leave it there."

✣ ✣ ✣

As they approached McNally Street, Mas's stomach turned. Parked in front of Mas's house was a sheriff's car with its blue lights flashing.

Mas and the boy were on the same wavelength. *"My obaachan,"* Yuki whispered, and Mas felt immediately ashamed. The boy obviously cared about Akemi. How could Mas have doubted him?

They ran into the house, fearing the worst. But there was Akemi, unhurt, standing there with two officers.

"What happened?" Yuki asked his grandmother, but before she could answer, the officers grabbed Yuki's arms.

"We have to take you into custody," said one of them, a tall black woman, fastening a handcuff around his wrist. Yuki started to resist, but Mas pressed his palm on the boy's back. Don't fight, he thought. You may think this is a land of black and *Nihonjin* TV newscasters, but it's more complicated than that. Before anyone could say anything more, the other officer, a short *hakujin* man, answered their silent questions. "We're charging him with murder," he said, "in the death of Junko Kakita." While murmuring something about rights and lawyers, they led Yuki out the screen door that Tug Yamada had fixed, down the driveway, and into the black-and-white squad car.

CHAPTER THIRTEEN

"One more time. Just tell me one more time." G. I. Hasuike's eyes were so bloodshot that they looked like red marbles. Mas didn't know who else to call at midnight. G. I. wasn't the best, but he, at least right now, was their only shot.

Akemi, sitting on Mas's couch, took another breath. "They came saying that they had a warrant for Yuki's arrest. That lady died in the hospital. They have a witness now, saying he did it."

"A witness," G. I. muttered. Mas hadn't noticed the first time, and now saw that his hair, fastened in a ponytail, reached his waist. "Who?"

Akemi shook her head. "I don't know. But you got to get him out of jail."

G. I. nodded. "He'll have to stay there overnight. The arraignment will be scheduled probably during the next few days, and then they'll move the case from municipal to superior court. That's what they do in felony cases."

Akemi pulled a pillow from the couch and squeezed it hard. Someone was knocking on the door, and Mas looked through the side window to check. It was just Haruo. Mas had called him; Haruo was attached to the boy and would want to be informed. Now, with four of them in the living room, G. I. kept going about first- and second-degree murder, involuntary manslaughter, continuances, and setting bail. Mas had little idea about the meaning behind the terms, but G. I. apparently did.

"They'll assign him a PD, but then I can come in. That is, if you want me to represent your grandson."

Akemi nodded again.

G. I. stood up and then clutched Akemi's shoulder. "It'll be all right, *Obasan*. *Gam-BA-re*," he said in broken Japanese. His pronunciation was terrible, but it didn't matter. They were all in this together.

Mas couldn't sleep that night. Even some two hours after G. I. and Haruo left McNally Street, Mas wandered the rooms of his house like a ghost. This was his fault. Why had he given Yuki directions to the mistress's house that morning at the hospital? And how could the mistress have just died like that? She had had all the answers, and Mas had been planning to get them from her in time. But now the time was gone.

Mas wanted to make this whole thing right. Somehow. He knew how to play the game in dingy rooms in Little Tokyo and other places across the country, and even Hiroshima circa the 1940s. But the police and courts—those were way out of his league. That was a world G. I. and other Sansei understood. They could swim in those waters. If they were any good, they could avoid becoming someone's next meal. If they were real good, they could pop out of a rock and bite unsuspecting prey right in the face. The next few days would reveal just how good or bad G. I. Hasuike was.

As Mas wandered to the kitchen, he noticed a sliver of light under Mari's old bedroom door. Akemi was still up, like him. He softly rapped on the door.

"Come in, Masao-*san*," she said.

She was wearing slacks and a nice blouse, as if she were ready to go to the courthouse with G. I. at three o'clock in the morning. She gestured for Mas to sit on the bed. He complied.

"Can't sleep," she said. "Every time I lie down, I picture Yuki there, alone. It must be cold in that jail."

"Heezu tough. He be *orai*." Mas put his hands on his knees and studied the looped rug on the floor of Mari's old bedroom. The rug had been from one of his customers. A widow who had been cleaning her attic. Mari had immediately fallen in love with it, remembered Mas. She'd said it reminded her of the pioneer days. What pioneer days, she didn't say.

"He's all I have, Masao-*san*. I still can't believe that his father is dead. The cancer just spread through Hikari's body in a matter of months. It's like that shadow that was following us for fifty years had finally caught up."

Mas regretted knocking on Akemi's door. This was the last thing he wanted to talk about now.

"Before he died, I wanted to tell Hikari the truth. About his father. But I didn't know his first name. Just the last. Sato."

Mas was jolted from his daydreams. "Sato," he said aloud.

"I know," Akemi continued. "There are thousands of Satos out there. I don't think you knew him. He was older. Part of the military police, at the time you three were working at the train station."

The MPs. They had come to the Hanedas almost once a week.

"You know they questioned us, right? My mother, Joji, even the maid. They wanted to know about our ties to America. If we kept in touch with my father in Los Angeles. You remember, Masao-*san*? You gave me the coals so that I could burn my English books one morning."

Mas nodded. He could still feel the coldness of that winter morning and feel the chalky charcoal on his face.

"He was just one among many. They accused me of horrible things. Sato wasn't as cruel, but he seemed as though he knew a secret. That he was above all of them. They poked me with their batons, and then began to jeer me. 'Is it true what they say about *gaijin* women?' they said." Akemi's voice remained steady but was softer, as if a volume knob inside of her had been turned down to low. "They did nothing the first time. But they kept calling me back in. I couldn't sleep at nights, Masao-*san*. I still can't."

Mas felt his blood stir. Those sonafubitchi MPs—what had they done to Akemi?

Akemi must have sensed Mas's anger, but she shook her head. "No, no, Masao-*san*," she said. "That's the thing. They said awful, terrible things, even slapped me once. But they didn't go as far as . . . You see, I ran into Sato one evening on my way to the bathhouse from my aunt's house. I lived at her place for a short time to be close to the factory. He must have lived downtown, I guess. I was afraid. I immediately put my head down, hoping that he would not recognize me, but he did. He wasn't wearing his uniform. Just simply a cotton *yukata,* and *geta* on his feet. 'Haneda-*san*,' he called out. And we talked. I thought in the beginning that it was a trick, so I said nothing. But then the next evening I met him again, and the next night and then the next."

Mas bit down on his gums. His dentures were still floating in some water in the bathroom, but he didn't care. There was no vanity between him and Akemi.

"I began to trust him. I know it sounds crazy."

Akemi brought her freckled hands to her face. "I was so lonely, Mas, you have to understand. Before I knew it, it had happened. Later on, it was almost worse than a physical rape. He ignored me, Masao-*san*. Like I was a piece of trash, or an animal. Like it was my job to service him.

"I tried to pretend that I wasn't pregnant. I denied it to myself. I tried to work especially hard in the factory, hoping that the baby would just dissolve and leave me. Just the stupid thinking of a nineteen-year-old. How could I tell my mother? She had suffered so much. But Joji knew. He told me not to worry. That he would take care of us. He had a plan, he said, but he never told me what.

"Even after the *pikadon* fell, I still expected that Joji would come back. I know that it sounds stupid, but I thought that my brother was more powerful than any bomb. We even went down to the train station, or at least where the train station used to be. We searched underneath every burnt limb, every piece of broken concrete. After hours and hours of searching, we finally ate the rice balls we had packed. Like a picnic in the woods—only this picnic was in the middle of a nightmare."

Mas continued clutching his knees. He felt dizzy, and now the loops in the rug seemed to swirl.

"I needed something, Masao-*san*. I needed some proof. Later on, they sent us a bone and said it was Joji's. We knew that it was the bone of a horse. But it helped Mama, at least. There was something she could bury." Akemi stared at Mari's wall full of high school mementos and photos of *hakujin* boys with long hair.

"I wanted to talk to you, but you were too weak, I guess. Within days, Mama finally noticed the obvious. I was at least three months' pregnant. Mama didn't ask questions, but she didn't speak of me to the neighbors, and told me not to go outside. I guess everyone assumed that I was dead. She took me away to our relatives in the countryside. We made up a lie, that I had married. My husband had been a soldier in the war. When they asked me his name, I just said Riki Kimura. I don't know why. I barely knew him. But what I knew, I liked."

Mas let out a funny hacking noise, and Akemi caught on immediately. "Mas, you didn't have it as bad as us," she said, almost angry. "You didn't know. Riki Kimura—yes, he was a troublemaker. But he also fought for us."

"Heezu just out for himself. Like a big shot."

"Maybe. Maybe for some reason he felt like an outsider, too." Akemi folded her hands together, and Mas kept his mouth shut. "When I came back to Hiroshima, when Hikari was only two, I heard that Riki Kimura had disappeared. That his family's house had been destroyed. It was so convenient—can't you see? Riki Kimura could officially be my son's father. I could even claim we were married. The records were all gone."

"So Yuki thinks Riki Kimura is his grandfather?" Mas remembered the square name tag that Yuki had proudly shown them that day of the medical exams.

Akemi nodded. "It all started with my son, Hikari. Having no father, no brothers, no sisters, he was lonely. I filled his emptiness with stories about Riki Kimura. Even in my eyes, Riki became bigger than life. I could say anything about him. That he was Japanese—not *Kibei,* like us—but he still stood up for us. That he was brave and good. I couldn't tell my son the truth. That I had had sex with a man I knew only as Sato. That he was a *rokudemonai hito,* a worthless person. And that I was even more contemptible, because I was so weak."

"It was wartime. Thatsu the past, Akemi. We all do things back then."

"And Yuki, he heard all the stories from his father. He can't know what really happened." Akemi dabbed at the wetness around her eyes with her fingers. They were bent, like crooked nails—from arthritis, no doubt.

"Akemi-*san.*" Mas had to explain. Akemi had a right to know how her brother had died.

But once again Akemi stopped him. "I'm very tired, Masao-*san,*" she said.

Mas himself was exhausted. He felt that he could sleep for days or even weeks. He rose to leave.

"Masao-*san*."

Mas waited.

"This is not your fault. If I didn't have that stupid hope that Joji was somehow alive, Yuki would have never come here."

Mas closed the door behind him and then checked the dead bolt on the front door. Then he remembered. The pink box. Tripping over the torn-up driveway in his bare feet, he opened up the Jeep. The dome light revealed nothing. Mas fervently traced the car floor with his fingers. But it was no use. The pink box and thirty thousand dollars were gone.

✣ ✣ ✣

The next morning, the sheriff's deputies were at the door again. Akemi called G. I., who came within twenty minutes in the same wrinkled outfit he had been wearing the night before.

Mas, Akemi, and G. I. stood on the withered lawn, the dandelions brushing their ankles, and watched through the open door as the deputies proceeded to dismantle everything from the couch pillows to frozen vegetable packs in the freezer.

"Whatsu they lookin' for?" Mas asked G. I.

"Any kind of evidence. The money." Dried drool left a mark like a snail's trail down his chin.

"Money?"

"Yeah, the authorities have information that the

dead woman had thirty grand in cash. And now it's gone."

Mas's chest began to thump hard. The money. Where was it? Had Yuki brought that pink box in? It didn't make sense. Or maybe some of the neighborhood kids.

In fact, a whole line of them sat on their bikes by the street as the police searched. Mas approached them, forgetting that he was still in his pajama bottoms and slippers. "You kidsu not come ova here last night?"

The boys, all around eight, looked at one another blankly.

"You don't play with dis car, huh?" Mas pointed to Yuki's rented Jeep.

"No, uh-uh," the tallest one said. He was wearing a black and red tank top with the number 32.

Mas studied their faces. Their skin, ranging in color from toffee to black-blue, was smooth and unblemished, like perfect plums.

"You pushin' drugs, mister?" number 32 said. "That's what my mama says."

On any other day, Mas would have shooed the kids away, but this day was anything but ordinary.

Another one piped up. "Hey, mister, was that kid livin' here some kind of gangster or sumptin'?"

Mas gave up and joined G. I. and Akemi on the lawn. Those kids were no help. They saw only what was right in front of them, when the truth was buried somewhere deeper.

✤ ✤ ✤

As soon as the police left, G. I. and Akemi headed for the courthouse. Mas stayed home and surveyed the damage. It was bad. Clothing and fishing poles spilled out of closets. Soup cans and ramen packages lay on the floor. The air conditioner in the living room had been taken apart.

Mas went into his room. The mattress had been overturned, and even the coffee can in the closet had been dumped, leaving a pile of change and a few balled-up dollars.

That damn Shuji Nakane. That guy was the one who had set up Yuki. But what could Mas say to Akemi and G. I.? That he had accepted hush money?

Within an hour, the house still looked pretty much the same. All Mas was able to do was put the mattress back on the bed frame and then lie on top of it.

That's the way Tug found him when he came over that afternoon. "Heard about the trouble." Tug stood in the doorway of Mas's bedroom.

Mas didn't bother to get up. "Yah, everybody 'round here, I guess."

Tug stepped over some overturned bowling trophies and sat down at the desk in the corner. There were too many things to be fixed. Besides, Tug didn't seem like he was in any mood to be putting things back together.

"Heezu innocent," Mas said.

Tug picked up a pen and tried to balance it on the side of his index finger. He did this for about fifteen minutes straight without saying a word. Finally, he got up. "Justice will prevail. The truth will come out."

Mas nodded. That was precisely what he was afraid of.

✣ ✣ ✣

It was already one o'clock, and no sign of either G. I. or Akemi. Mas had finished cleaning up as much as he could, and couldn't just sit around watching TV talk shows with crazy people yelling at one another. He had to do something. He walked outside and pulled at some dandelions. Studying the Jeep in the driveway, Mas got an idea. Why not? Rather than waste time, he might as well make some money.

Like a wartime medic, he patched what equipment he could from the garage. He still had a push mower, what the old-timers called a Pennsylvania, all rusty and blades dull. A rake with some missing teeth. A pair of hedge clippers with a busted handle. They weren't his finest, but good enough.

Today was Thursday, so it was the East Indian family in Arcadia. Arcadia was a wealthy city with a good supply of cash flowing from its racetrack and a large shopping center off Huntington Drive. There was plenty of new blood pumping in the residential neighborhoods, too, people who built mini-castles on sites that once held 1970s ranch-style homes. Mas's customers, the Patels, were among them.

Mr. Patel owned a small chain of chicken-bowl fast food eateries throughout San Gabriel Valley. He even sometimes asked Mas for advice. "This too sweet, you think?" he said, spooning some teriyaki sauce onto some rice.

It was Mas who had told Mr. Patel that he should have a spicy-bowl alternative. "Chili powda," he told him. "Maybe jalapeño peppa on side." P's Spicy Bowl was a hit. As a token of thanks, Mr. Patel had given him a case of P's Teriyaki Sauce. The unopened box was now collecting dust beside Mas's washer and dryer.

As Mas began to unload the Jeep, he was surprised to see Mr. Patel in the doorway of his house. "Hey, Arai, how are you doing?" He waved and walked toward Mas. He was wearing bright blue Bermuda shorts with a pink polo shirt.

"Betta," Mas said.

"Those substitutes you had were a little overeager with the clippers."

"Oh, yah." Must have been Stinky, thought Mas. He wasn't a detail man, and was notorious for cutting bushes down to their bare leaves. Mas kept unloading the Jeep. The push mower, the rake, the hedge clippers. Ugly, broken-down tools.

Mr. Patel picked up on it right away. "Hey, what's all this?" he said.

"Izu robbed. My truck gone. Have to do best with whatsu I gotsu."

"That's what I like about you, Mas. You don't cry when life throws you a curve. You get back in the saddle. I wish my partner could learn a thing or two from you."

"Partner?"

"Yeah, silent partner, I guess you call him. Well, things have been a little rough with the restaurant business. Now he says he wants his investment back. Wants me to sell half the restaurants."

Mas frowned.

"We're in litigation. Hell of a world, huh?" Mr. Patel hiked up his Bermuda shorts on his scrawny body. "You're in a good situation; you're a one-man show. Partners, they can turn on you at any time. And when money's involved, watch out. Money can destroy a friendship." Just then the Patels' shar-pei, a wrinkled caterpillar on legs, ran out the front door. "Max—" Mr. Patel called out. "Damn dog," he muttered, and excused himself before running down the street.

✣ ✣ ✣

The Patels' was a straightforward job. Prune hedges, which today, due to Stinky's buzz cut style, required little effort. Cut grass. Tend rosebushes. In less than an hour, Mas was finished. The sweat stung his eyes, and he felt good. He wasn't ready for the grave—yet.

It was rush hour, and time to take a shower, rest his feet, and watch the horse race broadcast. Yet Mas was heading toward Sawtelle on the Santa Monica Freeway. That was as smart as driving through Pasadena during the Rose Parade. Mas knew better, but he had little choice. To free the boy, Mas had to do his share. While G. I. tackled the courts, Mas needed to be in the field and come up with evidence.

He finally arrived in Sawtelle two hours later, his back sopping wet with sweat. He drove straight into the parking lot and was surprised that it was empty, aside from a twenty-year-old Toyota Cressida. Was Chochin's closed?

A Mexican man was in the back, throwing full trash bags into the rubbish bin.

"Not open?" Mas asked.

The man shook his head. *"No inglés,"* he said.

Mas tried to muster up all the Spanish he had learned in a city college class. He tried various versions but wasn't getting very far.

"La Migra," the man finally said.

"Girl, *de dónde?*" Mas tried again. His tongue seemed awkward as he tried to form words that sounded more Japanese than anything else. The man squinted and looked confused. Finally Mas returned to the Jeep and rummaged through the glove compartment. There was the Polaroid, the one with Yuki and the girl with the tadpole eyes.

Mas pointed to the girl and then himself. "Papa. *Mi hija.*"

The man must have had a daughter, too, because his face lit up in recognition.

"Uno minuto." He went back into Chochin's and then came out with a pink bag. On the handle was a tag, RUMI KATO, and an address in Gardena.

✣ ✣ ✣

Driving from Sawtelle to Gardena meant traveling on the 405 again. It was slow, and the setting sun blinded his right eye. But Mas was patient. He knew what had to be done.

Gardena was a cigarette burn below downtown Los Angeles. At one time, Mas knew, the Japanese had multiplied in Gardena like mold on month-old leftovers. Now most of them, or least their children, had moved south to cozy neighborhoods next to clean shopping centers and sanitized parks. The older and poorer ones had stayed behind, like passengers on a run-down boat. But the food was still good and cheap, and old gamblers still frequented local coffee shops. In other words, it was Mas's kind of town.

Finding Rumi Kato's apartment was no problem. Finding Rumi Kato, though, wasn't quite as simple. The apartment was in a cul-de-sac, a stone's throw from a large Asian grocery store that had changed hands at least two times within the last five years. It was a typical Gardena apartment—about seven units, with an upstairs and downstairs. Two sets of hedges were pruned Japanese-style, like floating orbs in the sky. A *toro,* a stone lantern shaped like a mini-pagoda, sat in between the hedges.

Rumi Kato's unit was on the first floor, smack in the middle. Mas rapped on the door, which was decorated with a dried flower wreath. No answer. Mini-blinds in the window were half-open, so Mas snuck a look. The unit was pretty much empty. Either Rumi Kato was immaculate, or else she was on the run.

Mas sat on the steps. He pulled out a pack of Marlboros and waited. After his third cigarette, a woman in the front unit poked her head out. "Can't you read?" she said. Her voice was rough and high-pitched at the same time, like feedback from a cheap audio system. She was small and chubby, with heavy arms that bulged from her polka-dotted blouse.

She then pointed at a row of signs that Mas had somehow missed. NO SMOKING, they said five times over.

Mas doused his cigarette on the stoop, which made the woman even angrier. She pulled out a hose that was rolled up near the *toro,* and nearly soaked Mas as she aimed a stream of water toward the cigarette ash.

This was some *urusai* mama, thought Mas as he leapt to his feet. He wanted to tell her off, but then thought better of it. A nosy landlady meant someone who knew what was going on. With everybody.

Before Mas could come up with something to say, the landlady approached him. "You got some business here with somebody?" she said after turning off the water.

Mas nodded. "Kato. Rumi. Gotsu delivery for her."

"Hah," the landlady said almost triumphantly. "That girl is finally out of here, and I'm telling you that I couldn't be happier. She had her loud parties—I called them orgies, only with women. Never listened to me. Was a disrespectful girl, typical of the young ones today. Used to be you could rent to a Japanese and expect no problems. Now I'm going to discriminate against the Japanese, and I don't care if the Fair Housing Authority tries to get me or not. I can tell them I'm Japanese, and I know."

Mas didn't react, which apparently fired up the woman even more.

"If you don't believe me, look." The landlady, with her strong arms, virtually pushed Mas into the empty apartment. There was no furniture, but on the living room wall was a large X painted in red. The paint had dripped down in areas, looking like spilt blood. "Can you believe she did this? Just to spite me, I think."

Mas pressed down on the red paint. It left a faint mark on his finger. Looked like it had happened at least a day earlier. "You knowsu where I can find her?"

"I would forget about it, if I were you."

"I really needsu to give sumptin' to her."

"Well, she's probably out of the state by now. But she used to spend a lot of time at the bowling alley. The coffeehouse." The landlady then tore the wreath off the door and crunched it up in her powerful hands. "If you find her, you can give her this," she said, handing Mas a ball of broken dried twigs.

❖ ❖ ❖

The Gardena Bowl coffeehouse was an old-time Japanese hangout that still served Portuguese sausage, eggs, and rice all day, as well as greasy chow mein and, if you were lucky, egg foo young swimming in gravy. Mari had once told Mas that real Chinese didn't eat such things, but Mas brushed her comments aside. He wasn't Chinese, and besides, it tasted good.

The waitresses were mostly middle-aged or older and had the menu memorized so you barely had to say two words before they took your order down. One greeted Mas as he walked in. "Counter?" she asked, but Mas ignored her. He could hear bowling pins crash against one another in the distance. Usually, it was a comforting sound, but now it seemed suffocating.

After walking down the worn carpet alongside the couple of dozen lanes, Mas went back into the coffee shop and ordered some green tea. It came in a plastic coffee cup and was hot enough to burn his tongue and cold sores. He sat at a table for at least an hour when he finally saw who he was looking for. She came through the doorway and settled down in a booth by the women's bathroom. Mas got up, getting the girl's attention. She immediately picked up her purse and jacket to leave.

"I'm not with Nakane," he said, but apparently the mere mention of the name terrified Rumi Kato.

"Dis yours?" Mas had brought the pink bag. The girl tried to grab it away, but Mas held on tight. "First talk. Five minutes."

Rumi relented. Sitting across from her at the table, Mas noticed that her eyes were constantly in motion. Next to her on the floor was a small tan suitcase.

"You goin' somewheres?" he asked.

Rumi nudged the suitcase with the edge of her foot. "What do you want?" she said in Japanese. "And who are you?"

Mas, for a second, was stumped. Yes, who was he? He was no friend to the dead mistress, and definitely did not represent the interests of Riki Kimura. "I Arai," he said. "Masao Arai. Dat boysu Kimura, my friend."

"I remember you from Chochin's. And Keiko's Ramen House, too."

Mas took out the Polaroid photo of Yuki and Rumi. "Just young kid. Straight from Hiroshima."

Rumi nodded. "*Hai*, that is what he said."

"Youzu there, *desho*? When Junko all beat up?"

Rumi's eyes continued to dart back and forth.

"Youzu went straight to ramen house afterward. Told Keiko sumptin', but not whole thing."

She took two quick breaths. "Two guys," she finally said. "One Japanese and a *hakujin*. And Nakane and a Japanese old man waiting outside. I was in the bedroom. They didn't know I was there."

"Whatsu they want?"

"They were going to give her big money. A hundred thousand dollars to keep quiet about that Joji Haneda. But she refused it. Said that she wasn't going to keep some secret. So the two began to hit her. I was so scared. I called the police, and when they heard the sirens in the distance, they ran away." The girl folded the edges of her napkin. "I went to her. She was trying to tell me something. 'What, Junko-*chan*, what?' I asked, but blood came out of her mouth. I heard footsteps from below, so I slipped out before they could find me. I just left her there to die."

That must have been when Yuki came in, thought Mas.

"In the hospital, I told her that I was sorry. That I should have never left her. But she said, 'Rumi-*chan*, don't worry. You still young. You make a life for yourself.' She wanted me to go back to Japan. Like she was planning to."

You should, thought Mas. Go back home to your parents before it's too late.

"Then that Nakane and his men came after me.

Told me that I had to tell the police that the young guy had killed Junko. Or else."

Mas could guess what "or else" meant. And now Rumi Kato was obviously going to take off to another American city. Maybe Las Vegas, Chicago, New York—who knows? There was a Chochin's in every big town. "You needsu to talk to police."

"And tell them what? I'll deny everything. I'll tell them that you're an old *sukebe* just coming after a young girl."

"So the boy go to jail for sumptin' he didn't do."

Rumi had folded the napkin into the shape of a samurai helmet. She propped it up in between the Tabasco and soy sauce containers. "They'll deport me back to Japan. If they do that, they'll take away my passport. I won't be able to leave for years," she said. "Or else Nakane. Who knows what that bunch will do."

The red X had frightened the girl; there was no doubt about that.

"They closed Chochin's down, did you know?" she said. "Someone called the INS. There's nothing in Los Angeles for me now. I'm sorry about your friend, but he seems smart. With me gone, he won't be in jail long." She gathered up her things and waited for the pink bag. It was no use. Like in gambling, Mas knew when to stop. And the time had come.

"You didn't look in here, did you?" she asked as Mas handed over the bag.

"No," Mas lied. In fact, he had searched the contents shortly after he had left Chochin's. Underwear, contraceptives, and a faded color photo of the girl, much younger, with her parents back in Japan.

Mas watched as Rumi headed for the glass door. "You won't get away," he called out.

"What?"

"It come back to youzu."

"What? What are you talking about? *Bachi?*"

Mas felt his breathing grow deeper, from the pit of his stomach through his sore lungs. It wasn't *bachi* or even a threat of *bachi* that was ruining him, he realized. It was something else entirely, a spirit he couldn't describe. "Your insides." Mas thumped his rib cage. "Your *kokoro* will neva be the same."

The girl, for the first time, smiled. "Then I'll just have to take my chances."

❖ ❖ ❖

It was late, past eight o'clock, but Mas drove past Tanaka's anyway. The lights were all on; the outline of a few heads, including someone in a pith helmet, could be seen through the dusty window. Mas parked the Jeep and went in. That's when he heard the news. Just like the mistress, the man called Haneda was dead.

CHAPTER FOURTEEN

In Hiroshima, gossip buzzed altogether like the nasty cicadas that bleated incessantly throughout the summer nights. You couldn't figure out where one of those pests was, but you heard them, all in unison. In L.A., it was different. Gossip moved around in small circles, mini-tornadoes whipping the landscape. The fake Haneda had had a mistress, had shamed his entire family. Shame, shame, shame. The same mistress was now dead, a victim of a suspicious beating. The twister of news multiplied, traveling down from Ventura to Sawtelle to Crenshaw to Gardena to Pasadena.

It was the next morning. G. I. and Akemi had already left for Yuki's arraignment, so Mas could take a good look at the *Los Angeles Times*. There were a few Japanese names among the obituaries, but no Haneda.

It made sense. The Hanedas would have a private family ceremony, away from the talk and the spotlight.

But later that afternoon, the L.A. Japanese newspaper *The Rafu Shimpo*, came in the mail, and there it was—two times, in fact. One was within the English pages, the other in the Japanese section, bordered by a thick black line. *Joji Haneda, 68, a Los Angeles–born Nisei resident of Ventura. Survived by wife Betty, son Jeff, and daughter Susan.* The next line shocked Mas, enough so that the blood rushed from his hands. *Also survived by sister Akemi Kimura, of Hiroshima.* How could they have included Akemi? But more important, why? Why make the connection so public, so clear to everyone? This was not a simple mistake. Mas knew how it worked with mortuaries; he had been through it with Chizuko. They went through the obituary, carefully selecting each word and going over the spelling of each name. You didn't want so-and-so in the obituary, fine. Leave out an *urusai* brother-in-law, ex-wife, whatever.

But on the other hand, this Betty Haneda wanted to make damn sure that everyone thought her husband was kin to Akemi. That meant only one thing: Shuji Nakane had gotten to the wife and two children.

Mas licked his lips. They were so dry that skin was peeling off of them like fish scales. He checked the date. Two days from today. Visitation at seven P.M. At Evergreen Cemetery in Los Angeles.

✣ ✣ ✣

The phone rang around noon. Mas figured it was Stinky pumping him for more gossip, but it was another voice. Lifeless, dull, as if she were lying in a coffin herself. "We lost," Akemi said. "No bail."

Mas felt sick to the pit of his stomach. He shouldn't have even mentioned the funeral, but he did. It had been a mistake, because immediately afterward, Akemi hung up the phone. A few minutes later, she called right back, reciting a set of numbers.

"Whatsu dis?" Mas asked.

"His booking number. You're going to need it. Yuki wants to talk to you."

✣ ✣ ✣

Finding the jail was no problem. Mas had once done a rose-pruning job for a Catholic church in Little Tokyo, just some blocks south. But visiting the jail was another matter altogether. A mini-mall was on the corner, selling bail bonds and breakfasts. Public phone booths stood like tombstones along the street. To the north were the twin towers, looking like any other kind of government building, aside from the thick windows and elevators lined with steel grids. What stayed with Mas the most was the quiet. Voices on the streets were hushed, as if everyone had a secret that was not worth celebrating.

Two lines of waiting visitors wrapped around two buildings named Los Angeles County Sheriff Men's Central Jail. Mas wasn't sure where to go, so he took a chance and picked a line with mostly men. He figured that this was the place for hard offenders, those who had killed and maimed. Judging from the visitors in line, he was right.

Nobody spoke, even those with friends. Then a man, maybe Chinese or Vietnamese, came up to Mas. He was a scrawny man, with thin hair that stood up like weeds. He asked something in a language Mas could not make out. Mas shook his head. "No understand," he said. The man was looking for some kind of connection, an explanation, maybe. But Mas had no answers himself.

Once his watch read five-thirty, the line began to move. Mas's stomach began to growl, but he lost his appetite. He had been in a jail only one time, back in Hiroshima.

Mas watched the others, most likely regulars. They put their belongings in lockers on one side of the waiting room and then got back in line toward a counter protected by thick glass. Two female officers wearing green uniforms and with their hair tied back in buns punched at a computer keyboard as each person passed by. Finally it was Mas's turn. "Yukikazu Kimura," he said. The officer asked him for the booking number, just like Akemi had said, and Mas pulled out an old receipt that he had used to jot down the number. He pushed the receipt through the glass, and in time she directed him to another officer, who stood by some sort of metal detector.

Before Mas knew it, the officer was patting him down and rummaging through his pockets. He took out Mas's Marlboros and matches from a local gas station and shook his head. "We'll have to hang on to these for you," he said.

At that point, Mas wanted to head back home. He felt trapped, off balance. Why had that stupid Yuki Kimura come to America? He should have stayed in the new, improved Hiroshima. Very few had the guts to make it here, and the young ones were only fooling themselves to think they could.

After going up the concrete steps, there was more waiting. What had the sign said—visitation only until six forty-five P.M.? There was only twenty minutes to go. Finally an officer directed him to a room separated from the other side by a thick glass window. There was a line of prisoners on the other side, seated next to red phones. Two chairs to the left, wearing an orange jumpsuit, was Yuki Kimura.

✣ ✣ ✣

Mas lifted the telephone receiver. It smelled funny, but he had no choice. "Hallo," he said, looking at the boy through the bulletproof glass.

"Hello," Yuki answered. The boy looked terrible. His red hair was parted in the middle and lay completely flat. His eyes were rimmed with dark, puffy bags. "You weren't at the courthouse."

"No. Had *yoji*," Mas lied.

"Doesn't look good," Yuki said.

Mas couldn't say anything to make it better.

"I have a request, *Ojisan*. A serious request."

"Whatsu?"

"Send my grandmother back to Japan. I don't care how you do it. Go with her, if you have to."

Mas almost felt like laughing. How could anyone force Akemi Haneda to do anything?

"I have a bad feeling about this. Real bad feeling. The police need someone to blame. They might cut a deal with the Japanese government, and I may be tried over there. I don't know which place will be worse."

Mas had heard about the high conviction rate in Japan, the aggressive questioning by police. More often than not, the suspect ended up confessing.

"All I know is that I can't put my grandmother through this. Better yet, take her to Hawaii, or even Guam. Somewhere safe and quiet. Away from all of this."

"You knowsu she not goin' anywhere."

"You don't understand. You can't mess around with these people."

Mas was confused. "Whatsu people?" As he stared at Yuki's face, the table between them began to shake. Down the line of jailed suspects, a man in an orange suit banged the telephone receiver against the Plexiglas at a visitor, a woman. In a split second, two guards had grabbed the prisoner and were dragging him toward a back door.

Mas and Yuki watched, saying nothing. The skin underneath the boy's left eye began to twitch.

A bell sounded, and then a voice announced over the intercom, "Visiting hours will end in five minutes."

"I must go," Mas said, relieved that his own time was limited.

But Yuki would not let him go so easily. "Come tomorrow, *Ojisan*," Yuki said. "And then I will tell you."

✣ ✣ ✣

As Mas got back into the Jeep, he began thinking about Riki again. Riki had been plenty sick, but the timing of his death seemed too convenient. With him out of the way and Yuki arrested, anyone could create a new history for Joji Haneda, U.S.A.

The traffic on the Ventura Freeway was light, so Mas knew that he was meant to go to the Oxnard City Hospital again. He went straight to the third floor and wandered around until he found the same Filipino nurse he had talked to the first time.

"Excuse, excuse," he said.

"Yes?" The nurse was holding a clipboard and seemed like she was in a hurry to go someplace else.

"I talksu to you a few days ago."

The nurse wrinkled her forehead and then had a moment of recognition. "Oh, yes, I remember. You were visiting—"

"Joji Haneda."

"Yes, yes." The nurse's voice took on a strange tone,

and she looked at Mas nervously. "How can I help you?"

"Well, I just wonderin'. I meansu, he looked bad, but still seemed to die all of a sudden."

The nurse glanced down the hall and then pulled Mas into an empty hospital room. "Who told you?" she asked. "What did you hear?"

"Nobody tellsu me anytin'. Riki—Joji, I meansu—an ole friend. I don't wanna cause any trouble. Just can't rest unless I knowsu the truth."

The nurse ran her hand through her straight black hair.

Mas tried again. "Just sumptin' funny, I think."

"That's what I thought." The nurse lowered her voice. "I told the doctors that it was very strange. The oxygen mask had been in place, at least when I saw him last. He wasn't strong enough to take it off by himself at that point. But after his monitors indicated that his vitals were taking a nosedive, I ran into his room, and his mask had been removed."

Mas bit down on his lip. He remembered Riki's gulping down air from the oxygen machine during their last meeting. "Where's mask?"

"Here." The nurse pointed to the vinyl chair in the corner, as it was set up in every room. "Now, you tell me—how did that mask get there?"

Apparently the doctors hadn't paid any attention to the nurse, and Mas understood. Doctors and hospitals were always worried about getting sued; at least that's what one of Mas's young doctor customers kept telling him. So if Riki's death had been helped along by someone else, who could it have been? The nurse didn't remember Riki's having had too many other visitors. Even the wife and children had stopped coming around.

"You can try to make your case with the hospital, even the police," the nurse said. "I'll lose my job if I make too much more of a fuss. But you, an old friend, that's different."

Mas shoved his hands in his jean pockets, thanked the nurse, and left the building.

✣ ✣ ✣

The next day, Mas knew what to do. He went to the jail early in the afternoon, and left his cigarettes in the Jeep. He brought the sports page to read in line. Finally, he was back in jail, with Yuki looking at him from the other side of the glass.

Yuki's skin, even the whites of his eyes, looked yellow and diseased. How long he would survive in jail, Mas didn't know.

Yuki didn't waste any time. "I haven't told you the whole truth," he said. "I didn't tell you about the land."

"Your property?"

Yuki nodded, his voice now barely above a whisper. "I made a deal," he said. "With this one development company. Ten million dollars."

"Nakane."

Yuki nodded again. "Of course, I wouldn't sell it to them while *Obaachan* was alive. I couldn't, anyway. It's all under her name. And she refused to deal with any developers. She's just like my father: wants to hold on to the land no matter what. But after my father died, money was tight. For both of us. *Obaachan* was too proud, but not me. So I made a deal with Nakane. He'd give me a hundred thousand up front, and I'd make sure that the land was undisturbed. We'd put a fence around it. Make sure that no one else had access to it."

"Fence?"

"I know; it didn't make sense. But I agreed. And then I started feeling guilty. What was I doing? *Obaachan* was my only family, and here I was, making deals behind her back. So I changed my mind. I even offered to repay the money in monthly installments. Nothing was on paper, anyhow. Well, Nakane was so angry. Threatened to get rid of me, and *Obaachan*, too. Next thing I know, he's on his way to America to find out about this Joji Haneda in California."

"Whyzu dis land so special?"

Yuki pressed his hair back. "That's what I thought at first. It's small; can hold only fifty apartment units. And it's right by some factories by the water. Who would want to live there?"

"Where's dis place, again?" Mas listened as Yuki described the location. Ujina. He knew it well. Full of factories back then, pumping out gray smoke while producing airplane propellers and other military equipment. He knew a couple of boys who had lived in the area. Mas pictured the makeshift shacks, the bald lightbulbs lighting up the shantytown at night. Why would such a piece of land be so valuable?

"I have some theories," Yuki said. "But I can't do anything locked up here. I need your help, Arai-*san*. Can you give it to me?"

✣ ✣ ✣

The last thing Mas wanted to do was make a long-distance telephone call, much less one to Hiroshima. But after a few tries and pressing a series of zeroes and ones, he finally got a funny dial tone that sounded like blips more than rings. About the fourth blip, a male voice came on. "*Moshi-moshi*, *Shine* magazine. Noguchi speaking."

Mas took a deep breath and put all his energy into speaking the most proper Japanese that he could muster. "Excuse, is this Noguchi Nobuhiro? Kimura Yukikazu's friend?"

"Yes, who is this?"

"Ah, Arai Masao. Calling from America."

"What's happened to Yuki? We heard about his trouble; we've been trying to call the police and sheriff's departments, but no one can give us a clear answer."

"Ah, yah, he's in some trouble. Needs your help."

"Yes, of course, anything. What can I do from way over here?"

Mas swallowed before speaking. "Land. Haneda land in Ujina."

"Where they are hoping to build some new mansions?"

"Yah, Yuki needs you to do research, find out about that land during World War Two."

"So—" said Noguchi. "I believe there were a lot of defense factories in that area."

"Ah, yah, well, I think Koreans working and living there, too."

"Of course, of course."

Mas could hear the reporter typing on some kind of keyboard.

"I'll do some nosing around and then I'll call you back." The reporter jotted down Mas's Altadena phone number and then ended the phone call.

About an hour and a half later, the phone rang. Mas had placed the tan telephone on the middle of his kitchen table, right next to a half-eaten rotisserie chicken.

"Hallo, hallo."

"Arai-*san*? It's Noguchi. I've consulted with another reporter, and we've discovered something very interesting."

Arai's hand grew wet as he held the telephone receiver tight to his ear and heard the *Shine* reporter's findings. The conversation was short but fruitful. Mas now understood why everyone was in a rush to find a Joji Haneda in America.

CHAPTER FIFTEEN

The funeral was set for seven P.M., so that meant Mas and Haruo had to leave by six P.M. Punctuality was key for every Nisei, and no one was ever late to a funeral. But Mas was in fact behind schedule. He had called Haruo to go on ahead, so he was surprised to see his friend waiting for him on the porch at six-thirty.

Haruo was wearing a polyester brown suit and thick tie from the seventies. His hair had been oiled and combed back, fresh teeth marks at the side part. Mas could smell a healthy dose of aftershave lotion, probably stored in Haruo's family medicine cabinet for decades. Haruo Mukai was looking good enough for a funeral.

As Mas wrapped a skinny tie around his neck on the porch, Haruo held out an envelope.

"Whatsu dis?"

"Koden," said Haruo.

"Koden?"

"I put thirty in yours. Figured you knowsu Haneda for a long time."

Koden? Mas felt like laughing. Why help out the very family who was cheating his friends out of millions of dollars? "I not gonna give *koden,"* he declared. "Not gonna give nutin' to those people."

"Mas, you gotsu history."

It was no use. Mas didn't have time to argue with Haruo.

"Betta put your name on back," said Haruo.

Retrieving a pen from the kitchen, Mas wrote in block letters JOJI HANEDA and then the Hanedas' old address in Hiroshima.

✣ ✣ ✣

Mas had not been to Evergreen Cemetery for a few years. They passed Mexican bakeries, closed for the night, and liquor stores, open but windows barred. On the sidewalk, a middle-aged man pushed a small cart, a bell ringing.

He remembered his friend Ichiro "Itchy" Iwasaki, who had worked a brief time at a nearby mortuary after getting laid off from his job as a janitor at City Hall.

"Terrible work," he'd told Mas, describing a midnight trip to pick up a 103-year-old woman from a nursing home, weighed down by all her money and paperwork tied around her waist. There was the middle-aged man who had committed suicide in a deep freezer, alongside iced shrimp and Fudgsicles. The most heartbreaking was an infant, not even two months old, who had died in his sleep with a mobile of sheep and clouds overhead.

Itchy, like the other mortuary workers, had had the option to watch a cremation. Might help in explaining it to the loved ones, his boss explained. But Itchy had declined. "Hey, this is just to tide me over. Not a career move or nutin'."

The cemetery itself still looked the same, except the grass from the outside of the iron gate looked a little brown and sparse. Haruo steered the car into the driveway, following a line of new Hondas and Toyotas—tan, light gray, and wine-colored—waiting to park near the chapel.

The lot seemed to be filled. "Many people come to say good-bye to Haneda," said Haruo, his suit jacket overwhelming his skinny shoulders and arms. He followed a loop in the road lined with palm trees, and parked next to a giant sphere, someone's strange grave marker.

Mas told Haruo to go ahead inside, and then walked outside the chapel. A tall monument stood in the back next to a patch of grass. It was skinny and pointed; at the top was a concrete man, helmet on his head, hands at his sides, and a rifle hanging from his shoulder. There was a plaque with a verse:

Those who lie here gave their lives,
That this country,
beset by its enemies,
might win out of their sacrifice
victory and peace.
—Dwight Eisenhower

Surrounding the monument were plaques set into the ground with names of dead Nisei veterans, some marked with the Buddhist chrysanthemum; others, the Christian cross.

Beyond the soldiers were more graves of mothers, daughters, fathers, sons, all Japanese. Beyond that were black families, even a good number dating back more than a hundred years. Some tombstones had oval photos of older black women wearing corsages, and black men in felt hats. There were cement angels looking over the graves of babies, born and dead within the same year. The markers weren't lined up straight and perfect, like at some of the high-tone cemeteries in the hills. Instead, the ground had shifted, causing some to rise like crooked teeth.

It took Mas a good ten minutes before he found it. A headstone, short and squat, shaped much like his late wife herself. The letters were filled with dirt, and Mas felt a pang of shame. He should have come earlier, he thought, trying to scrape the letters clean with the edge of a matchbook.

After Mari had been told of Chizuko's cancer, she

didn't want to go back to school. But Chizuko insisted. They didn't know how long she had—maybe six months, maybe another twenty years. "You can't do anything here at home," Chizuko said. "You study hard, get good grades. That's best medicine for me."

Chizuko was fine during the winter and spring quarters, but experienced a setback in the summer. It was as if she could let down her guard because her daughter was on academic break.

"What's wrong with you?" Mari was wearing a dress with nylons. She had gone to the hospital right after her job at a law firm downtown. She now stood in the doorway of the den.

Mas lowered the volume on the television. "Huh?"

"Why don't you support Mom more?"

"I go, ebery day." He went religiously to the Beverly Hills hospital, seven days a week, from three to six o'clock.

"But you don't talk to her. You just sit there, watching old TV shows. And when you do talk to her, you guys end up fighting."

"What can I do? She has plenty of doctas." Mas squeezed the television remote.

"Why don't you tell her thanks?"

Thanks? Why I have to say thank you? thought Mas, but he dared not speak. He knew enough to keep quiet when the women in his household got mad.

"She's not doing well, Dad. Can't you tell? You're not going to have another chance."

"Chance for what?"

"Fourth stage. That's what she's in, Dad. The fourth stage. It's not good, okay? You know that as much as me." Mari gestured wildly with her hands. "Are you that out of touch? Are you that dense?"

Mas turned up the volume on the *Gunsmoke* rerun.

Mari glared, her eyebrows arching down. "I'll never marry a man like you," she said, leaving the den.

Mas felt as if he'd been stung by a bee, like the time he'd been clipping an orange tree for an Indian businessman. Her words cut into his skin, but after the initial pain, Mas felt nothing at all.

✣ ✣ ✣

The letters were almost completely clean when Mas sensed a presence standing over him. Akemi, wearing a black pantsuit, handed him a handkerchief from her purse.

Mas shook his head. *"Kitanai, yo."*

"Go ahead," Akemi said. "Please."

The sun had dipped halfway down, filling the cemetery with shadows. Mas could barely tell if the headstone looked any better. He should have come more regularly, maybe brought some cymbidium during the summer months. But the fact was that he hadn't. There were no excuses. He had had the time.

Until recently, he had had transportation. He should have never let her be forgotten, in front of all the others buried at Evergreen Cemetery.

✣ ✣ ✣

Akemi, meanwhile, had her own agenda. She was on the far edge of the Japanese graves. Clutching her soiled handkerchief, Mas made his way to where she was standing. In spite of the darkness, Mas could still make out the letters on the headstone: SUSUMU HANEDA, 1898–1946, HUSBAND, FATHER, BROTHER, HE WAS OUR HERO.

"We had the mortuary handle all the arrangements," Akemi said, taking the handkerchief from Mas. "They even sent me a picture and a map. But this is the first time for me to see this in person."

Mas stayed quiet. He had had no idea Joji's father was buried right here in Evergreen.

"He died in a camp in New Mexico after the war. Somehow he contracted TB." Akemi folded the handkerchief in half. "A family friend had hung on to his ashes. I wanted to bury him in Hollywood, near the movie stars. They wouldn't let me. It's just as well, I guess. Here, he is among friends."

Mas averted his eyes and then noticed that the plot next to it had been recently dug up. That didn't need any explanation. It was there that the fake Joji

Haneda would be making his new home, this time forever.

✣ ✣ ✣

The funeral must have been halfway over when Mas and Akemi finally entered the chapel. Mas could already smell incense from the small lobby area, where two Japanese men and one woman arranged *koden* envelopes on a long folding table. One wrote numbers on each envelope, another recorded names in a ledger, and finally, the last one looped rubber bands around bundles. Only the last worker looked up and tipped his head. Mas reciprocated and slapped down his envelope without stopping to sign in.

The public offering of incense had already begun. A line formed in the middle of the aisle; Mas could see Tug's white hair somewhere in the front. A woman, her purse hanging from her arm, stepped forward to a pot smoking with incense sticks. Shiny rosary beads hung from her clasped hands as she bent toward the Buddhist altar, a black box with gold decoration. She then pinched ash and released it into another pot. She bowed again. She walked over to the coffin. One half of it was open, and Mas could see the outline of Riki's hooked nose. A large framed photo was set on the closed portion of the coffin. It was Riki, smiling, outside his Ventura nursery.

Tug was next. Devout Christian that he was, he avoided the pot of incense and Buddhist altar.

Instead, he went straight to the coffin and bowed to Riki's body. The top of Tug's hair was still sparse, and a gauze bandage was placed over his bruise. Are you nuts? thought Mas, licking his lips. This guy hit you, maybe even could've killed you if he got the right spot. And here you are, bowing to him.

Tug's next action surprised Mas even more. He went right to the front row of the pews, where the family sat, and shook hands with each one. The widow, her permed hairdo shaking. The pale son periodically wiping his hooked nose. The daughter weeping into a handkerchief. Tug looked sincere; in fact, Mas knew that he was sincere. For a second, Mas almost hated his friend.

Tug slid back into his pew, and the ritual continued. Row by row, the mortician tapped the shoulders with his white-gloved fingers, and the people rose and lined up.

Shuji Nakane was nowhere to be seen. Perhaps, with his dirty work completed, he was already on a plane back to Hiroshima.

Finally, it was Akemi and Mas's turn. They stood with the others on the right-side aisle. As the priest chanted, they stepped closer and closer to the pot of incense and the coffin.

✣ ✣ ✣

Akemi approached the body first. Instead of keeping her distance of three steps back, she got so close that her hips touched the coffin. She bent over and studied Riki's face for a good minute and a half, long enough for old women to nudge their sleeping husbands in the pews. The heads of the family members, minutes ago bent down in grief, were now upright, eyes still on Akemi.

Go tell them, Mas thought. Go tell them all, *this is not my brother. This is not Joji Haneda.*

But Akemi instead quietly backed away from the body. Her cheeks were shiny with tears, and Mas was confused. Why be sad over Riki's death? He was a fraud; Akemi must have figured it out by now.

It was Mas's turn, so he took a few steps toward the coffin. Riki's skin was a strange peach color, his age spots covered up and his thinning hair carefully combed back with oil. Are you really dead, Riki? he thought. Is this really your end, or another beginning? Mas half expected Riki to rise any minute, brush off his face makeup, and sneer. But the hooked nose remained still. He looked so peaceful that Mas realized that his friend and nemesis was indeed gone.

After the whole room had made the procession to the incense pots and Riki's coffin, another speaker took the microphone. A familiar long face, cheekbones, the nose. The son was giving the closing comments, addressing the crowd. "Again, my mother, sister, and I thank all of you for coming. I know that my father would be grateful to see your presence here tonight."

Before Mas heard more, he stepped outside, leaving Akemi standing alone in the back. The sun had almost set, and a film of gray rested on the parking lot. He ached for a cigarette. He patted his windbreaker and pants pockets. Nothing.

"Tobacco?" a familiar voice asked from the side of the building. It was Shuji Nakane, holding out an open package of filtered cigarettes. In his other hand was Mas's *koden* envelope. "The clerk for the mortuary had come to me, confused. It seems that someone had not written their own name on the envelope. Just Joji Haneda, and an address in Hiroshima. I told him that I would take care of it." Nakane took out a silver lighter, flipped it open, and then placed the tip of the envelope on the flame. When he saw the fire had taken hold, Nakane released the burning envelope. It eventually landed on the dirt next to some weeds.

"Youzu wasted thirty dolla," Mas simply said.

"And how about that thirty thousand dollars, Arai-*san*? You got rid of that money a lot quicker than I thought you could."

"You killsu that girl."

"I did? Oh, no, Arai-*san*. It wasn't me. My associates are responsible for that. But there's absolutely no proof. The American way, right? We are all innocent until proven guilty."

"I knowsu. Someone tellsu me. I go to police."

"Now, that would be a tragic mistake, I think. And who would they believe?"

With the toe of his fancy shoe, Nakane crushed the burnt envelope, which looked like a large piece of dried seaweed. For a second, Mas felt afraid. This man could kill him, right then and there. In fact, murder would be quite convenient, because Mas's body could then go straight into the ground.

Mas heard a murmur of voices from the front of the chapel. The funeral must be over, he thought, and then, before he knew it, Akemi was heading right toward them. "Nakane, I must talk to you," she said.

Mas stepped in front of Akemi's path. "No, no," he whispered.

Akemi acted as though Mas weren't even there. "You can take the land," she said to Nakane. "I'll sign it over to you. I don't care. But my grandson. Spare him."

"I wish you had made this offer back in Hiroshima," said Nakane. "But there's nothing I can do."

More people filed out from the front, and then the side door of the chapel burst open. The mortician and five other men carried the coffin toward the small, square building with the chimney. The men disappeared through a door, and then quickly emerged without the casket.

The mortician with the white gloves firmly locked the door with a huge metal key. After peering into the room again through a small window on the door, the man left for the front office.

"Thatsu not Joji Haneda," Mas said as loudly he

could. A few couples in the parking lot stared at him. "Thatsu not Haneda."

"What are you doing, Masao-*san*?" Akemi asked.

Mas went to the crematorium and pressed his face through the window. His eyes slowly adjusted to the darkness. The coffin, looking less grand than it had in the chapel, lay in the middle of the giant gas oven.

Mas felt a wetness down his collar. He began pounding the door. "Stop!" he cried out. "Stop!"

Someone pulled at his arm. "He's dead. He's gone."

The crematorium then rumbled like an earthquake, and Mas began to smell something foul, like burning fish. He turned toward the square window in time to see the coffin explode in flames.

CHAPTER SIXTEEN

In a matter of minutes, most of the casket had burned away. All that was left was the vague rectangular frame, and then Riki's body, engulfed in fire, began to rise.

The person tugging on Mas's arm had let go. It was stone quiet, aside from a police siren in the distance. Mas stood transfixed as the flames licked the frame of the casket. With each layer that burned, another layer appeared.

✣ ✣ ✣

The air raid siren had rung early that morning, about seven-thirty, Mas remembered. There were four of them—Mas, Riki, Joji, and a younger boy, Kenji—in the basement of the train station. Like all the other boys, they wore school uniforms even though they had stopped going to school long ago. Sewn on each uniform was a square cloth with a name and blood type: Mas was AB; Riki, A; and Joji, O. Mas couldn't recall much about Kenji; he was one of those boys you noticed only when he was gone.

Mas hid underneath a shelf in the corner, Joji scrunched in a doorway, and Kenji pressed himself against the floor, covering his head with his hands. Riki, however, remained in the center of the room. He flung his arms out and wagged his tongue as if he were catching raindrops in his mouth.

"Have you gone mad?" Mas couldn't believe that Riki was acting so foolish.

"I'm tired of ducking each time we hear that siren. I've decided to dance instead." Riki then started kicking up his legs.

Riki looked so ridiculous, Mas couldn't help but laugh. Soon he himself was in the middle of the cement basement floor, leaping up and down like a frog. Joji remained in the doorway, waiting, while Kenji lay still. Minutes passed, and they heard just the droning of the cicadas. Not even the sound of a lone B-29.

"You know—" Riki said in between deep breaths. "I believe that our old principal, Naito-*sensei*, is actually in charge of that siren."

"Naito-*sensei*?" Mas pictured the bald, soft head with round-framed glasses.

"Yeah—whenever he has to go to the toilet, he just rings that siren."

The two of them broke down in laughter. It was

very unpatriotic of them, Mas knew. Many bombs had fallen; many people had been killed. But it was still funny to imagine Naito-*sensei* squatting and declaring a raid.

Joji finally moved from the doorway and began changing his shoes. He was one of the few teenagers who actually owned a pair of work boots—probably from America, Riki had sneered jealously one day. They were all familiar with Joji's routine by now, how he carefully transferred some folded-up papers from his sock to the inside of his left boot.

"Always so serious, Haneda," Riki finally said.

"You think that all of this is a joke?"

"A joke?" Riki mimicked Joji's American accent. "War is a joke."

"You won't be laughing when America wins the war." Joji patted the side of his boot. "With these papers, I'll be on my way home."

"Home to what? A prison camp?" Riki said.

"What are you talking about?"

"Didn't you hear? The Japanese in America are in camps."

Joji furiously laced his boots. "Liar."

"Yeah, I heard it from one of my neighbors. Their relative was sent back on a boat as part of a prisoner-of-war exchange. That's what they think of you back in America, Haneda. As a thing to be traded for one of their own."

"You don't know what you are talking about," Joji

said, but even in the dim morning light, Mas could see the glimmer of doubt on his face. They all had heard the stories. There had even been talk of Joji's father's being a spy, maybe even a double agent, trapped in America.

Joji climbed up the staircase. "It's past eight. You guys can fool around, but I'm going to work."

"Go ahead, Haneda. Work, work, work. Just know that you are working for your enemy."

Joji paused at the top of the stairs, shook his head, and then turned the doorknob. As the door opened, a flash of light flooded the basement and Mas felt himself being knocked to the ground.

✣ ✣ ✣

Mas pressed his face against the door of the crematorium. The burning body was moving now, as if it were alive. "Joji, Joji, is that you?" he cried. He felt feverishly hot, salty drops of sweat stinging his eyes and falling onto his funeral suit.

But the body was not Joji's. It twisted back in time and now Mas saw the body of their supervisor at the train station, his black boots still remaining on his burnt legs.

"Masao-*san*, Masao-*san*."

Someone was calling his name. Who? It came like a faint whistle through the orange flames and smoke. The whole world was on fire.

"Help us, help us. We are so thirsty."

Mas climbed up the rubble. There were people everywhere, running, weeping, their flesh melting away from their bodies. "Water, water," they all seemed to say.

"Masao-*san*, over here, over here."

There was Kenji, the boy that no one noticed. Only now his face, arms, and even scalp—what had happened to his hair?—were strangely dotted with dark spots. "Water, we need to go to the river. The river by the bridge," said Kenji.

"Wait, wait," Mas called out. He looked down and was shocked to see that his uniform had been torn to shreds, exposing his thin gray underwear. His toes were bleeding, but he felt no pain.

Mas was being pushed by the crowd to the bridge, the same bridge where he, Joji, and Riki had posed for a local photographer. Now people were throwing themselves into the black water, their scorched bodies seeking some sort of relief. Mas thought some were wearing their pajamas, but he realized that they were naked; the checkered pattern of their pajamas had been burnt into their skin. After their bodies touched the water, their faces shone for a moment with pleasure, then the current swept them away.

"Come on, Masao," said Kenji, standing at the edge of the bridge. He jumped into the rushing currents, and Mas closed his eyes to follow. He leaned forward to make the plunge, but suddenly someone grabbed on to his shoulder.

"What—" Mas dangled from the bridge and looked down to see bunches of logs rushing down the river. They seemed to be of every size, some short and stubby, some long and thin. One was even connected to a pair of shoes, noticed Mas. How strange.

Then Mas understood. "Kenji," he screamed, someone still hanging on to his shoulder. "Kenji, it's poison. The river's poison." But the spotted boy was long gone. Families were bent down by the banks, cupping their hands into the water and gulping enthusiastically. "No, no," Mas yelled.

Mas heard a voice from behind. "They won't listen to you." He allowed the person to draw him back onto the bridge, and turned to see the familiar hooked nose.

"You're alive." Mas blinked hard at Riki, whose hair was completely singed away. Only a few bristles stood up on his high forehead.

"At least half of me," said Riki, revealing his backside. The back of his uniform was gone, as if someone had purposely designed his clothing that way. On his neck was a huge, bloody gash that exposed the nubs of his spinal column.

Mas felt the remains of his breakfast, a roasted sweet potato, come up his throat. He vomited as people continued to push toward the river and bump him from all sides.

"No time for that, Masao," said Riki, gripping the shreds of cloth around Mas's neck like a leash.

"Joji—" Where was Joji?

"This way, this way."

At the edge of the bridge lay a long, skinny body. Riki placed the burnt body over his shoulder as if it were a sack of rice. The arms and legs dangled lifelessly, and then Mas recognized the work boots. "He's alive," said Riki, "barely."

It seemed as though they walked for days. All the landmarks—the corner drugstore, the stationery shop, the public bath—had disappeared. Only one wall of the once-majestic government office stood—now a giant tombstone marking a mass grave. The body of a man, who apparently had been resting on a cement stoop, remained burnt in place.

Is this all we are? Bits of dust, ash? How could life leave so quickly? Mas wiped his face with his black hands and, for the first time in a long time, felt tears spring up to his eyes. Were his parents still alive? What about his brothers and sisters? All he wanted was his flat, hay-filled futon, lined up with the others. He wanted to rest, close his eyes, and wake up to a new, bright Hiroshima day.

Mas's legs, which had been numb, were starting to buckle underneath him. "Let's rest for a while," said Riki, lowering Joji onto the ground. Joji's broken body was singed black, but his eyes were alert and wide open.

"He's trying to tell you something," said Riki.

"Aa—" Joji rasped.

Mas placed his ear by Joji's blistered lips.

Joji tried again. "Aa-ke—"

Mas understood. "Akemi, right? Don't worry, Joji. I'm sure she's all right." But Joji would not be comforted. "I promise you," Mas finally said, "I promise to find her." Rain then began to fall, softly, almost kindly. At least Joji would have some water to drink, thought Mas. Then he looked down at his bare hands and arms. Black streaks. Black rain.

Mas glanced at Riki. They did not say anything, but they both knew. This was no ordinary bomb.

"You go ahead," Riki said. "Go home. Get your brothers to help."

"No, I can't leave you and Joji."

"I can't go any farther. I'll watch him. We'll make it." Something in Riki's voice sounded strange, but then, everything was off balance and unfamiliar. Mas nodded and continued on to the hills, to home. When he finally saw a patch of green, he began to run until he could touch the blades of the tall grasses. When he turned back toward Riki and Joji, he could barely see them—mere stick figures in the steaming, ravaged landscape. Was one of the figures walking away from the other? Mas tried to focus but could not. He knew that he should turn back and check on Joji. But instead he collapsed and immediately fell asleep in the bed of green grasses.

✣ ✣ ✣

Masao-*san*, you okay?" Mas could smell Akemi's sweet perfume behind him.

"I was supposed to find youzu."

"I'm here," she said softly, stepping beside him.

"No, no." Mas shook his head. He explained his promise to Joji and how he had eventually abandoned the two Hanedas. "I sleep for days. When I wake up, Joji neva come home. You neither."

"But I made it. I survived."

"But Joji—"

"You were fifteen, sixteen, Masao-*san*. A child. We all were. You have to forgive yourself. Forgive yourself for living." Akemi's tears lay on her cheeks like fresh rain.

Akemi understood, as did Haruo and maybe Riki Kimura. But it was only a matter of time before all of them would be gone, and the past could be erased and completely forgotten, for better or for worse.

They waited until all of the mourners had left for a Chinese restaurant in Monterey Park. The remains in the crematorium had been removed by two men wearing breathing masks, gloves, and paper gowns. The lights around the cemetery grounds were dimmed, and a security guard was waiting by the gates.

"It's time to go," Akemi said.

"*Chotto.*" Mas asked for some more time. In total, he spent a good half hour by Chizuko's grave site. He wished he had brought a couple of stalks of the cymbidium that Chizuko had nurtured in planters in their backyard. At least two of them still had the waxy flowers, their petals open like lips singing.

As he headed to the parking lot, he was drawn to one of the headstones. It was white, and glowed in the moonlight. HIROSHI YANO, it read. The Pasadena grocery man who had been shot to death in a fifty-dollar heist.

As he read the inscription, Mas's toes tingled in his good shoes. Of course, he thought to himself. This is what Joji Haneda was trying to tell the world.

✣ ✣ ✣

When Mas reached the edge of the parking lot, he called out to Akemi, who had been joined by G. I. Hasuike, Tug, and Haruo. "We need to contact police," he said. "I knowsu how to prove dat man no Joji Haneda." In his excitement, Mas tripped over a cement parking lot bumper, and the four rushed to help him up.

"You okay, Masao-*san*?" Akemi asked.

Mas said again, "Heezu not Joji Haneda."

"Then whozu he?" Haruo asked.

Mas ignored Haruo's question. "Itsu the blood. Rememba the blood type on us at all times during war?"

Haruo nodded. "Yah, on name tags, in case we get hurt or bombed."

"Look on records back in Hiroshima. It should say Joji Haneda, type O. But that man today—he type A."

G. I. looked dumbfounded but promised to check it out.

"That'll helpsu you, Akemi-*san*, at least with the land. But I guess that has nutin' to do with gettin' Yuki outta jail."

"Don't worry, Masao-*san*." Under the fluorescent parking lot light, Akemi's face looked soft and unwrinkled, as if she had gone back in time at least thirty years. "That's all worked out." She turned back to the funeral chapel, where a slim woman dressed in a short-sleeved sweater and tight pants stood carrying a small bag. It was the witness, Rumi Kato.

❖ ❖ ❖

Apparently Rumi Kato had been on her way to Vegas, traveling 85 miles an hour on Interstate 15. But then her tires lost their traction, and the whole car flipped over two times. Her Toyota Corolla was a total loss, but she was unhurt, not a mark on her.

"I went to the police. Told them about that morning, when Junko was beaten," Rumi told Mas. "I could have died today—that's what I deserved. My life was spared for a reason, I know. It was like you said at the bowling alley. That it wasn't just about *bachi*."

"Bachi?" G. I. looked amused. "You mean what goes around comes around?"

Rumi nodded and then attempted to speak in

English for G. I.'s benefit. Pointing at Mas, she continued. "He said that I need to speak the truth. Or my insides not good."

"You say dat, Mas?" Haruo seemed genuinely happy, and Mas could only shrug in response.

"So you knew that you needed to come back to clear Yuki," Akemi said.

Rumi nodded. "No matter what happens."

Mas bit down on his dentures. Back at the Gardena bowling alley, the girl had been intent on running. Yet here she was, returning to the scene of the crime, ready to make things right.

✣ ✣ ✣

As soon as Mas got into the passenger's seat of the Honda, Haruo began his grilling. And finally Mas relented. "I knowsu him, Joji Haneda. And that man today, heezu not him. Heezu name is Riki Kimura."

"Riki Kimura . . . Kimura," Haruo murmured. "Same name as the boyzu."

Mas nodded. "Heezu same class as me. And Joji, too. After the war, dis Kimura became one of those no-good gangsters, *chinpira*."

"Black market?"

"Yah, only he good at it. Real good." Mas paused. "I made it ova here to America on his dirty money."

Mas had been desperate. There was no future for him in Hiroshima. He wasn't going to stay and become a mere field hand below his three brothers. He was destined for something more, and he knew that it lay in the country of his birth, America, the victor.

When he met Riki on the streets of Hiroshima months after the bombing, there was no talk about Joji Haneda. Mas figured that Joji had met a bad fate that had somehow been helped along by Mas himself. Riki's old downtown home was gone. Both his mother and grandfather had been killed, and his father was still missing. Riki now hung out with the other street orphans who had turned to the black market, alcohol and drugs, and prostitution for money. Mas didn't know which vice Riki was resorting to—perhaps all—but whatever his choice of illicit activity, it was making him rich. Riki even showed Mas a whole set of Australian army jackets he'd bought from a soldier, all stashed in a corner of an abandoned factory that somehow had survived the blast.

Mas stayed away from Riki as much as he could. He spent his days in the country, harvesting rice, trying to save as many yen notes as he could, but they were practically worthless, more valuable for firewood than anything else.

In his desperation, Mas starting thinking: What was wrong with stealing from a thief? I'm an American citizen, anyway. I have the right to leave this place. So one evening he returned to that abandoned factory, and sure enough, hidden in an Australian army jacket were two hundred American dollars and also some folded-up papers in an envelope. When Mas saw the name Joji Haneda on the papers, he could only imagine what had happened. He ran out of the dilapidated factory building with the army jacket and two hundred dollars, but not the papers. Those papers were cursed, he felt—and as it turned out, so was the jacket. When Mas was eventually caught selling the jacket on the black market, he told the military police what they wanted. Riki Kimura. Seventeen years old. Hooked nose. A scar on the back of his neck.

Mas explained to Haruo, "The MPs lookin' out for these black market gangsters. They let me go, but I neva tell them about the two hundred dolla. I use that to go to Kobe and then get the hell out of Japan."

"And dis Kimura?"

"Stuck in jail for a while, but I guess he finally make it out of Hiroshima on Joji Haneda's papers. I neva say nutin', even when he showed up in California. I kept Joji's death a secret. Nobody needsu to know, I thought." But that was before Akemi Haneda had returned to her birthplace, Los Angeles.

"Dis Kimura one bad guy," Haruo assessed.

"Well, he lookin' for a place for himself. Just neva found it."

✣ ✣ ✣

Before going home to McNally Street, Mas had Haruo stop by Tanaka's. "Wait here," he told Haruo in the car. "I be just few minutes."

An old dome desk light was on by the cash register.

There Wishbone stood, straightening out some nails in wooden compartments. He wore a baseball cap advertising a brand of lawn mower. From a distance, he could pass for any skinny Nisei guy, even Haruo.

Mas said, "You not at the funeral."

Wishbone turned, the light drawing shadows on his pockmarked face. "Wasn't in the mood."

Mas waited, hearing the tired crickets outside. He couldn't stand this feeling inside his gut. It was like making a bad bet you couldn't face up to, like assuming a jockey was steady but finding out later he was a drug addict. Everything became clear in that darkened shack. So clear that it hurt.

"You the one who killsu him. Joji Haneda."

"What? He died of cancer. Any fool could tell that he was only a few steps away from the grave."

"No." Mas shook his head. "He not wearin' his mask. Nurse tole me everytin'."

"You have no proof, Mas, and neither does that nurse."

"No proof, but I knowsu. Afta that card game, youzu out to finish him off."

"Why would I want to take his life when he owes me money? Can't get cash from a dead man. Think, Mas, think."

"Yah, Izu thinkin', Wishbone. Thinkin' that you mad enough to kill."

Wishbone placed a nail on the counter. "What if I told you that he asked me to take his mask off? That he begged me to end it all. That with every breath came pain. Not only his body but things in his head."

"Youzu no right," Mas said weakly. But he knew that pain well. He was just surprised that Riki had succumbed to it.

"I tried to put the mask back on him. But he kept turning his head, fighting me off. Didn't want to breathe anymore, I guess. Once the monitors started beeping loud, I got out of there. But nobody saw me. I made sure of that."

Mas somehow believed Wishbone, but he wasn't going to let him off scot-free. "You the one at the mistress's house that day," Mas said. "You the one runnin' 'cross street. And then, later, you were there when she all beat up."

Wishbone jiggled a box of nails.

"Youzu the one who set dis up. With Nakane in first place, *ne*."

"I don't know what you're talkin' about, Mas."

"Nakane here in June, askin' questions. Waitin' for me. Youzu tole him about me."

Wishbone said nothing.

"Not Haruo at the mistress's house. Was you. She had a load of money to give to you." That envelope had been meant for Wishbone, Mas knew now. Wishbone had been playing both sides, and Yuki was now the fall guy. "Youzu probably behind my truck gettin' stolen, too."

Wishbone came out from behind the counter.

"How much do you think I'm gonna get for this place? Don't own the land. Just the business. Fire sale. Chump change. How am I gonna live, Mas? Can't depend on my kids; they have their own lives." He placed the tip of one of the nails in his mouth and bit down. "You'd do the same. If the price was right."

"You were gonna let innocent boy go to jail?"

"Hey, wait a minute," Wishbone interrupted. "That was not my doin'. And the girl, too. Didn't know they were going to do that. All I was paid for was to hook you up with Nakane. I even told them not to hurt you. Haneda wanted to see you, too, but on his own terms. I was a matchmaker of sorts. Nothin' criminal about that."

"And these people from Hiroshima?"

"I owe none of them," said Wishbone. "They owe me; that's what I think. We are the ones who were locked up, stripped of our manhood, because we looked like them. Now they can pay us for what we sacrificed."

"Youzu crazy, Wishbone."

Wishbone's eyes seemed to burn like coals. "We the ones who opened the door for them. Even my uncle was a liaison for a Japanese bank here in L.A. Those guys used him, said he was some kind of bridge, and then threw him away when he got too old."

Mas understood. It hadn't been easy starting over in the 1940s and '50s. For those Nisei, you could see the world divided by race: Japanese, *hakujin*, and the others.

But Wishbone didn't know the whole story. He hadn't seen the ravaged bodies, the burning flesh. One minute friends laughed, full of life; next minute, destroyed. Those things never escaped one's mind. Once you witnessed that, you saw evil, and it didn't live in just Americans or Japanese. It lived close by, in friends, in neighbors, and, most frighteningly, inside yourself.

Mas circled the lawn mower shop. Finally he stopped by a beat-up corkboard fastened to the wall near the door. "You gotsu grandchildren." Mas gestured to some wallet-sized photos pinned to the board. "I see them, all fat, cute. Izu gonna be grandpa, too." Wishbone looked up, curious. Even in the darkness of the shop, he was always ready to hear some fresh gossip.

"I knowsu that baby gonna be *orai*. Or I say I knowsu, but don't really." Mas remembered meeting Yukikazu Kimura for the first time at the medical exams. *"My white count abnormally high,"* the boy had said. And he was two generations removed from the Bomb.

There also had been those damaged babies born to the survivors immediately after the war. Their heads bloated, their limbs withered and useless. Mas didn't know which was worse for them—to die or to live. The image of those babies had stayed in the back of Mas's mind all throughout Chizuko's pregnancy. Chizuko recalled it, too, Mas knew. They never spoke of their fears, because if they gave voice to them, their fears would somehow become true.

But Mari had been born perfectly normal. And her child, his grandchild, would be healthy, too, right?

Mas stayed quiet, listening for some kind of answer, a sign. The crickets stopped their chirping. It felt cold in the doorway.

"About your truck," Wishbone finally said. "I didn't know what they were going to do with it. They just asked me what was important to you. The only thing I could think of was the Ford."

Mas merely nodded and stepped out of Tanaka's Lawn-mower Shop. That was the last time he would go through its doors.

CHAPTER SEVENTEEN

It took G. I. Hasuike one day to free the boy. The only thing was, Rumi, the witness, had to stay in town for a while. Her parents were coming to America for a long visit, she explained. "Good," Mas said. "Youzu needsu to talk."

Nakane, meanwhile, was on the run. The authorities thought that he had escaped to Japan, or even to Mexico, under an alias. It was only a matter of time before he was caught, Mas figured. Lies like that rarely lasted beyond a lifetime.

✣ ✣ ✣

Akemi and Yuki, on the other hand, got the green light to leave the country, as long as they checked in with the Japanese authorities when they arrived in Hiroshima. They didn't waste any time, and booked a flight directly to Kansai International Airport for the next day. Everybody was supposed to go to see them off at LAX—everybody, that is, except for Mas.

Mas didn't like anything about airports. The crowds, the airport limousines, the constant hubbub. It was a place on the go; except Mas wasn't going anywhere. And it wasn't even so much the good-byes. What made Mas feel so empty was seeing the lovers, old friends, fathers, and daughters meet up again after being separated by time and distance.

He didn't expect Akemi and Yuki to understand. They stood on his porch, their bags in hand.

"I'm forever indebted to you, *Ojisan*." Yuki's politeness embarrassed more than flattered Mas. He almost preferred dealing with the old Yuki.

"I did nutin'."

"If you hadn't figured out the blood-type connection, we wouldn't have a chance to hold on to the land."

G. I., through some backdoor shenanigans, had been able to verify the blood type of the Joji Haneda who had died at Oxnard City Hospital. Type A, it was, just as Mas had predicted.

"And I heard back from my buddy at the magazine, the one I had you call, *Ojisan*. I don't know why we didn't check sooner. But our land used to be next to this shantytown full of Koreans who had been forced to work in Hiroshima. Practically kidnapped and brought over.

"People were using it as a landfill, and some attorneys for the former laborers want to conduct an investigation. There's something down there. Evidence.

Something worth a lot more than even ten million dollars."

Mas nodded. He'd read of the lawsuits filed on behalf of men and women who had been captured and forced to work in Japan during World War II a few years back. At the time, he'd thought the lawsuits were pure foolishness. Just a way for lawyers to make another buck, he figured. But if someone was hiring fellows like Nakane to nose around and even kill, it was certainly worth looking into.

"Well," Akemi said, "it's up to us, isn't it? We'll find out what's going on." She then turned to Mas. "Masao-*san,* I wish you were coming with us to the airport. Tell me that we will see each other again."

Mas blinked hard two, three times. "Oh, yah."

"You come and visit us in the new, improved Hiroshima."

"Of course," Mas lied, standing stiffly as Akemi gave him a brief hug.

Yuki knew enough not to touch Mas, and bowed instead. "If there's anything I can do—"

"Oh, yah, send me a copy of that drawing."

"Drawing?"

"The one of the man with one leg."

Yuki unzipped his day pack and took out the illustration. "Here, you can have this. It's a copy."

"Wait." Mas went into the bedroom and returned to the front with another image. The black-and-white photograph of the boys on the bridge.

"What's this?"

"Joji Haneda. Your grandmother's brother." Mas pointed to the tall boy on the left-hand side. On his uniform was the white ID tag with a letter O faintly readable.

"And the others?"

Mas hesitated. "Schoolmates. Friends."

Yuki didn't bother to ask where Mas had obtained the photo. He took the snapshot and placed the drawing in Mas's hands. Yuki then bowed again, picked up the suitcases, and headed for the Jeep. When he reached the middle of the driveway, he turned around. "*Ojisan*, I'll take you to a pachinko parlor or, better yet, boat racing. We'll see how well you'll do in that."

"Orai, orai." Mas waved from the porch and stood there until the Jeep disappeared from McNally Street. In the balmy sunshine, he studied the color drawing of the man without the leg. This is what Joji Haneda was trying to tell the world. That he wasn't Riki Kimura, type A, but Joji Haneda, O. The circle that he was trying to draw was his identity, a message that lasted more than fifty years. Mas was just happy that he was around to figure it out.

Mas was in the garage when Tug came by, five hours later. He seemed a little more subdued than usual, and Mas figured it had to do with the boy's leaving.

Tug gave a brief report about going to the airport, asked a few questions, said a few words, but pretty much revealed nothing. It wasn't like Tug. He wasn't the kind to hide his thoughts. He was direct and big, in body and spirit.

Mas made some comments about a new gadget they were selling at the local hardware store, but still little response. Mas expected Tug to show some interest, but he merely sagged on the Coleman cooler.

"Youzu okay, Tug?"

Tug took out a handkerchief and mopped up the sweat on his forehead. "I had to get out of the house. It's Joy. She's back home for a week."

"Oh, yah." Must be nice for her, thought Mas, get a break from hospital work.

"She and Lil have been at it the whole time. She's thinking about quitting medicine, Mas. She's done all the course work, internship, almost done with her residency, and now she says it's not what she wants to do with the rest of her life."

Mas felt numb. Even though the Yamadas weren't the type to *ibaru*, make a big deal of it, Mas knew that they were in fact very proud of Joy.

"What she wanna do instead?"

"Paint." Tug kicked a piece of wire Mas had left on the garage floor. "We should have never enrolled her in those Pasadena art classes."

"Maybe she just feel dis way now. Temporary."

"It's not just a phase, she says. How are you going

to pay off your loans? I ask her. Those are going to have to be some damn good paintings."

Mas flinched. For Tug to curse, even say a word like "damn," meant he had reached his limit.

"It's not even the worst of it, Mas," Tug said. "I wouldn't normally tell just anyone this, but I know you'd keep this under wraps." Tug took a deep breath. "She says that she's been in therapy, counseling. For a year now."

This counseling was an epidemic, thought Mas. Good thing Haruo wasn't around to talk about how great it was to dump your feelings onto a complete stranger.

"She says that she's been trying to be a good Japanese girl her whole life, and she needs to break out of it. I don't get it, Mas. We tried to be good parents. I don't know where we went wrong." A bus paused at a stop down the street; the door folded open and then shut. It spilled exhaust as it left. "I guess what hurts the most is that she didn't come to us with her problems. She didn't trust us. Now she's telling someone about how terrible we are as parents."

"No, Tug," Mas interrupted. "You and Lil are good parents. You take care of her, take her to church, tell her what's wrong, what's right. She a nice girl. Itsu just that we all got problems. May have nutin' to do with mother, father. Sometimes sometin' happens, changes everytin'."

"Maybe, maybe." They remained quiet while Mas

cleaned his tools. "By the way," continued Tug, "I wanted to ask you. Haruo's not back gambling, is he?"

"Whatchu mean?"

"Well, I went to pick him up to go to the airport, and what do you know, he was running that incinerator in his backyard."

Mas balled up his cleaning rag.

"He was smoking up that entire block. Neighborhood kids were in his driveway. They thought he was burning a body or something."

"Howzu they get dat idea?"

"You know kids. So I was a bit worried. He put it out as soon as I came, but when he went back into the house to make sure he had turned off the stove, I checked."

"And?"

Tug pulled out a bill from his pocket. It was only about half a greenback, burned, yet still clearly showing Ben Franklin's face.

"Money."

Tug nodded. "Now, I don't know what he was doing burning one-hundred-dollar bills. I didn't say anything, but wondered if you could talk to him. You're his best friend, after all."

This time Mas didn't hesitate. "No worry, Tug," he said. "I take care." So it had been Haruo, thought Mas. He had been there that night after Yuki was arrested. Haruo was the king of second, third, and fourth chances. And now, by getting rid of Nakane's thirty-thousand-dollar bribe, he was trying to give a chance to Mas.

After a few more minutes, Tug rose to go home. "Well, Mas, life's going to be a lot quieter, huh? What's next?"

"No idea," Mas said. "No idea."

✣ ✣ ✣

The house on McNally Street was especially quiet this evening. Mas picked up his usual routine—a cold Budweiser, and the horse race broadcast. This is what he wanted, right? For the dust to resettle in the corners of his room.

Mas turned off the television set and sat at the kitchen table for a while, maybe a full hour. Crickets chirped, and children called out to one another on the street. Mas picked up the message that Akemi had apparently written to him a few days earlier. MARI CALLED, it said in capital letters.

It took Mas three tries. On the first attempt, he forgot to dial one before the number. On the second, he hung up before anyone could answer. On the third try, he let it ring and ring, until he heard her voice. It sounded so real that he began to talk, and then realized that it was only the answering machine.

"Itsu Dad," he finally said, and before he could add anything else, a beep sounded, ending the message.

✣ ✣ ✣

The next morning, Mas did what he had always done on Fridays for most of the past thirty years. He went to the Witts' in San Marino.

As he eased Tug's pickup truck into the driveway, Mrs. Witt waved her hands from the back doorway as if she were directing a train to stop. "Mas, I need to talk to you," she cried out. Mas noticed that her fingers were dark purple. Dying those T-shirts in her vats again, he noted. "I'll wash up and meet you in the orchard," she said, her hands dripping purple.

Mas got out of the truck and opened the rear door. Tightening his grip on his wooden toolbox, he headed for the broken branches. Weeds and dandelions everywhere. Most of the trees had been chopped down, except about a half a dozen. And then, in the back row, he saw it. A branch that remained fused to its new home. Mas tripped over some extended roots and checked the connection. Fine. Fine. The leaves were waxy and bright green. He yanked a leaf to get a better look, and then, hidden by a bend in the branch, was a small persimmon the size of a baby's fist.

"They found it." Mrs. Witt was a bit breathless. She was wearing a white gauze top and loose blue shorts. Her hands were still purple, but dry now.

"What?" Mas released the leaf.

"They found your truck." Mrs. Witt wiped some sweat with the back of her hand. "Can you believe it? They just called me, about ten minutes ago. Good thing you gave them my number. Tried your place first, but couldn't get an answering machine. They want you to go in. It's the police in South Pasadena."

"Get my truck?" Mas blinked hard and adjusted his baseball hat. Sonafugun. The Ford was still around. "So nutin' wrong with it, huh?"

"I didn't say that. I don't know the condition of your car; you got to go to their impound lot for that. But they did find it. How did you get here, anyhow?"

Mas gestured toward Tug's pickup in the driveway. "My friend's. I just come to see the broken branches."

"Well, Mas, you don't have to worry about that. I called in some tree people, heavy-duty guys with tractors and that sort of thing. I knew you were recuperating, and I had to get moving on the house."

"So you gonna move for sure."

"Yep. Sure looks like it. Even found a condo in Colorado Springs. It's for old people. Retirees."

Mas wrinkled his forehead. Neither Mrs. nor Mr. Witt—Mas had seen him recently on a television commercial—had aged gracefully. They were barely sixty, if even that, and their skin had lost all its luster.

"I'm working on a project now, tie-dyed pajamas for my grandkids."

"Thatsu nice." Mas didn't know what else to say.

"So, you are coming back, right? There's loads to be done. I've got algae all over my koi pond, and hedges have to be recut. I want to put the house on the market by August."

"Next week," said Mas. "After I getsu my truck."

Mrs. Witt seemed satisfied and headed back toward the brick house. "By the way . . ." She turned. "How are you doing?"

Mas reached up and grabbed hold of the tiny persimmon. "Fine," he said, pulling down. "Just fine."

✣ ✣ ✣

The police headquarters in South Pasadena had recently been renovated. It was in a desert style, with a fake adobe facade and tile in green and blue, looking more like a Southwestern Holiday Inn than a den of cops and robbers. Mas had been there once, when he needed to get information on getting a license to work in the city. A young girl, her brown hair tied up in a ponytail, sat behind the glass window. Wearing a black uniform, she spoke through a slotted plastic circle. "On the other side, sir, in City Hall."

This time, there was no ponytailed girl, but a dark boy who looked like a Hawaiian. Mas followed the boy, whose leather holster squeaked as he passed by a couple of offices and then entered a wide room lit up by long fluorescent bulbs. "Detective Benjamin, this is the owner of the truck that was found this morning," the Hawaiian boy said before returning down the hall.

Detective Benjamin was a solid man with damaged red hair like Pacific Ocean seaweed. His face was marked with a million freckles, which from a distance made him look tanned. "Mr. Arai, is it? Here, have a seat." He pulled out a hard wooden chair next to his metal desk.

Mas felt nervous—guilty, even. I'm the one whose truck was stolen, he reminded himself. This isn't about the money.

The detective rummaged through a pile of files in a wire basket and pulled out a manila folder. "Well, a 1956 Ford, huh?" he said, holding the folder open. "A classic. One of my friends restores these beauts. Even provides the cars for our annual Fourth of July parade."

"Izu my truck here?" Mas squeezed the sides of the wooden seat.

"No, we had to send it down to the impound in Alhambra. But I'll get to that in a second."

Mas bit down on both lips and waited.

"Yep, your truck was just collecting parking tickets on the edge of town near the L.A. border. They did get some fingerprints off the vehicle." Detective Benjamin flipped through the pages in his file.

"Well, here's one suspect." The detective tried to smooth out a flimsy piece of paper on the flat surface of his desk. "Recognize him?"

Mas squinted and wished he had his five-dollar reading glasses from Thrifty's. It was a typical mug shot, photographed against a white background. A *hakujin* man in his fifties with dirty-blond hair.

"Daniel Hawthorne," the detective said. "Also known as David or Dale."

Hawthorne. The man who had visited Haruo in the beginning of summer.

"Has a record." Detective Benjamin read from his folder. "Filed phony immigration papers. Accused of identity fraud but not convicted."

"I-den-ti-ty—"

"Ya know, identity theft, like stealing money from credit card accounts. False identities and so on."

False IDs? Mas tried to keep himself from laughing. There was no doubt that this Mr. Hawthorne was in league with Shuji Nakane. "Probably wear fancy shoes," Mas mumbled.

"Excuse me?" the policeman asked, and Mas just pretended that he was clearing his throat. The detective continued to go on about police procedures, but Mas was more interested in the found truck. "My lawn mower not in there?"

"Lawn mower?" Detective Benjamin laughed harshly. "No lawn mower. Actually, I don't think you'll find any extras on your vehicle."

Mas swallowed. Phones rang on other metal desks. Other men slurped down mugs of coffee and chewed crumbling cake donuts while taking notes.

"Here." The detective slipped a piece of paper with a yellow attachment in front of Mas. "This is the release form. Show me some identification, sign it, and then you can get your car."

✣ ✣ ✣

Mas tried to prepare himself for the worst. He imagined the truck's body almost stripped, the door handles yanked off. The smog was especially thick that day, and Mas could barely read the hand-painted sign on Main Street in Alhambra. He circled the fenced lot and parked a block away from Saul's Towing, almost afraid that the impound would suck in Tug's truck like a gigantic magnet.

The clerk was most likely the owner of the lot, judging from the way he flipped down his reading glasses and studied Mas's paperwork with weathered hands. "Seventy-dollar charge for the tow, and fifteen dollars a day. That'll be eighty-five dollars." The clerk wrote the figure on a white form complete with carbons in pink and yellow.

"Eighty-five dolla? But my truck was stolen. The police brought it ova here." Mas pressed his work boot against the foot of the counter. It was a high counter that reached up to Mas's chin. He noticed that it was bent in a few places.

The clerk held on to the forms. "Did they get who did it?"

"They found fingerprints. Thatsu all."

"Well, sue him, then. But you still have to pay the fee."

Mas felt the anger rise to his head. What the hell? Why did he have to fork out the money to retrieve his own property? He felt like adding another dent to Saul's counter.

"Look, someone's gotta pay," said Saul. "I'm offering the service, but I'm not doing this for free. You can't expect the police to pay. That's taxpayers' money. That leaves you. You want the car, pay for it. Think of it as a deduction on your income taxes."

"Letsu me see the truck." Keys hung in rows from nails on the wall behind the clerk.

Saul shook his head. "Look, this is not a used-car lot. I'm not doing this for my health."

Mas pulled his wallet out of his back pocket. He already knew that he had only two twenty-dollar bills and a couple of George Washingtons, but he looked anyway. His thumbs extended the torn lining of the wallet. "I don't have eighty-five dollars right now."

Saul shrugged. "Nothing I can do for you, sir. Just come back with the cash. We accept Visa, Mastercard, too. And remember, it's an extra fifteen bucks each day."

✣ ✣ ✣

Mas returned to the house and rummaged in his closet for his Yuban coffee can. His stash was down to almost nothing, but he was still able to put together sixty bucks. With the forty in his wallet, he was covered. The Ford was going to come home.

Mas drove back to Alhambra and reentered the one-room office of Saul's Towing, where an oily-faced kid had replaced the middle-aged owner. After handing the kid his paperwork and cash, he waited in the gravel-covered driveway. He looked down at the toes of his work boots. They were getting worn out; he'd be needing a pair by this fall, he thought, and then heard a familiar squeak of metal hitting metal. The Ford.

The engine sounded the same, but the body had gone through hell. The kid jumped out of the driver's seat, like he was tumbling out of a hay ride, when Mas noticed there was no door on the driver's side. Or the passenger's, either. "Sonafugun. Sonafugun," Mas muttered, as if he were saying magic words to turn the Ford back to the way it was. The front grille had been ripped off, as well as the front bumper. Wires that had been attached to the headlights had been cut and now poked out like slashed veins. The Ford had been blinded.

Mas circled the truck. The flatbed was still in place, but the tailgate had been disconnected. Aside from a rake that hung from a wire clip Mas had installed, all the equipment, including the Trimmer, was gone.

Mas was afraid to look inside the cab. They had tried to carry out the seats, but failed. The steering wheel, nicks and all, was still in place, but the end of the stick shift was missing. And the ashtray—what the hell were they going to do with that?

As he surveyed each piece of destruction, Mas felt the rage build up inside of him. It was like they had stripped him naked and paraded him around the city. Their grimy hands had gone through the glove compartment, the seats, and the bed of the truck. Even though Mas couldn't see their fingerprints, he felt them everywhere.

"Please sign, sir." The oily-faced boy had left the engine running and now held out a final piece of paper on a clipboard.

Mas carefully guided his signature with skinny loops beside the *X* on the bottom.

"It's all yours," the boy said, glancing at the hood, which was bent in the middle as if the thieves had tried to pry it open with a crowbar. "Well, at least it still runs. Most of them don't, you know."

Mas remembered how Mari and her friend had accidentally smashed the hood when they had jumped from their neighbor's fence. The hood had never been the same; Mas was the only one who had mastered the trick of opening it.

Mas hit the left side of the hood three times and lifted it open. There, in the center, was the magnificent, greasy engine like a black pearl in the middle of an oyster shell. It whirled and purred, the valve cases and air cleaner all intact. Mas had to laugh. Those sonafugun vultures had stripped the Ford, but left behind the most valuable part. The heart of the machine.

ABOUT THE AUTHOR

NAOMI HIRAHARA is the Macavity Award nominated author of two other Mas Arai mysteries, *Gasa-Gasa Girl* and the Edgar winner, *Snakeskin Shamisen*. A writer, editor, and publisher of nonfiction books, she previously worked as an editor of *The Rafu Shimpo*, a bilingual Japanese American daily newspaper in Los Angeles. She and her husband reside in her birthplace, Southern California. For more information and reading group guides, visit her Web site at www.naomihirahara.com.

Don't miss the second
Mas Arai mystery,

GASA-GASA GIRL

by

Naomi Hirahara

On sale from Dell

Please read on for a preview.

A MAS ARAI MYSTERY

GASA-GASA GIRL

In the shadows of a long-forgotten past is a secret worth killing for. . . .

NAOMI HIRAHARA

Author of *Summer of the Big Bachi*

BEFORE

Gasa-gasa. That's what Chizuko called her. Their *gasa-gasa* baby, constantly restless, constantly moving. Once, when Mas Arai returned from his gardening route to their home in Altadena, California, he found her in the living room chewing on the leather case for his favorite pair of pruning shears. Five minutes later she had gotten into his bowls of Japanese *go* playing pieces, a spray of black and white stones all over their linoleum kitchen floor. And five minutes after that, she had moved into the hall closet and pulled down all of Mas's long-sleeved khaki work shirts.

"She movin' all the time," said Chizuko. "Can't watch her every minute; I have enough to do around the house."

Mas didn't dare criticize Chizuko's mothering skills, because what could she say about him as a father? It was one thing when they were at home, when the walls of their McNally Street house could contain her. But out in the larger world, Mas and Chizuko had to keep their eye on their daughter at all times. If they didn't, Mari would have for sure stumbled into a dry ravine in Elysian Park during a gardeners' association picnic, or run away with a band of ravenous deer at the old Japanese Deer Park, in Orange County. Mari always seemed to be on the move, yet she still somehow escaped falling off the edge. Where, Mas often wondered, would the *gasa-gasa* girl end up next?

chapter one

To go far from the noise of civilization, to live the simple country life and breathe deeply of pure air—that is the cleanser of life.

—Takeo Shiota
New York City, August 1, 1915

March 2000

Mas knew that New York City wasn't for him as soon as he saw that its gardens were under lock and key. Even in the best neighborhoods in Beverly Hills or San Marino back in Southern California, lawns lay open like luxurious carpets to the edges of sidewalks, beckoning guests and the glances of envious passersby. Of course, back home there were also visual threats and warnings—the blue and yellow Armed Response signs on metal stakes. But it was one thing to pierce grass with a sign, and quite another to put a garden behind bars.

"It's called a community garden," Tug Yamada explained. "Everyone pitches in to make it green." They were stuck in traffic on Flatbush Avenue. Tug had picked Mas up in a white Mercury rental car, a pearl amid the black Town Cars that had circled JFK Airport. Mas could always count on Tug to help him in a pinch. But then again, Mas guessed that Tug was behind this recent turn of events. It would take an outside force—specifically a six-foot Nisei, a second-generation Japanese American—to push Mas's daughter, Mari, to place a call from Brooklyn to his home in Altadena.

"Community? Like Japanese ones back in Los Angeles?"

"No Japanese gardeners over here, Mas. At least no more than you can count on one hand." Tug stretched out his palm, magnifying the missing half of his forefinger, a remnant of his war injury in Europe.

This was no place for Japanese gardeners and no place for a Kibei like Mas, who was born in the U.S. but raised in Japan. *Kibei*—"ki" meaning "return," "bei" referring to America—was a word made up by Japanese Americans to explain their limbo. So while America was actually home for the Kibei, many of them weren't quite comfortable with English; on the other hand, they weren't that comfortable speaking Japanese, either.

Mas was used to not belonging, but he felt an especially strong sense of displacement the minute he'd gotten on the plane. A bunch of *hakujin* and blacks, and a few young Chinese. There were a couple of Japanese, but they were business types who wore blue and black suits with ties and hard shoes even on the airplane. They sat in the front, behind a curtain that separated the first class from the rest of the plane, called economy but really meaning *bimbo*, for the passengers with no money, like Mas. Even when Mas returned to America from Hiroshima in 1947, he bought the third-class boat tickets, which turned out to be a large open room full of other teenage dreamers lying on *goza,* straw mats, on the bottom of the ship.

In the streets of New York, there were black and brown teenagers with the same look in their eyes. Wrapped in puffy jackets and their heads topped with knit caps, they seemed to hold their dreams casually, maybe recklessly, as if those dreams could never dry up.

"Everyone *gasa-gasa* ova here, huh?"

"Yeah, everyone moves around in New York, Mas. You should see where Joy lives in Manhattan. It's like rivers of people walking at night."

Tug had been in New York for a couple of weeks now before the opening of his daughter Joy's art exhibit. In Mas's eyes, Tug was the closest thing to an expert on Manhattan. "Joy live close to ova here?"

"You have to go over the Brooklyn Bridge, but it's just a short subway ride away."

"Fancy place, dis Manhattan?"

"Well, Joy lives in a postage stamp of an apartment. The water comes out all brown." Tug stroked his white beard. "And you know how I love baths, Mas."

Tug, in fact, had installed a Jacuzzi tub, his and his wife Lil's only extravagance, in their modest home just two miles east of Mas's. There was no doubt that this love for baths started when Tug was a child simmering nightly in the family *furo,* the huge Japanese wooden tub, on their red chili pepper farm.

Mas asked a few more perfunctory questions about Joy, then cut to the chase. "So you knowsu whatsu goin' on with Mari?"

"I'd better let her and Lloyd explain."

Lloyd? Mas had barely thought of his new son-in-law. "Not the baby—?" Mas couldn't even say the name: Takeo Frederick Jensen. It was too long; and why had they named the child Takeo, anyhow?

Mari had sent a photo back in December of a little red monkey-faced infant with fists curled up like cooked shrimp. You couldn't tell if the baby looked more Japanese or *hakujin* or something in between. Mas remembered when Mari had been that small. He was almost afraid to touch her, and even Chizuko told him to keep his distance. But, in time, he got the hang of it—support the neck, watch the soft spot on top of the head. The first and only time he gave Mari a bath, he noticed a dark-blue mark above her buttocks and thought he had done something wrong. "Masao-*san*, most Japanese babies have that," Chizuko said, laughing. Later Tug's wife, Lil, explained that doctors called it a Mongolian spot, which seemed like a fancy term for a temporary birthmark on a baby's behind.

Tug stopped the car at another light, and Mas noticed another one of the community gardens. This one was a triangle of green trapped next to a fancy white store that looked like it sold overpriced basketball shoes and jerseys. Mas could make out a Japanese cedar, and even some kind of makeshift pond. It was still cold in New York, a good thirty degrees lower than L.A. Were the people of New York City so hungry for trees and flowers that they had to create this spring oasis in the middle of melting snow?

Tug seemed to read Mas's mind. "Lloyd was telling me about that place. Even has a name, Teddy Bear Garden, or something like that."

Teddy bear? Kids' stuff, thought Mas.

"A developer was going to get rid of the garden, so the whole community, even Lloyd and Mari, protested. Early on, somebody had thrown a teddy bear into the area, so I guess the name stuck. You know about these community gardens, Mas. There's one across the freeway from Dodger Stadium, I think."

Tug was a die-hard Dodger fan, so it was no wonder that anything remotely involving his baseball team would stick in his mind. Mas himself recollected seeing the small clumps of flowers and vegetables against a hill right above one of the tunnels of the Pasadena Freeway. And there was another garden in Alhambra, a few towns south of Altadena, where Chinese immigrants dressed in cotton pants and sometimes straw hats tended stalks of corn and vines of cherry tomatoes. But those gardens were primarily vegetables, while these ones on Flatbush Avenue were filled with trees and flowers struggling to bloom. In L.A., everybody had pride of ownership in their personal flower gardens—a concept that had led Mas and several thousands of other Japanese Americans to get jobs as gardeners, whether they could actually grow anything or not. Everyone assumed that Japanese had green thumbs. If only they knew the truth: that most of them starting out could hardly tell the difference between a weed and an impatiens plant. But they had caught on fast enough, making money to feed their families and send their kids to fancy schools as far away as New York.

"How long youzu gonna stay?" Mas asked.

"Well, Joy's exhibition opens in a couple of weeks. You, Mari, and Lloyd are all invited, you know. I don't know about the baby, though. I don't know what people do at art gallery openings."

Tug's daughter, Joy, had recently traded in her white coat and stethoscope for poverty and paintbrushes. It had been a bad blow, but in typical Yamada fashion, Tug had bounced back, in full support of his daughter's new career. Mas had never been much into support; at least that's what both Chizuko and Mari told him time and time again. That's why he had been surprised to hear Mari's quavering voice on the other end of the line from Brooklyn: "We're in a bit of trouble, Dad. We might need your help." Help? When had Mari ever asked for help? Mari didn't want to get into the details but told him that she and her new husband, Lloyd, were going to buy him an airplane ticket. "You'll need a driver's license to board. And don't forget a credit card, just in case," she said.

But there was one problem: Mas didn't have a credit card. He'd had one briefly, when his wife, Chizuko, was alive, but that had been about fifteen years ago. So he went to the bank, and within a week, he had his own shiny piece of plastic bearing on it his full name, MASAO ARAI.

Now, with his driver's license and new credit card

in his worn leather wallet, he had both an identity and money. He wasn't sure whether they were enough to help Mari, but he knew if he didn't come through this time, he probably would never get the chance again.

✤ ✤ ✤

They passed a few more corner pizza shops, a line of leafless trees in a brown park, and some small grocery stores that looked like the old produce stands in Little Tokyo. Tug finally turned right onto a smaller avenue called Carlton. On both sides of the street were three-story brick buildings—brownstones, Tug had called them. They all had heavy metal gates on the doors, but no Armed Response signs. These Brooklyn people chose to fight their crime the old-fashioned way, thought Mas.

Cars were parked bumper to bumper along the curb, so Tug double-parked in front of one of the brownstones, pressing down a button to open the trunk. "I'm sorry I can't wait with you," Tug said. He left the car running while he got out and lifted Mas's hard plastic yellow Samsonite suitcase from the trunk. Mas clenched his arthritic hands as he waited out on the curb in the cold.

Tug handed Mas the suitcase and a set of keys. "Lloyd asked me to give these to you. One's for the gate and the other's for the door. He'll come home right after work."

And Mari, what about her? Before Mas could get any more information, Tug was back at the driver's-side door. "See you, old man. I'll call you tomorrow."

Mas hesitated for a moment in front of the brownstone. Clutching his suitcase and keys, he started up the concrete steps, only to have Tug honk his car horn. Shaking his head of white hair back and forth, Tug lowered the passenger's-side window. "No, Mas," he said, "not up there. Down."

Mas pointed to a gate on the right that seemed to submerge below street level, and Tug nodded in response. With that, the white rental disappeared down Carlton Avenue, leaving only a brief trail of steam and exhaust.

This was worse than Mas had imagined. He knew making ends meet for a freelance filmmaker and—could he even say it—modern-day gardener in New York must be tough, but was it tough enough that they had to live underground? Even the small window, no higher than Mas's knees from the street, was heavily barred. You couldn't tell if it was meant to keep people out or keep people in.

Trying the keys a couple of times, Mas was finally able to open the gate. Beyond the gate was a dark and damp entryway leading to a large door. Mas's eyes had trouble adjusting to the dim light, so he pulled out his new Rite Aid reading glasses from his shirt pocket to pick out the key for the door.

The apartment was cool and musty, much like his garage after a winter rain. There were layers of smells: the familiar staleness of old newspapers and books, a lingering memory of meals made by Mari and Lloyd, and maybe decades of households before them, and a faint sweetness of talcum powder. Mas felt the side of et the drizzle wet his hair, which had been back with Three Flowers oil, like always. He the collar of his jacket and went up the steps niserable garden. Its condition didn't surprise ost gardeners were too busy with other people's s to put much energy into their own. Mas's front ad its share of dandelions, and the backyard d have been completely grim if it had not been for uko's leftover buckets of cymbidium. As he stum- over some icy gravel, he thought he heard the ing of a telephone in the distance. Not my phone, thought, going over to examine a fancy iron bench d some metal rabbits and ducks. The square of green oked like last season's Bermuda grass.

Someone had attempted to plant a few daffodils, nd they were bravely breaking through the choco- ate brown soil. The plum blossoms on the garden's sole tree were still tightly closed, awaiting the warmth of the spring sun.

Before Mas could take further inventory of the hi- bernating plants, he noticed a figure at the open door. The son-in-law, a skeleton of a man, his dirty blond hair hanging down his head like seaweed. His face was ashen gray. Mas shoved his hands in his coat pockets and walked back to the apartment, preparing himself for the fake niceties that relatives who were virtual strangers said to one another at holidays and funerals.

But the son-in-law didn't even bother to smile. "Mari and Takeo aren't here," Lloyd said. "And I'm not sure exactly where they are."

the wall by the door—wood paneling, but no light switch. He could make out the outline of a lamp shade, found the knob, and turned it two times.

The front room was small, about fifteen feet by fif- teen feet. There was a long couch along the wall on the left side, but what caught Mas's eye first was a set of wooden stairs that led not to a door or room but to an- other wall. Stairs that went nowhere, an underground apartment—what *was* this house? Tug had explained that the neighborhood was called Park Slope, but Mas hadn't seen any sign of anything green other than the Teddy Bear Garden. He noticed that unlike in typical Japanese American households, no shoes were left anywhere near the doorway, so he went ahead and stepped onto the hardwood floors, leaving his suitcase on the threadbare brown rug.

There was a mini kitchen in the corner, a wire dish rack holding a couple of coffee cups, a plate, and a few upside-down baby bottles. A desk by the hollow fireplace was overburdened by papers and books—it seemed almost as if it were spitting out and rejecting the weight of the information it carried. Mas turned on another lamp by the desk and peered at the books. Most were in English, but a couple were in Japanese. A Japanese-English dictionary, the fat kind that Chizuko had used when she was writing official let- ters, sat on a shelf. Even though Mas and Chizuko had sent their daughter to Japanese school every Saturday, Mari wouldn't have anything to do with the language and had forgotten the little that she had learned. Chizuko was offended and sometimes hurt when the teenage Mari had hissed at her in public places: "Speak English, Mom, speak English."

These couldn't be Mari's books: but then again, who else's would they be? The son-in-law's?

On the shelf next to the dictionary were a couple of photographs: the same one of the baby Takeo that Mari had sent to Mas, and a large one of Mari with her pale and scraggly husband, Lloyd, standing on some cement stairs leading to an official government building. Mas had not seen Lloyd for years, and that absence hadn't done Lloyd any good. Instead of looking more refined and clean-cut, his hair was down to his shoulders and barely combed. He wore wire-rimmed glasses and a tan suit, but he wasn't fooling anyone. He was a no-good gardener, just like Mas. But while Mas was a Kibei, Lloyd was a *hakujin* man, over six feet tall. He had absolutely no excuse for falling into the same line of work as desperate men.

Taped to the wall over the desk was a grainy photocopy of a man's image. Mas adjusted his Rite Aid glasses. A Japanese man wearing a straw hat and suit. A shadow fell on half the man's face, but he looked important. *Erai:* a big-boss type. The image was black-and-white and had obviously been taken more than half a century ago, maybe in the 1920s or 1930s, about the time Mas was born.

The disorganized books and papers on the desk didn't make much sense: Mari had always been like Chizuko, who'd kept their home in Altadena spotless. Every kitchen knife was sharpened (that part done by Mas after much nagging from Chizuko) and arranged

by size in one of the kitchen
paid immediately and filed awa
Mari herself had lined up her p
the top of the pink desk Mas had b
them were those strange white Japa
in colorful cardboard sleeves. At one
like sugary flowers, but now, still left
in Mas's silent house, they were virtual

Something else was wrong with th
apartment. Mas had taken on a new cus
months ago, a young couple with a baby,
Their wood-framed house had a sloping fr
something Mas would have never taken on i
day. But now competition was worse than
he couldn't afford to be choosy. Every time he
at the door to talk to the missus, he noticed th
of blocks, overturned plastic toys, and aband
blankets. A disaster that only a baby could create. This front room had little sign of that.

Mas went into the back room, the bedroom. Again he turned on a light, the lamp beside the bed. Sure enough, a small crib stood in the corner. A few stuffed animals and packages of disposable diapers. By the crib was a large fluorescent lamp, almost like the ones Mas had seen in orchid greenhouses. What kind of strange life was Mari leading with this giant *hakujin* gardener?

A door in the bedroom led to a small backyard outside. Through the bedroom window, Mas could see that it had started to rain. He turned the double lock and opened the door. Finally, a faint patch of green, mixed in with dirt and gray.

the wall by the door—wood paneling, but no light switch. He could make out the outline of a lamp shade, found the knob, and turned it two times.

The front room was small, about fifteen feet by fifteen feet. There was a long couch along the wall on the left side, but what caught Mas's eye first was a set of wooden stairs that led not to a door or room but to another wall. Stairs that went nowhere, an underground apartment—what *was* this house? Tug had explained that the neighborhood was called Park Slope, but Mas hadn't seen any sign of anything green other than the Teddy Bear Garden. He noticed that unlike in typical Japanese American households, no shoes were left anywhere near the doorway, so he went ahead and stepped onto the hardwood floors, leaving his suitcase on the threadbare brown rug.

There was a mini kitchen in the corner, a wire dish rack holding a couple of coffee cups, a plate, and a few upside-down baby bottles. A desk by the hollow fireplace was overburdened by papers and books—it seemed almost as if it were spitting out and rejecting the weight of the information it carried. Mas turned on another lamp by the desk and peered at the books. Most were in English, but a couple were in Japanese. A Japanese-English dictionary, the fat kind that Chizuko had used when she was writing official letters, sat on a shelf. Even though Mas and Chizuko had sent their daughter to Japanese school every Saturday, Mari wouldn't have anything to do with the language and had forgotten the little that she had learned. Chizuko was offended and sometimes hurt when the teenage Mari had hissed at her in public places: "Speak English, Mom, speak English."

These couldn't be Mari's books: but then again, who else's would they be? The son-in-law's?

On the shelf next to the dictionary were a couple of photographs: the same one of the baby Takeo that Mari had sent to Mas, and a large one of Mari with her pale and scraggly husband, Lloyd, standing on some cement stairs leading to an official government building. Mas had not seen Lloyd for years, and that absence hadn't done Lloyd any good. Instead of looking more refined and clean-cut, his hair was down to his shoulders and barely combed. He wore wire-rimmed glasses and a tan suit, but he wasn't fooling anyone. He was a no-good gardener, just like Mas. But while Mas was a Kibei, Lloyd was a *hakujin* man, over six feet tall. He had absolutely no excuse for falling into the same line of work as desperate men.

Taped to the wall over the desk was a grainy photocopy of a man's image. Mas adjusted his Rite Aid glasses. A Japanese man wearing a straw hat and suit. A shadow fell on half the man's face, but he looked important. *Erai:* a big-boss type. The image was black-and-white and had obviously been taken more than half a century ago, maybe in the 1920s or 1930s, about the time Mas was born.

The disorganized books and papers on the desk didn't make much sense: Mari had always been like Chizuko, who'd kept their home in Altadena spotless. Every kitchen knife was sharpened (that part done by Mas after much nagging from Chizuko) and arranged by size in one of the kitchen drawers. The bills were paid immediately and filed away. When she was a child, Mari herself had lined up her pencil erasers by size at the top of the pink desk Mas had built for her. A few of them were those strange white Japanese ones wrapped in colorful cardboard sleeves. At one time they smelled like sugary flowers, but now, still left on the pink desk in Mas's silent house, they were virtually odorless.

Something else was wrong with the Park Slope apartment. Mas had taken on a new customer a few months ago, a young couple with a baby, in Pasadena. Their wood-framed house had a sloping front yard—something Mas would have never taken on in his heyday. But now competition was worse than ever and he couldn't afford to be choosy. Every time he waited at the door to talk to the missus, he noticed the trail of blocks, overturned plastic toys, and abandoned blankets. A disaster that only a baby could create. This front room had little sign of that.

Mas went into the back room, the bedroom. Again he turned on a light, the lamp beside the bed. Sure enough, a small crib stood in the corner. A few stuffed animals and packages of disposable diapers. By the crib was a large fluorescent lamp, almost like the ones Mas had seen in orchid greenhouses. What kind of strange life was Mari leading with this giant *hakujin* gardener?

A door in the bedroom led to a small backyard outside. Through the bedroom window, Mas could see that it had started to rain. He turned the double lock and opened the door. Finally, a faint patch of green, mixed in with dirt and gray.

Mas let the drizzle wet his hair, which had been combed back with Three Flowers oil, like always. He drew up the collar of his jacket and went up the steps to the miserable garden. Its condition didn't surprise Mas. Most gardeners were too busy with other people's gardens to put much energy into their own. Mas's front yard had its share of dandelions, and the backyard would have been completely grim if it had not been for Chizuko's leftover buckets of cymbidium. As he stumbled over some icy gravel, he thought he heard the ringing of a telephone in the distance. Not my phone, he thought, going over to examine a fancy iron bench and some metal rabbits and ducks. The square of green looked like last season's Bermuda grass.

Someone had attempted to plant a few daffodils, and they were bravely breaking through the chocolate brown soil. The plum blossoms on the garden's sole tree were still tightly closed, awaiting the warmth of the spring sun.

Before Mas could take further inventory of the hibernating plants, he noticed a figure at the open door. The son-in-law, a skeleton of a man, his dirty blond hair hanging down his head like seaweed. His face was ashen gray. Mas shoved his hands in his coat pockets and walked back to the apartment, preparing himself for the fake niceties that relatives who were virtual strangers said to one another at holidays and funerals.

But the son-in-law didn't even bother to smile. "Mari and Takeo aren't here," Lloyd said. "And I'm not sure exactly where they are."